I0673106

THE
SPACE SIEVE

David Smith

THE SPACE SIEVE

Published by Lehi David Smith
Available from Lulu.com, Amazon.com
ISBN: 978-0-6152-0502-1

THE SPACE SIEVE

CONTENTS

✿ CHAPTER 1 ✿

THESE FEW WORDS

YOU WILL WANT TO KNOW MY NAME, but it is unimportant. It suffices that I am the one who is relating this story. Were I to give you my name, you could not pronounce it in any case. I am a being from another dimension – and another universe – than the one in which you are living. And while you may be curious about my universe, it will also remain unknown to you, as will my physical form. These are not things you need to know in order to read this book. What this book *is* and why it came to be, on the other hand, *is* something you will need to know.

It might have occurred to you that within the total expanse of all creation there are beings that are outside your comprehension. You might have surmised further, that such beings might have ways of amusing themselves that are also beyond your power to imagine, and that their "toys" so to speak, could be rather unusual. And while this is true and interesting, that alone it is not the reason for my producing this account.

Think what would happen if one of you left something he liked to play with –something such as a chain saw, a welding torch, a lawnmower, a motorcycle etc. – in the company of less-intelligent creatures – in a monkey cage at a zoo for instance. Think of the death, of the mayhem. It would be interesting, wouldn't it?

Think now what would happen if someone in my realm – someone of true intelligence and power – left his plaything where it could fall into the hands of a lesser creature – indeed, into the hands of a creature such as *yourself*. That too would be interesting, wouldn't it?

1

In the case I wish to document here, there *was* a device left in the world of a lesser creature – *your* world – and it was most unusual, even by my standards. Indeed, it was the most powerful toy ever conceived by anyone, anywhere.

And what happened to it? Well, let me simply say that you should be happy you are still around to read this document.

And so, why did I write it?

It is something that I *do*, so to speak. I like to catalog those instances where unusual playthings are left lying around. It's a pastime for me. And as I said, this particular one was most unusual. (Moreover, in this case there was an *additional* reason for this book which I will make note of at the appropriate time.)

So in creating this document, my intention was to create something for my own kind to enjoy.

No, I am not referring to the book you are now reading – such written work would be far too crude for my kind to take notice of. At the same time I produced my document for my *own* kind, I also spawned *this* one, in your language, almost instantly, sort of like a burp after a meal. You may want to know *how*. Think about it this way. Suppose you have a thought. You are thinking about a place you have been. You can visualize it fully in your mind. And indeed, using my language I can convey such images instantly, and simultaneously. But now, imagine how long it would take you using *your* language to describe a location about which you are thinking, to another person. It would be so slow. It would be imprecise. It would be inadequate.

And it would certainly not be worth my while. When I produced my document in my own language, I also spawned this crude one in your language in an instant, merely as a byproduct. How could I do something like that, you may wonder? To explain, I must digress to discuss your concept of *time*.

Like so much else of what you take for granted, "time" is perhaps the greatest constant of your existences. It completely dominates and limits every one of you. It is your constant companion throughout your life as it stalks you, like a wild creature destined always to vex you. And then, time will ultimately kill you.

Remarkably, it does not occur to you that this thing you call "time" is something relatively limited to your own existences, and to the reality in which you live. While time for *you* may be one of the most powerful and immutable aspects of your existences, it may not have occurred to you that it – time – does not constrain most creatures within the total sphere of existence, and indeed it is not even perceived by them. The only occasion for which they take notice of it – of time – is when dealing with creatures that exist within a realm of existence (a "universe" if you will) that *contains* time. In any case, now that I have digressed to explain something so basic, I reiterate that due to the abilities that I possess, the book you are now reading took me very little time to produce, after your manner of understanding.

You should also recognize that while your kind has a rudimentary cognitive or "thinking" ability that has allowed you to develop primitive technology in a variety of areas, many of you also have an ability which you call "intuition" that allows you to understand much more. In other words, intuition can accomplish far more than thinking, for those of you who know how to use it. This ability plays a key role in this book. And yet intuition – for all its value – is entirely mysterious to your kind and indeed, cannot be described by your language! What a remarkable state of affairs.

So therefore, I cannot give you a direct sense of the events in this book nor can I relate any of them to you simultaneously using something as singularly simple and linear as your language. I can only endeavor to describe them as best I can, using your words.

Having then produced this book, I simply left it somewhere in your world in a place where it should eventually be discovered – in a place where it was, or will be, found. (You see how difficult it is to describe events in something as contrived as time, using something as simple as your language!) Someone of your kind will eventually come across my book, will read it, then will copy it, hand it out, and so forth. He may even take credit for having written it himself.

Let him (or her) do so. It is of no consequence to me.

And so as you read this book, and sit there like a baby it its crib looking out at the world around you and feeling yourself to be so well informed about what you can see and hear and sense, and confident in what you know and believing that you also know all that you don't know, you will perhaps appreciate this momentary opportunity to take a brief glance out the window, if only that the wiser ones among you can begin to understand what inept and naive creatures you truly are.

So now after having related these few words, I can begin this narrative. As you read, you should remember how difficult it is to describe the unusual events recorded herein using only your crude language. Your language at its best – and your kind does not use it at its best – is wholly insufficient to describe even those things about which *you* are familiar. You can imagine how inadequate it is to describe the events that *I* will now relate.

✿ CHAPTER 2 ✿

THE THANKSGIVING PARTY

THE SUBJECTS OF THIS STORY – the key players if you will – were all adolescent children.

This – adolescence – is an interesting time for your kind; still containing all the innocence and simplicity of youth, but beginning to have increased levels of adult-like abilities, as far as humans go. And yet, with this newly-emerging capability there is enough youth left that there is still the capacity for wonder and imagination, which seem to leave your kind soon after you reach adulthood. These qualities of childhood are one of the most useful, and indeed most appealing, characteristics of humans. The change that happens from childhood to adulthood, when these qualities are lost, leaves most of you about as interesting as a piece of dry pastry, with all of the filling squeezed out of it.

Their names were as follows: Sally and Chip, brother and sister, ages thirteen and fourteen years respectively, Diane and David, not brother and sister, also ages thirteen and fourteen respectively. You will also want to know their *last* names, but this information is irrelevant.

And while you will get to know these children better as a natural course of this account, it has come to my attention as a result of other works I have done for others of my kind, that most readers like to know a little bit about the subjects of the story "up front," as you would say. So while this information would seem unnecessary at this point of the story to *me*, for the sake of others I will here give a few details regarding them.

Both Sally and Chip were blond. Diane was blonde to brown and David had dark hair. As far as eye color: Sally and Chip, blue; David brown, and

Diane greenish brown. (Of course, had you asked any of them, none of them would have been able tell you any of this. One wonders why someone reading this document would need to know, when the actual people themselves never noticed. But I suppose you wanted to know, *didn't* you?)

I could also mention each of these children were what one would call attractive for your kind. In fact, Sally and Chip (largely due to genetic reasons but also partly due to lifestyle choices) would grow up to be noticeably beautiful. Diane too would grow up to be beautiful, if a little heavy-set, and David would also be acceptably attractive in his adulthood, if a little on the thin side.

As far as their personalities: Sally and David both were similar to each other, as were Chip and Diane. Sally and David were the type of people who had a tendency to do things the hard way, by which I mean they tended to resist advice and therefore had to find out for themselves the way things actually are. This trait is referred to by your kind either as "courage and independent thinking," or as "foolhardiness and bull-headedness." Whether it is referred to as one or the other, is entirely a question of whether those persons, in doing just whatever they want, turn out to be *right* or not. Chip and Diane on the other hand tended to be more conventional, tended to accept and appreciate advice, and tended to conduct themselves in a manner in which they thought others would want them to.

Diane and Chip tended to be cautious, whereas the other two children tended to be more impetuous. Diane and Chip tended to be conservative, whereas David and Sally were more inclined to seek the advantages and opportunities that can come from taking risks – in some cases excessive ones.

These four were all related to one degree or another by "family ties" and as such, found themselves all together on this day at Thanksgiving party, at the home of some grandparents. And yet, other than for Sally and Chip, the four children were not actually related by blood. This is worth noting, as what the future held for Sally and David, and for Chip and Diane, is that they would one day find themselves joining as is typical for your kind, in your ritual of marriage (And suffice it to say this ritual is not uncommon in my realm either. And you did just wonder about that, didn't you? Well, you should have.)

In any case, what the future held was that Sally would marry David, and Chip would marry Diane. Both marriages would prove highly successful, although Chip and Diane's would be far more tranquil than David and Sally's.

Or at least, that's what the future *would* have held for all of them. (You see how difficult it is for me to describe matters involving time, using your language.)

Finally, David was unusual in that he had a rare intuitive sense that will become evident shortly. This tended to isolate him from others to a degree, since difference sometimes leads to isolation from that which is more common. Why this is true may seem interesting to you but I have already paused far too long in this descriptive foray and I have no intention of prolonging it any further

On the occasion of this family get-together, comprising on the order of 40 members of the extended families and relatives, the customary events were transpiring. While the adults busied themselves with preparing the foods and drinks your kind find pleasant and which are customarily prepared and consumed on such an occasion, and while others of the party were occupying themselves with tedious conversation, observation of various electro-mechanical devices in the home and so forth, the four mentioned children were running around through the rest of the house. In this sense, they were having the most fun and stood the chance of doing the most good, as nothing worthwhile at all was being accomplished by the adults, other than for preparing the meal. And indeed, the children's activities were far more interesting as well. For the parents, while they could have been engaging themselves in interesting conversation regarding the intimate details and secrets of their lives, chose not to do so, as adults almost always choose.

For instance, Chip's father, Duane, was a single parent who lost his wife, Ginger, to a strange illness that was never correctly diagnosed. Therefore, Duane was left to raise his children – Chip and Sally along with their younger brother Donny – all by himself. While that is in itself not all that interesting, there is something interesting about Duane that he could have talked about at this Thanksgiving party had he chosen to do so, along the following lines:

Having lost his beloved wife, Duane was inconsolable for a great long time. For his wife had not only been his love, but had been his fondest, truest, and deepest friend. Her death left a vast space in his life that could perhaps never be filled.

And yet, as your kind often does, Duane's mind attempted to fill this space in his life through imagination. Interestingly, Duane became convinced that the spirit of his wife had come to occupy the body of his youngest son, Donny, and on one occasion he had confided this to a group of

7

friends. In his living room, Duane had described how little Donny was showing so many of the traits of his deceased mother that Duane was sure Ginger was somehow inside of Donny. The little boy even seemed to have many of his dead mother's mannerisms. This was a great relief to Duane, knowing that his dearly departed wife had taken up residence inside his youngest son.

Duane expressed the concern however, that there were a few traits of his wife's personality that were at the present time only partially expressed in little Donny's personality. This, he confided, left him distressed and wondering whether his wife was really in there at all.

Upon hearing this, his friends' feelings ranged from skeptical, to concerned about Duane's state of mind. Strangely one of them, trying to be helpful, offered that there was a possible explanation for why the boy did not seem entirely like Ginger. Little Donny, the friend pointed out, had only an immature brain, whereas Duane's wife had been in possession of a fully mature brain at the time of her demise. Naturally therefore, if Duane's wife had taken possession of little Donny, she would seem a little altered, inasmuch as inside little Donny she only had the brain of an immature boy through which to express herself. Obviously, this would make her seem a little different than she had been when she was alive. The friend offered this explanation as a solution that could relieve Duane's concern.

It is an interesting emotion that your kind calls, "love." To some of you this word means physical attraction. To some it means a sense of devotion. To some it means a sense of responsibility. But perhaps the most common and compelling definition of what that word means for your kind, is a powerful urge merely to be in the physical presence of the one you love – a need to be simply *near* them. Thus, Duane's mind imagined his wife was inside his little son.

Similarly is your habit of locating the physical remains of your deceased in a safe and certain location, so that you can then imagine that you can "visit" them, imagining yourself to there be in the presence of the one you love, even though you must know that there is really no one there at all.

Of course, these involuntary self-delusions of Duane's were all nonsense. But they were somewhat novel, weren't they? They were something Duane could have talked about to make the party interesting, but he chose not to do so. In fact, nobody talked about anything personal, private, or secret at all. Therefore, the party (where the parents were) was entirely nondescript and pointless.

But the four children I mentioned previously on the other hand, were about to happen upon something extraordinary. Indeed, they were about to happen upon something that was simply one of the most remarkable creations that has ever been in your universe.

As they rummaged throughout the house, the four children had come upon a closet with double doors. Giving in to curiosity and devilishness, they all (these four children) opened one of the doors and endeavored to climb inside. This was actually a large utility closet and as such it contained the furnace and hot water tank, along with such accumulated detritus as the owners of the house had placed there.

But it was not all worthless material, it turns out. As Chip tried to close the door with the four of them inside, David moved further back into the closet and unbalanced a pile, which fell over. A number of objects fell against the other door, pushing it open, and the objects and the children spilled out of the closet.

Among the objects that fell out was one that was much larger than the rest.

It was the Device. (Hereafter then, one of the words I will use to refer to this object will be: the "Device.")

There are various Devices, and they have various names. They are created by, and used to amuse, beings who are on a higher plane of existence than your kind. This Device is the particular toy that I mentioned previously, created by a being outside of your world and your reality. I mentioned it was left such that it found its way into your world. In addition, *this* Device was unique in the sense that it was substantially more than the usual plaything, even for those creatures that would consider it to be a toy. As I stated before, it was the most powerful Device ever conceived.

For three of the children, as they watched the items fall out of the closet, what they saw was junk. And what they thought was that they would get into trouble if they didn't get it all back into the closet before they got caught.

But one of the four children saw something different altogether. What David not only saw, but focused upon, was the largest object that fell out of the closet.

For you see, David saw only, the Device. And what *he* thought is that his eyes and mind were looking at something unique in his world – nothing like he had ever before seen.

In one of those rare moments of clarity, his mind reached to another place, a higher place, and somehow achieved a realization that this object was different – valuable – even wonderful. This is a rare quality some of your kind has – the ability to see that to which all others seem blind.

The party, the other three children, and indeed, the rest of the world now essentially, all disappeared for David. And while the other three children scrambled to return the items to the closet, David – in what the children would later recall as an almost reverent, trance-like state – approached and put his hands on the Device.

Let us digress now. The Device was laying on the floor, on its back. When upright, it looked vaguely like a small, upright piano: the base, 22 inches wide, and 15 inches deep, and overall, 50 inches tall. The entire back of the Device was essentially straight and flat, with the upper half only about half as deep as the base. So about 28 inches up, the front surface tapered back. Picture an upright piano about that size: about half-way up, a keyboard slopes down toward you as you sit at it, and behind the keyboard there is a surface, sloping slightly back, where you would put the music if it were a piano.

The entire Device was essentially smooth, and dark, almost glossy black. I will refer hereafter to the back, sides, base, and so forth of the Device, but the important parts I will refer to as the "keyboard" and the "screen." The "keyboard" is the sloped part of the Device where the "keys" would be if it were a piano. The "screen" of the Device is the surface behind the keyboard, where one would put the music, if it were a piano. I say these are the important parts – the keyboard and the screen if you will – but that will only be evident *later*. For at this time, the object had no keyboard, no screen, and indeed, looked like a black object with no obvious features other than for its overall shape. The lines were extremely simple – with minimally rounded edges at the intersections of the sides of the Machine, with no embossing or embellishment of any kind.

I note I just said "Machine" instead of "Device." Within your range of understanding both words are reasonable ones to use for it. In any case, you know what I'm talking about.

Here is a test: did you wonder why a being such as I would describe the Device with measurements in "inches" as I did? Did you feel that a being as advanced as I should have used measurements such as "centimeters" or some such metric? Well if you wondered about that, you will want perhaps to feel good about yourself for a moment – but only for moment – after which I must remind you what a silly creature you are. What difference should it make to me which of your absurd systems of measurement I should use? Indeed, if "inches" are the units which would make the most sense while I am trying to use your language to describe things as best I can, would not measurement in "inches" be the most reasonable for me to use? In any case, I now resume the story.

By the time the other kids noticed, David had already begun to drag the Device down the hall into his grandmother's bedroom. The Device has no weight per se, or, another way to look at it is that depending on the situation, it weighs different amounts. When on your planet, and when dormant, as it is at this moment, it would seem to weigh on the order of about thirty pounds. (Yes, I said pounds, not kilograms, didn't I?)

"Hey David, what are you doing with that?" Sally asked. "Get it back in the closet with this other junk before somebody finds out!"

It's worth noting that David was already becoming fond of Sally, but you would never have known that right now. He said nothing. Instead, he dragged the Device over to the back side of his grandmother's bedroom by a rarely-used sewing table, and he stood it up near the window. The sun was blazing outside in a perfectly clear day.

To the other three, the strange object cast a dark sense about the room, and shadows seemed to dart among the knick knacks and other objects that were cluttering it. But this was just their imagination. It was David's odd behavior that was really troubling them.

The grandparents, like most of you, were packrats, and they came into possession of the Device at an auction. Seeing it there, Grandma thought it was a cabinet and would make a nice addition to the bedroom. She bought it before realizing it had no drawers or openings of any kind. It was simply a black object, seemingly useless for any purpose. And so like most of you would do in a similar situation, finding herself in possession of an object for which she had no conceivable use, she took it home, put it in a closet, and forgot about it.

How the Device got into your world in the first place, is beyond your capacity to understand, and is irrelevant to the story at this point, but I will tell you that the Device will sometimes have a tendency to *drift*. This involves a type of slippage that you cannot understand, but that you may have some sense of later.

David knelt in front of the Machine, and began to examine it with his hands.

Chip looked at David. "Hey David," he asked in his usual friendly tone. "What are you doing? We need to get that back in the closet before somebody finds out."

Then Chip looked at the Device. "Hey, so what is it? Do you know what the heck it *is*?" He reached over and rubbed his hand on its smooth surface. As the girls gathered around, David pushed Chip's hand away.

"Leave it alone," David said quietly. He had not even so much looked at any of the other kids since exiting the closet.

"David," Diane said politely, "are you all right?"

After hesitating for a moment, she reached over and shook him a little, "David?"

Finally, he looked up. "Yeah," he said, "Hey, can you all *leave*? I mean, can you all go back to the party or go *play* or something? I mean, it's okay with me if you . . . . I mean . . . . can you just . . . . I, I don't want to be rude, but . . . . ."

"You want us to what? You want us all to *leave*?" Sally frowned indignantly. "Well, it *is* rude," she said. Then turning to the others, trying to get ahead of the conversation she said, "Well let's leave then if that's what he wants." But David seemed not to be listening.

"Wait a minute," interjected Chip. "What are you going to do, David – stay here all alone in here with this – this wooden rock thing?" He reached over and rubbed the smooth surface again.

David was deep in thought. Without looking at him, he started to push Chip's had away again. But then he looked at Chip, and his voice was neither friendly, nor polite. "You can just go ahead and go. I mean, you can come back after awhile . . . but right now, can you just . . ." then he looked back at the Device, and without taking his eyes off it, he said softly, "just leave. . ."

"Okay this is too weird," Diane said.

Sally was giving directions again. "Okay well if that's what he wants why don't we just leave him here with his – his *box*? *I'm* going." She moved toward the hall, then stopped and looked back at the others.

"Let's *go*." And she headed down the hall, with the other two following.

And they went into another bedroom, closed the door, and then stood around and talked about, and wondered about, what David was doing, and what that strange object in which David was so strangely and so intensely interested, was

If at this point you are wondering about details such as what the other people in the house were doing, what they said, what the rooms looked like etc., I can tell you: these things are unimportant. Let us proceed.

You may also be interested in what happened to David, and this *is* useful to tell. His mother, when the appointed time came for their Thanksgiving feast, went looking for him, and upon finding him she fairly had to pry his hands off the Device and force him to go to the table with the rest of the family.

After first taking a mother's interest in what her son was doing, but finding David unwilling to accede to her wishes to leave the object and come to dinner, she first lowered her tone somewhat and commanded him. This having no effect, she threatened him, informing him that his father would be called. Growing more disturbed than angry, she grabbed his arm and pulled him down the hallway. David's mother, in addition to being unusually strong for a woman, was not one to stand much on excessive talk and entreaties where the obedience of her children was concerned.

As David subsequently turned and pulled away to go back to Grandma's bedroom, his mother's gritted teeth and a mild slap to his face together with her reciting his full name to him, convinced him that his mother would not be trifled with any more in the matter, and so he went with her to dinner.

David didn't pay much attention to dinner, and didn't eat much of it either, in spite of his mother's unhappy protestations about the time she had taken with the others making the dinner, and couldn't David at least notice how nice it all was – a few of the foods were among David's usual favorites after all. But David seemed odd and distant to her. And so, in addition to essentially missing the dinner his mother had helped prepare for him, David largely ruined it for her as well.

Later in the evening as the Thanksgiving party began to conclude, David surprised everyone when suddenly he demanded that he be allowed to take the Device that he had found, home with him. But in spite of the fact that for Grandpa and Grandma it was nothing of any particular use, they were not inclined to give it to David – they had bought it at an auction after all, they asserted.

David, having been thrifty in his life, had accumulated a fair amount of money for a child his age. And although not a lot of money *per se*, when he offered the entire sum to his grandfather in exchange for the Device in front of the other members of the family (and thereby shocking everyone, and continuing to further shock his three playmates, Sally, Diane, and Chip) his

13

grandfather, for appearance's sake, could not see denying the boy, and he relented to let David have it – for free.

(It should not however be overlooked that during the process, David concluded that Grandfather could either take the money, or David would come later and *steal* the Device. This was unusual for David, as he had always been rightfully regarded as among the more upright and responsible of all of his Grandfather's posterity. Or at least, up until now, he *had* been.)

Anyway, the Device ended up in David's bedroom.

☼ CHAPTER 3 ☼

TOO FAR FOR THE TIC

AFTER THE PARTY, which had been on a Saturday, David told his mother he was sick and as a result he missed school for several days. This too was odd, as David had always been a diligent and interested student. During those days, when his mother left him alone in his room, David sat and studied the Device – which you will recall, in terms of any exterior trappings resembled more of a solid object than a Device. Initially, he ran his hands over it, looking for a seam, a flaw, some distinction – but he didn't find any.

He studied it for hours at a time while everything else about his life melted away. He became obsessed with it. He carefully considered the Device, and he pondered over it. As time passed, he grew tired and fell asleep in front of it. After several minutes passed he awakened and pored over the Device anew. This process – studying, falling asleep, awakening, studying – repeated time and time again. When his mother came to see him, he told her he was sick. He began more and more to look like he *was* sick. As the days passed, his mother and father became more and more concerned.

As this continued for still more days, one evening David became exhausted and fell asleep as he had done so many times before. But when he awoke, he felt something was different. As he looked around his room, everything appeared to be where it was before, yet it was as though something had changed. He looked out the window. The sky, the ground, everything seemed unusual – as if he was living in a world that was similar to the one in which he had been, yet somehow it was not the same. (I will point out for you, that the world had not changed – but something about David *had*.) David now felt that somehow, he understood something about the dark

15

object in his room that he hadn't before. He moved near it, kneeled, and placed his hands on what I have referred to as the "keyboard." And although I have called it that, the surface had been smooth.

But it was smooth no longer. As David pressed his fingers on the flat space of the keyboard, the surface under his fingers became textured. And although he didn't notice it at first, all over the surface of the Device patterns began to appear - broad swirls changing to a faint mosaic pattern, then swirls, other shapes, and so forth. The Device also became ever so slightly warmer, and for a few moments it expressed a faint hum. David didn't notice the sound at first, until a single pitch penetrated the room, like a soprano hitting a single high note, a long-way off. Still unaware that there was a texture all over the Machine, David continued to focus on the keyboard, and the shapes and patterns that formed and flowed upon it.

Then suddenly, he *did* notice the shapes and patterns all over the Device, and when he did, he began to move his hands differently upon the keyboard.

This young person, David, was one of you who had *intuition*. What had happened here, for those of you who need everything explained to you, is that David's mind had finally assimilated enough data that it had begun to make sense regarding the seemingly disconnected features of the Device. While someone such as David could never explain what was happening, his mind was working subconsciously, connecting what would have seemed to David like unrelated facts, and it was formulating a process to enable David to accomplish his goal. Each bit of data added to the intuitive process. David's was beginning to obtain an inkling of the fact that this seemingly nondescript object was actually a Mechanism, and his subconscious mind was beginning to make sense of it.

It would continue to make more and more sense of it. As David continued to press his fingers on the keyboard, the texture on the Device continued to move. But now, it began to move more deeply, or perhaps it would be accurate to say, more *intensely*.

The Device all the while, remained essentially black. But in the light, shining from the window at the side of the room, the patterns and shapes could be seen all over it. David watched this, and he could see and feel the texture moving on the keyboard.

I have mentioned part of the Machine that I called the "screen" that is above the keyboard. Once, while David was pressing his fingers on the flat, minimally-textured keyboard, a tiny yellow shape briefly appeared on the screen – on that part of the Device above the keyboard. Unlike the rest of the Device, the screen had no texture but was still completely smooth.

Downstairs, David's father (whose first name was "Leland") was sitting in the living room with a friend from down the street. The friend's name was Mike, and he was Leland's best friend, meaning naturally that Leland and Mike were friends from their own youth.

You are perhaps wondering what this has to do with the story. As I told you before, interacting with your language is unpleasant for me. I have no intention of spending any more time than is necessary in doing so. Telling this part of the story is important, as are all the other parts that I will relate.

It is also worth mentioning that although the present events took place just after Thanksgiving, this particular evening was mild and pleasant. People were outside. Windows were open. David and his family live in the southwestern part of the United States (as do the other three children I mentioned previously). For those of you who are unfamiliar with this part of the country, suffice it to say that this time of year is considered to be very appealing for those who live there – very similar to a pleasant fall in the cooler parts of your world.

Completely unaware of what David was doing, Leland sat in the dim light of the living room with Mike and they passed the time talking. Mike gestured as he talked about a bedroom of his that he planned to paint over the weekend.

"I got four brushes last week," Mike said. "I don't clean 'em when I'm done with them. I just throw 'em away. I got four rollers too. Same thing – don't clean 'em." He chuckled. "Life's too short."

"Yeah," Leland replied. "Well I clean the brushes. I don't know. It just seems a waste *not* to."

"Well I don't," Mike replied, "I just use 'em once and throw 'em away. And I don't use oil paint either. It's too much work to clean up the brushes with solvent."

"I thought you said you didn't clean 'em." Leland observed. "If you don't clean the brushes then what difference does it make?

A mockingbird began to sing in the distance, and a dog barked for a few moments.

"Oh, yeah," Mike realized. "Okay, yeah. I get it. Yeah."

The sound of a screen door slamming punctuated the conversation.

Mike thought for a moment. "You know, it makes me wonder if I could have been using oil all these years instead of latex."

"Well look, Mike," Leland pointed out, "I like latex anyway. I've used oil, but really, latex works better. It seems to make a nicer . . . hey but listen, what about rollers? I usually use those bigger, puffier rollers that soak up more paint. That's how I get the job done fast. You know the more paint you have on the roller, the longer you can go before you have to dip it again."

"Yeah, well," Mike continued, "I like the rollers that have a low pile – the thin ones. It takes longer, but I like the texture that you get better."

Upstairs, David continued to press his fingers on the keyboard.

But now it was no longer entirely black.

Colored buttons now covered the surface of the keyboard. I say "buttons" but they were really small, glassy, glowing forms that were somewhat elevated from the surface of the keyboard. Each button had a color and a texture, as well as a shape, and they ranged in from about the size of a pea to a grape, each one rising about half way from the keyboard. David pressed his fingers against these shapes now, in a deliberate, intense way.

Had you seen him, you might have thought it looked almost like a virtuoso playing the piano, as David's fingers danced upon the flashing keys.

His abilities were remarkable. But as he progressed in his understanding, intuiting more and more as each minute passed, David began to grow weak, and he started to look exhausted. In what was becoming a growing euphoria to him, David was pushing his mind forward – faster and faster, and still faster it ran. David was hurling his consciousness into the effort at an ever-increasing rate, and as he did so he drew more and more energy from his body – and he pulled that energy far faster than his brain and body had the capacity to replenish.

David was also having trouble seeing. Tears welled in the corners of his eyes. Beads of sweat tracked down from his hairline.

Leland paused, considering. "Well, so what about *brushes* then?" he asked. "Do you like skinny *brushes* too?"

"You know it's kind of funny," Mike replied, chuckling and leaning forward with his hand to his chin like he had just discovered some profound truth. "Actually I like the *puffier* brushes. Y'know it's kinda weird. I like the *skimpier* rollers, but I like the *puffier* brushes."

"No, not really," Leland replied. "I like the puffier brushes *too*. It makes sense that you . . ."

"No wait," Mike interrupted. "It *doesn't* make sense. Maybe I *do* like the skinny brushes – you know for some things puffy, for some things, skinny. I guess it depends on if I'm painting trim, or if . . ."

Just then – for only a moment – a faint but definite sound broke the stillness of the evening. It was like the sound of a thousand car horns all honking simultaneously, far in the distance.

"Hey, what was that?" Mike said, as he turned his head, listening.

But it was not clear where the sound had come from.

In David's bedroom, the screen on the Device now flickered with dim, yellow shapes. Imagine a checkerboard of black and yellow, squeezed left-to-right, so that the yellow squares are tall and thin, like vertical pieces of macaroni. These yellow shapes were flashing and moving rapidly – left-to-right – right-to-left – on the screen. The keys under David's fingers glowed and changed shape and color, illuminating his palms as David's finger tips scampered upon them. As the yellow figures danced on the screen of the Device, their reflected, distorted shapes glinted like shooting stars in David's wide, glassy eyes.

Somewhat absent-mindedly now, David occasionally wiped a tear from an eye, and increasingly, he also had to wipe the sweat that was running into his eyes when he felt it sting. Each time he lifted a hand from the keyboard, the lighted buttons clustered to the side of the keyboard underneath the one hand that was still on the keyboard. When he returned both hands to the keyboard, the buttons spread back so they were again under both hands.

The stillness of the evening in David's room was disturbed now by a faint roaring sound, and the objects upon his dresser trembled slightly. Occasionally, the gathering darkness was punctuated by brief, intermittent tones.

The usually innocent face of the boy was turning grim and grey now, like a drug addict craving his next injection. His body and his brain were becoming depleted. As his eyes scanned the yellow colors sweeping across the screen, the expression on his face became disturbing to behold. For one more minute of progress with this Machine, David would have traded his entire existence. He would not have been right to do so, but he would have. There was now for David, nothing else that mattered in the world, past, present, or future. This was everything to him – and far more than anything that he had ever known. It was all that mattered to him now.

Obviously, his behavior had become self destructive and inexcusable. It would be of little use to David if while he gained a greater understanding of the Device, he *died* as a result.

I say "obviously," but I mean it is obvious only from *your* standpoint, inasmuch as you are creatures which must come to terms with the fact that

19

you can die. But on another level, from *my* standpoint his willingness to sacrifice to gain further knowledge of this Machine was a great tribute to his intelligence. For while you all must die, David on the other hand had discovered something unique and more incalculably vast than anyone in your world could ever conceive. And moreover, David not only *had* it, he was quickly learning how to *operate* it.

Pausing briefly to wonder about the sound they had just heard, the two adults downstairs quickly resumed their inanity.

"Well but," Leland continued, a puzzled look on his face, "for me, painting is something I do just because it needs to be done. The thing is, Mike, you actually *like* to go paint a room."

"Yeah, I guess so," said Mike, "I do like to paint. But I leave wallpaper to my wife."

At this moment, David's mother, Sharon, was just outside the living room window – outside the room where Leland and Mike were talking. She was digging in the flower bed there, next to the house, planting some bulbs for next spring. A few small children were playing down the street.

"I generally use a fine finish brush for around windows and stuff," said Mike. "I've never been one to *tape*."

"Well," replied Leland, "That's what I was saying. You like to do the job, so you use a finish brush. I use tape because it's faster and I just want to get it over with."

Mike crinkled his nose, thinking. "No, no I don't know if I would say that using a finish brush is the harder way to do it. Maybe it's slower, maybe it isn't. I just like to use them."

"Yeah well," Leland followed up, "anybody who uses a finish brush is going to be . ."

Suddenly, Leland leaned forward in his chair and looked out the window of the living room into the gathering darkness of the evening.

"What . . . what is that?" He said, as he stood up. "What in blazes is that?!"

Mike looked blankly at him, at first unable to shift from the idle satisfaction of the evening. But when he realized the level of concern clearly evident in his friend's face, Mike turned to see what Leland was looking at.

But by then, Leland had already leapt to the window. Instantly, Mike also saw what Leland could see, and he jumped into a crouching position very close alongside him as they both cast their concerned stare out the window.   Indistinctly, they could feel each other's body heat, and could smell each other's rising emotion.

Leland's mouth moved, and he mumbled faintly. "Mike, what is it?" Mike turned to Leland briefly, and Leland could tell Mike was breathing very fast, and he noticed that Mike's breath smelled bad.

Then Mike saw something even more terrifying.

"Leland," Mike said, and his voice shook. "Look … your *wife*." And then Leland too saw that his wife Sharon was just outside the window, kneeling in the flower bed.

And although the ghastly apparition that had transfixed Leland and Mike was lowering itself very near to Sharon, she had not seen it yet. Nor had she seen Leland and Mike in the window, gape-mouthed and motionless.

But now I need to digress again.

The Device that David was beginning to operate upstairs in his room – in cases such as this it will spawn another Mechanism, and I would like to take a moment to tell you about it. This ancillary Apparatus – the one that Leland and Mike were looking at – the one that was now only inches from David's mother – actually 21 inches from her at its closest point – this Apparatus was created as a direct result of David's actions with the Device that he was operating in his room. It is called a "Tic."

As the Tic lowered, inching closer to David's mother, Leland began to turn white. He felt a huge lump in his throat – as if it were the size of a baseball and as hard – and it was getting bigger. It hurt a lot, and he could hardly breathe.

Mike, for his part, felt his lower parts – the parts or your bodies where you emanate your bodily wastes – contracting and relaxing involuntarily, very rapidly.

And now, here I must stop and tell you more about the Tic, while you might wish I would continue with the story. So you see the problem I have, don't you? I have to describe things for you every so often, yet how can I do it without stopping the story? The problem is with your *language*, not with me.

But here I do need to tell you what the Tic actually is. I need to describe it to you. It is an interesting and important Mechanism, and it will play an important role later in this story.

You might want to say that creatures such as I and such as others within the total sphere of existence who have the ability to create powerful Devices for our amusement are irresponsible to let them fall in the hands of lesser

21

creatures, and in a sense, you are right. What I am about to say is no defense of that. Yet, perhaps it does offer some redemption for us.

Each major Device has a safety feature. Nobody makes anybody include it, but they do anyway. The Tic then is that safety feature for the Machine that David is beginning to operate in his room.

But now I begin to tire of calling it only the "Device" or the "Machine" and I also need to differentiate it from the Tic. Yet while the "Tic" has a name you can pronounce the name of the Device that David is operating cannot be pronounced by your kind. Therefore hereafter at times I will call the Device one of the names that David will give it. He will call it many things eventually – one of them being the "Infernal Contraption" – but this is not the one I wish to use right now. David will first come to call the Device "the Space Sieve," and this is the name I will now sometimes use for it also.

And so, David sat in front of the Space Sieve, and pressed the glowing, ever-changing colored buttons, and gazed captivated at the yellow shapes flickering across its screen.

I say "sat" because while he *had* been kneeling in front of it, he did so no longer. The Device has the ability to create, and David used it to create a stool: the seat of which was about an inch thick and about a foot in diameter, with a metal frame under it that curved over to the Device. And while this stool may have at this moment appeared to be part of the Device, it was not. David simply determined that he needed it, and so he created it, based on his understanding of the Device, and his increasing ability to use it.

And he *was* increasing in his ability to use the Device. Indeed, of all the lesser creatures who have encountered a Mechanism, I have never seen *anybody* gain knowledge of its operation as fast as this boy was doing. And that is saying something. For you will recall that chronicling the unfortunate occurrences when a Device such as this is left lying around is something I do as a hobby. So I've seen quite a few cases where a Device falls into the hands of an inferior being and that being learns a sufficient amount to be able to start to use it. And in all of it, I have never seen another case where any being obtained this knowledge as fast or as fully as this boy David did - all the more distinctive and indeed disturbing, in view of the fact that *this* Device was the most powerful one that I have ever seen. And I have seen them *all*.

Previously, I mentioned that there were two unique reasons that I produced this document. This then, was one of those reasons: the magnitude of this Device, combined with this particular boy's skill in using it, his abilities being such that it's almost unnecessary to tell you more about the

Tic. But since the Tic will appear later in this story, this is as good a time to talk about it as any.

When a Device such as the Space Sieve detects that someone has begun to figure out how to use it, it creates – spawns if you will – the Tic. The Tic forms therefore, when the Space Sieve detects that it is beginning to be operated by a novice. The Tic has one function, and one only, and that function is as follows: the Tic completely neutralizes the external effects of the Space Sieve. The Space Sieve can still perform internal functions, such as the lights, buttons, and the chair that David is sitting on, etc., but it cannot operate on its external environment while the Tic is present. The Tic can do only one thing, but it can do that one thing perfectly. It renders the Space Sieve ineffectual.

That anything can render the Space Sieve ineffectual is truly remarkable but it is particularly so, given the unique scope and power of this particluar Device.

Once a Space Sieve has spawned a Tic, there is one, and only one, external function that the Space Sieve can do. That one remaining function is that it can be used to *remove* the Tic.

Once – indeed *if* – the Space Sieve detects that it is being operated by a skilled operator, as opposed to a novice, the Space Sieve can then be used to remove the Tic. This allows the Space Sieve to regain full functionality. Typically, this does not ever happen, as a novice typically cannot ever become a skilled operator by himself. This is because once the external functions of the Space Sieve have been neutralized by the Tic, the educational feedback to the operator is eliminated – the operator can no longer learn new information about it. The operator of the Space Sieve, when there is a Tic present, no longer sees things happening as he operates the Device. He therefore can derive no further experience about how to operate the Space Sieve.

Let me make an analogy. Perhaps I should have done so earlier. But here will do. Can you tell me how to ride a bicycle? Can you explain it? Try telling someone how to ride a bicycle then have them go right off and do it. Of course, you can't, and *they* can't. The only way to ride a bike is to *try* it.

As you push the bike, as you feel the inertia, the gravity, as you sense the movement, the pedals, the wheels, the handlebars, your mind begins to draw intuitive connections between all this information even though you have no perception of this at all. The feedback you obtain from trying allows your mind to formulate what to try next and more information is obtained as you

23

continue to try. Your skill advances, and as it does, your mind receives still more information, and you improve further. Even though riding a bike, water skiing, ice skating, etc., would be very complicated operations for you to do by *thinking*, almost anyone can do it, if they keep trying. Your mind, working with your body, makes the necessary adjustments to be able to do it. You don't even realize it is happening. This is the intuitive mind I described earlier.

Now suppose you tried to ride the bike, but you couldn't see, or feel, or hear. In other words, suppose you got no feedback as you tried to ride it. You could never learn how, could you?

Do you see the almost-foolproof genius of the Tic? Up until this point, David had examined the Device carefully and then he had placed his hands on it in a certain way, which had caused the texture to appear. This texture and the way it shifted in response to David's hands provided his mind with enough information to bring out the illuminated keys I mentioned, and then various lights on the screen. *This* provided yet *more* information to him, as he touched the keys and watched the lights. As the process continued, he learned more, made the Device do more, learned more, etc. But once the Device detected that David was a novice – inexperienced – it created the Tic as it was designed to do.

The effect of the Tic was then to stop the external function of the Device. This lack of external function was intended to stop the learning process.

Now here you might wonder whether all creatures would have the same senses as humans do, and whether the Device was emitting *only* stimuli that *you* could recognize. The answer is: it was not. But the question is irrelevant. The point is that it *was* emitting stimuli that you *can* recognize.

The idea then, was that once the Tic appeared, David – or whoever – could push the buttons all he wanted as he tried different things, but nothing *new* would happen. Since nothing new would happen, nothing new would be learned, and the learning process would stop. So the Device thereby, would have been rendered effectively inert, and harmless.

At least that is what is supposed to happen, and it's what almost always does happen when somebody accidentally comes across an advanced Machine.

But with *this* boy, that is *not* what happened. By the time the Tic was spawned, David already knew too much about the Device.

The Tic looked like a large duffel bag, 73 inches tall, and 21 feet in diameter, with the bottom round, and the top more pointed. It materialized in a vertical orientation, and was a dull white color overall. Randomly (or so it appeared) over the surface, were colored lights every 6-12 inches or so, each light one solid color. The lights were hemispherical in shape, about 1 inch in diameter, like colored, illuminated ping-pong ball halves stuck to the sides of the Tic.

One of the lights was different, however. What *that* one looked like was this: Hold out your hand and extend a finger horizontally, then make the end of this finger point down. Now imagine a light on the end of it, shining down. While all other lights on the Tic were colored, this one was white.

The Tic just hung there in mid-air, silently beside David's mother, unseen by her.

But now, the children down the street saw it. Two of them were riding bicycles. When the one in front saw the Tic lowering beside David's mother he stopped his bike suddenly and the other child crashed into him. A little girl in the yard nearby looked at the boys for a second, and then she turned and saw the Tic too. Her eyes grew wide for a moment, and then she became concerned and began to scream in short, high-pitched bursts. This screaming caused David's mother to turn and then she saw the Tic, silently hovering only inches away from her, there in the dusky evening, its lights glowing disinterestedly.

David's mother caught her breath, looked the Tic up and down and then threw down her trowel. While the appearance of the Tic is not frightening *per se*, it is sufficiently unusual to cause some concern in lesser creatures such as yourselves. Sharon first held one hand toward the Tic (but not touching it fortunately), and then screamed a long, full, continuous scream. She immediately took another breath, and she screamed again.

At this point, Leland suddenly threw himself against the screen of the window, attempting to attack the Tic that he perceived was threatening his wife. (And may I just comment here: this was brave of him.)

But fortunately, he missed it. When he collided with the window screen, it momentarily caught him and before giving way, held him back just enough that he fell down next to the house. His wife momentarily looked at him, and he at her. But as their gazes both whipped back toward the Tic, it had disappeared.

(Incidentally, when a Tic is spawned, it forms proximate to the Space Sieve, but its exact location is random. Its appearance next to David's mother was a coincidence.)

The Tic was gone, because it had been removed. If you've been paying attention, you know what that means. And if you haven't been, what it means is that the Space Sieve, tragically, now believed it was in the hands of an experienced operator. David had learned enough to operate it with sufficient skill to remove the Tic. The Space Sieve was now operating with full functionality, in the hands of someone who had sufficient skill to get past the Tic.

While very interesting, this was a great tragedy. It was a tragedy for David, for his family, for the other three children I mentioned previously who were at the Thanksgiving party, and for their families. And it was even more of a tragedy for many other beings of which you are presently unaware.

Upstairs in David's bedroom now, the screen of the Space Sieve had changed completely. In place of the yellow parallelograms that had been moving across it, the screen first glowed crystal blue, then black, and then it had images – and the images that appeared now were very easy to distinguish. If you have ever seen images of stellar phenomena, such as nebulae, galaxies, planets and the like – this is what blazed upon the screen of the Device, changing from place to place, from scene to scene, at David's will.

What he now saw so vividly on the screen of the Space Sieve – and as it all lay waiting obediently and patiently for his next whim and for the next movement of his fingertips – was nothing less than the totality of all creation.

Except these were not images. Although still in his bedroom, and although I seriously doubt that you can comprehend it, David was looking directly at the actual stellar objects themselves. To repeat: As David's view through the screen of the Device skipped from place to place, galaxy to galaxy, reality to reality, like a child flipping through channels of one of your televisions, what David was seeing were not images. Through the power of the Device, David was looking directly at the actual objects themselves as if through an open window.

If you can't comprehend how that is possible, you needn't try to, nor worry about the fact that you can't.

David's eyes, while still eager, were glazed now, and he looked very ill. His skin had a lifeless yellow cast, his clothes were drenched with sweat and his clammy hands trembled. His level of obsession and skill with the Device had continued to increase, but his physical mind and body were depleted. He would have given everything to continue, but the sugars, nutrients, cells, and energy levels inside his own physical body had reached their limit. His body could go no further.

To his dizzy dismay, David's shaking hands involuntarily fell to his side. The Space Sieve immediately turned dark and smooth as it had originally been, and the stool upon which David sat – the stool that he had created with the Space Sieve – disappeared – and David fell onto the floor.

Outside the house, his parents frantically looked around for the just-vanished Tic. Until they heard the thump from upstairs they had been so preoccupied they had completely forgotten about that which they considered most precious – their children.

Sharon and Leland, together with Mike dashed up the stairs to find their little ones. They quickly identified the locations of their other children, but when they found David they became hysterical.

He was lying on the floor in an unnatural position near the strange object, his mouth open, his hair wet.

☼ CHAPTER 4 ☼

ECLIPSE OF THE MORNING

QUICKLY REVIVING HIM, they cleaned David up and put him to bed, confident that he had no fever or illness that they could detect.

But unfortunately, David did not honestly tell them what had been going on. In fact, he lied to them, telling his parents he had passed out from exercising – not a very credible story really. Moreover, on this evening, having lied to them, he now continued a pattern of lying to his parents. This began innocently at first – he didn't feel he *could* tell them what happened. But lying, it seems, once begun, becomes easier for most of your kind. He began to deliberately mislead his parents, and indeed, began to actively plot their deception.

Had he not done so, a great deal of sorrow would have been avoided. For his parents, while completely inadequate to assess the capacity and function of the Space Sieve, were capable of recognizing dangers to their children, and were certainly more capable of doing so than was David for himself. At a minimum, his parents had the prudence that comes with age, and would not have allowed David to venture nearly as far with the Device as he ultimately would venture with it.

David, for his part, after that first evening recognized he was obsessed with the Machine. He also knew that to give himself over to that fixation as he had been doing, would ultimately lead to destruction of his health and more importantly to him, to the Device being removed from him. He could not allow that to happen, and he knew that this is exactly what *would* happen if he was too preoccupied with it. He realized this shortly after he found himself lying on the floor next to the Device with his hysterical parents

29

leaning over him. Later, he realized it even more as he heard them talking about the days of school he had been missing, about how odd he had been acting at his grandfather's house, and about how distant and strange he had been lately. And he could see they were making connections about where the problem really was.

But he felt the pain of his obsession most of all the next morning, when he awoke and found the Device had been taken out of his room.

This presented a difficult situation for him. He *had* to have it back. But if he was too eager, too persistent, he knew his parents, fearing for his health, would recognize his obsession, and would never give it back to him.

He got up and went downstairs. It was Thursday, and breakfast went normally. But he could see his parents eyeing him, waiting for him to ask about the Device, and so he didn't.

But finally his brother broached the subject.

I will point out here, as I have done in the past that I do not give irrelevant details in this account. I have not mentioned the names of David's siblings, nor have I even related their number. These details are no more relevant to this account than what David had for breakfast, what he was wearing, what his parents were wearing, where in the house they ate their breakfast, the color of the chairs, etc. I have no intention of prolonging my ordeal in using your manner of communication any longer than necessary.

If you want to read details such as those in a story, I would suggest you go get a work of fiction and read it. In the area of giving tedious, irrelevant detail, most of them will not disappoint in that regard.

"Mommy," David's younger brother said, "Why did you put that thing that David got from Grandpa in the garbage?" At first, David felt a rush of adrenaline-enhanced concern, and he could sense he parents were studying his face carefully. But his powers of reason quickly took charge.

"Ah," he thought, "now I know where it is – the garbage." He resolved he would simply retrieve it later. He began to formulate the rationale he would use when he did.

But then he felt a cold chill. He heard the throbbing diesel engine of a heavy truck in front of the next-door neighbor's house, and then he heard its brakes squeak as it stopped in front of his house. It was garbage day.

As he now ran to the window, David could see that among the rest of the family's garbage, was the Device. It looked unique – its dark form sticking out of the garbage container, contrasted against the brightness and color of the sunny morning.

David froze for a moment – he had resolved after all, to appear indifferent about the Device. But he instantly realized this artifice would be irrelevant if he lost it, and in seconds it would be loaded into the garbage truck. Running through the kitchen he crashed through the door and ran outside. By the time he reached the street the truck had already lifted the garbage container and it was beginning to tip into the truck.

David ran to the driver's door, and screamed, *"STOP!!"*

Unfortunately for David, the operator of the truck heard him, and did indeed stop the hydraulic arm. The operator had always imagined this happening – lifting a garbage container that held a child's valued possession, and having the child come running out of the house like this. Many men would have relished the opportunity to crush a child's hopes by dumping the garbage and continuing on. But this man had a kinder heart, and he saw the parents run out of the house behind David, besides. When he stopped the arm it was very near its highest point.

As he did so, the jarring caused the Device to come loose, and it fell. It crashed against the side of the truck, and David watched in horror as it struck the sidewalk. It hit hard on one of its corners, and raised a small puff of dust as it chipped the concrete.

He saw it all happen in slow motion, and being acquainted with the sorts of devices that your kind makes he believed the Space Sieve would be wrecked by the jarring impact.

Breathing heavily, he immediately up-righted it, and found the impact point where it hit the sidewalk. The curb had been chipped, and on one corner of the Device was the white concrete dust.

But as David ran his fingers along the Device and he wiped the dust away, he felt no chip, no dent, no scratch.

It remained unchanged, undamaged, perfect.

When Leland saw how robust it was, in hindsight he regretted having thrown it away. It was old, after all, and it had been Grandfather's.

He looked at his wife sheepishly. "You know Honey they really don't make stuff like that anymore. Look at the thing – not even a scratch."

(I might mention here, that there is nothing in, nor associated with, your universe that can damage this Device – there is no hard object, no energy in your reality that can mar it. Even the heat inside the core of your sun, cannot harm the Space Sieve.)

"Maybe," he continued, "we shouldn't have thrown it away after all."

Sharon looked back at him. "Lee, we *talked* about this," she said softly. "He's been missing *school* . . ."

31

But they agreed to let David keep it, so long as he would play with it for only an hour a day, and only after he had done all of his homework and the other tasks he was supposed to do were completed. In return, David secured from his parents the agreement that when he would play with it, he would be allowed to do so alone. (But he used the word "study" to refer to what he did with it. After all, who would believe a boy would play with what appeared to be an inert object? But his parents were able to accept, at least to a point, that David might want to "study" it. After all, he had pointed out, don't people study inert objects all the time?)

And so David kept his end of the bargain in exchange for his hour each day, and this went on for seven months, by which time David had become dangerously practiced in the use of the Machine, along the lines of which I will now begin to relate. As an introduction, and since you have probably already forgotten, it would be worth reiterating that when David first saw the stellar phenomena on the screen of the Device – the planets, the other worlds, the galaxies and the like – he wasn't seeing transmitted images. Although still physically sitting there in his bedroom, what he saw – looking at them directly – were the actual places themselves. It was as though, as I said, he was looking out an open window, directly at a tree, at the sky, or at any actual thing. That the objects he observed were billions of miles away or in alternate dimension of reality altogether, is irrelevant. He was in fact looking directly at them, and doing so from any angle he chose.

By the time summer came, David had already determined what he wanted to do, using the Device. He had chosen some first worlds he would visit and which, from his bedroom, he had explored in a general sense, many times. He resolved to start tomorrow, and to so begin the new life that the Space Sieve would provide him.

☼ CHAPTER 5 ☼

THE FIRST WORLDS

THERE IS A SAYING among my kind whenever the young begin to play: "The first worlds are always the hardest."

But as was the case with so many things, this did not hold true in David's case either. For David, the first worlds to which he traveled were by far the easiest.

However, David's first experiences *were* comparable to that of many other creatures in the sense that he initially chose to travel to realities that resembled his own – some with people like himself in them, and some without.

From each reality to which David traveled he was able, using the Device, to return to home very near the time he left, always complying, of necessity, with the 1-hour limit that his parents had placed on him.

As soon as David arrived at the first world to which he chose to travel (and details about how he did this and how he returned will be described later) he sat on his stool next to the Space Sieve and anxiously looked around the large, darkened room in which he found himself. The walls were made entirely of old concrete and there was a noticeable dampness. The gray surfaces were streaked and spotted with black slime, as was the floor, where the slime alternated with numerous black, hairline cracks.

As he glanced around, David saw tiny balls about the size of grape seeds here and there on the floor. They were solid, clear, and perfectly spherical, and were a reddish color. None of the tiny balls were stacked; each ball was resting directly on the floor, but while some of them clustered in large groups, many were scattered individually here and there.

David got up from the Space Sieve and began to walk across the room, taking care not to step on any of the balls. Momentarily however, he did happen to step on one of them. As it crushed under his shoe, it seemed to David as though the tiny ball had been only a thin shell filled with fluid. As he walked into another part of the dark room he noticed more balls – these about the size of BBs – that were translucent green and black. As he looked at them, David wondered whether they were the same sort of objects as the small red balls that he had just seen.

Just about then, he saw several of the balls move. They quickly rolled to one side, and then began to roll back and forth. The balls that had been clustered together in a group dissociated themselves from each other and also began to roll around on the floor of the room. For the most part they rolled in essentially straight lines, back and forth although some briefly moved in curved paths before resuming a back-and-forth direction. Neither the balls nor their movement concerned David, but it now began to appear obvious to him that these balls were some kind of living creatures, and it troubled him that he had accidentally crushed some of them.

David walked back toward the Space Sieve, and passing it he traveled to the other end of the room, where he found a ledge that dropped several feet. Near the edge clustered still larger balls – about the size of small peas – and these balls were a pale, clear blue color. As David watched, these balls too began rolling back and forth on the floor. Walking back to the Device, David activated it and used it to examine the balls that he had found on the floor.

He discovered the balls *were* a life form. They existed in this dark, damp world, and served the function of cleaning flat surfaces of the slime and various other forms of organic matter. They had no intelligence to speak of. Essentially, they just rolled around eating whatever they could find.

Another world to which he traveled had a large, indoor pool. The pool was 300 feet long, 100 wide, and 50 feet deep at one end. Oddly, the water in the pool was perfectly clear, except for a slight bluish tint, so clear in fact that David could see the bottom of the pool as easily as if the pool had been empty. This was something David had not realized before – until he saw truly clear water he had never realized how cloudy most water usually is. He realized that even the water in the clearest pools of his own world were actually relatively cloudy by comparison.

Around the pool near the deep end, glass walls and doors separated the pool area from dressing rooms also made of glass, some clear, some opaque, and there were bright chrome accents. Seeing only a few people around,

David helped himself to a swim suit which he put on, and he slid into the pool at the deep end.

But once in the pool, David felt an increasing sense of foreboding, although he couldn't tell why. A decent swimmer, David tried to swim out across the pool. But as he did, he felt terrified, and he returned to the side of the pool once again.

He resolved then to swim to the bottom of the pool. As he went deeper and deeper the water, he noticed that the pressure building on his body, and especially in his ears, was distressing. He stopped, and looked back up. He could see the surface of the water above and the light shining through it. He thought it looked like he was a mile underwater, and he once again felt the same sense of fear. He swam back to the surface, climbed out of the pool, changed back into his clothes, and left.

As he wondered what had been so frightening, he concluded that it was the perfect transparency of the water that struck him with trepidation. His experience in swimming pools had been in water that was much less perfect than that which was in this large pool. He concluded that the perfect clarity of the water enabled him to see more than he truly wanted to see.

Later, using the Device, he returned to the same pool again, but this time when it was night there. The room that enclosed the pool was largely dark, and the pool itself was only very dimly lit with a yellowish-green light. Once again David tried to go for a swim, but this time he couldn't even generate enough courage to get into the water. It seemed troubling how easily he could *see* how deep and large this pool was, and that he could still see the bottom of it, even at night. On another occasion he made a final attempt to swim in the pool during the daytime there, but once again found little success.

Having gone swimming in a lake before, and even in the ocean, David had been in much deeper water, including at night. But it was easier for David to swim in deep water when he couldn't see how deep it really was. By the same token, you are fortunate that in your present world your abilities are also limited.

You see, for your kind it is often better that you do not see everything. When you can, it frightens you. But since your sight is limited, you are able to be more bold. If you think back about your own lives, you may realize that in many cases had you known what awaited you – had you known what difficulties lay ahead of you – you would never have tried to accomplish some of the things that you did. And so, without being able to see the difficulties that lay ahead, you proceeded. Sometimes you have even taken what you call a "leap of faith."

If you always knew what lay ahead of you, you would become afraid, and you would venture far fewer things. And since you would try far less, you would therefore, accomplish far less.

In your present reality, your limited sight allows you to accomplish far more than what you would, if you could see as clearly as I do.

In another world David found himself on the top of a tall building, standing on large gray tiles. A few potted plants, attached to this surface, stood decoratively here and there. But momentarily, a chill swept over David when he saw that the edge of the surface on which he stood had no railings of any kind. Basically, if David had rolled a marble, it would have rolled right off the top of the building.

There were other people there too, sightseeing. As some noticed David, they did not perceive him as being different from themselves, nor did David perceive them as different from persons to whom he was accustomed, although he did not try to talk to any of them.

When a little breeze began to blow across the building, all of the people quickly left. As David stood there, he felt the building sway gently. This seemed mind-boggling to David, if not completely asinine. He wondered, "Why were there no railings?"

But the reason is simple: It is because the people he had seen there were immortal. Why protect themselves from falls when railings would obstruct their view and serve no useful purpose?

Another building David explored was a vast, brick one. Opening a door to a forum, he stepped out onto the dais, which was pitched downward at a severe angle, toward the audience which was 30 feet below and close in. On the dais were large, heavily-padded maroon chairs with high backs, and a few were occupied with people.

Strangely, the dais curved sharply away from the audience to the left and right, such that the chairs on those parts of the dais were not visible to the audience below.

As he looked down, David saw that the audience chairs, also sparsely populated at that moment, were also large and plush. Strangely, the chairs in the audience numbered only about 40 chairs – only about half as many as were on the dais. A disproportionate number of those who would attend this forum, it appeared, sat upon the dais, rather than in the audience.

As David explored the building further, he found signs with arrows, which he followed.

(You may be wondering: As David was roaming about, where was the Space Sieve? Whenever he went on his excursions he would simply, carelessly hide it somewhere – in a closet, behind a bush, or what have you. Was this irresponsible? Yes it was, and for myriad reasons that are so obvious I will not take the trouble to describe them.)

After climbing a distressingly-long staircase, David stood in an ante-chamber. At the opposite side an opening led into a large room. As he crossed to the opening and traveled through it, he found it to be a short corridor which appeared to be made of rubber. He emerged onto a smooth wooden floor in a room which he recognized as a dance hall, measuring 200 feet by 200 feet.

David walked to one of the vertical windows that were located at regular intervals on all the walls, and looked out. He could see far down to the street below. Tall buildings lined the street on each side. It appeared the room he was in was hanging from a bridge that was spanning the street between two of the tall buildings. As is the case with many boys, he was interested in engineering feats such as this appeared be, and so he looked out the window and upward, trying to determine how this heavy room was attached to the bridge, but he was unable to see any connections from the window.

As David headed off to the other side of the large room to take in the view from those windows, he broke into a sprint. When he stopped, his shoes squeaked slightly, and he noticed an odd sensation, like the floor under him had *moved* slightly.

It occurred to him that the room itself may have moved as a result of his coming to a sudden stop. He sprinted a short distance, and again came to an abrupt stop. Once again, it seemed to him that the room moved slightly.

Two young men each appearing to be in their early 20's saw David, smiled and came over near him. In unison, they began to step forward, stop, step back, stop, step forward, stop, etc.

This time David definitely felt the room swaying, if only slightly, in rhythm with their movements. Soon, another joined them. As the threesome now stepped forward and back, David could see through the windows of the room that it was now indeed swinging slightly back and forth. Some excitement was heard outside the room, and then a large group came into the room and also started stepping and stopping in unison. Everyone but David was nicely attired.

As the room swayed more and more and the people became more and more delighted, David began to realize that the entire room was hanging from the bottom of the bridge by a single point. The entire support for this heavy, hanging room was a solitary shaft, so that the whole room could swing in response to the crowd inside. And the people currently in this room were now having quite a time dancing and stepping, as the room itself swayed more and more.

Picture a street in a large metropolitan city lined with skyscrapers, and a bridge, crossing high above the street, connecting two buildings. Picture a square, one-story room hanging from the bottom of this bridge, like an apple hanging from the branch of a tree.

David was neither dancing nor stepping, but was just trying to keep his balance while watching the buildings outside the windows as they seemed to move and twist. It was scary to David, if not sickeningly, to be inside a large room that was full of people who were making the whole thing rock back and forth while it was essentially just dangling in mid-air, far above the street below. It occurred to David that he didn't want to be there, and didn't want to be around these people, and so, with a cross expression on his face, he left.

Of course, had he been in a different frame of mind, David could have seen all of this as being fun.

Other realities to which David first traveled included other worlds like your own, but with slightly lower gravity. David liked these worlds as it made it much easier for him to walk around and explore them, in some cases walking for miles along long, winding mountain trails. Once he saw a deep, perfectly-clear river that led to a terrifying waterfall. In some cases he would follow steep trails up vast mountainsides, climbing until the air became noticeably thinner (indeed, as the air was often thinner to begin with on some of these worlds.)

In one world there were transportation devices that to David resembled cars, and so they were. After watching people using them it occurred to David that nobody seemed to own any of the cars per se, but rather they simply existed for anyone who wanted to use one. Upon realizing this, David climbed into one of the cars. It was nighttime and in the darkness he saw that the controls of the car were different from the ones he'd seen his parents drive. But he was sufficiently intuitive that soon, off he went. As he traveled along, he turned into a drive that wound along the edges of a large cluster of buildings. Following this drive, he found its course was a long circular path around the buildings. Parking it now, David left the car and walked into the center of the structures. There he found a large, concrete plaza. He walked along, and as the night had now turned to day, more and more people were walking through the open space. Eventually, David came to a long concrete foot bridge that arched over a wide river. As he walked up the rising side of the bridge he saw the flowing water below – a wide, swirling, eagerly-moving mass of brown, drifting fluid.

Walking down the far side of the bridge, David first came to a wide dirt field and then he crossed a street. Standing at the curb beside a listless-looking tree and looking around, he was soon joined by three girls on heavy, two wheeled vehicles. These machines were laden with chrome and were accented with scarves tied to various locations. The girls seemed somewhat rough and masculine – although they were clearly female – and they took a level of interest in David that he found disturbing. As they climbed off their bikes and approached him, David smiled, but winced. Upon seeing this, they immediately lost interest, climbed back on their machines, and left. David quickly retraced his steps back over the bridge and returned to the place where he had begun.

Once there, David came upon a being that was clearly not from that planet. This particular individual was an ambassador from a distant world – one that had an ecosystem based on oxidation by fluorine, rather than oxygen. Therefore this creature could not be exposed to the air on this planet, but since he was required to visit it in his official duties, he wore a "rendezvous" suit. The shiny black, skin-tight garment covered him completely and was not so much an outfit as a device in itself. It provided his body with the fluorine he needed to breathe, nutrients, and the appropriate temperature, as well as removing his bodily wastes, all the while perfectly separating him from the oxygen-rich environment around him. It made it possible for him to see, hear, smell, and to experience the other forms of sensory contact that were particular to his species. Wearing this device, the ambassador was to interact on this world in performing his duties, all the while being completely separated from it. But remarkable as it was, the suit was uncomfortable and so constraining that it often became oppressive for him even to move while in it.

Perceptively, David recognized this suit as a mechanism, and marveled at the technological miracle that it was. And yet, using the Space Sieve, David himself could have created a rendezvous suit that not only performed all the functions that the ambassador's did, but would do so while being entirely imperceptible to the ambassador and to every one around him.

As gifted as he was, David never obtained even the slightest inkling of what the Space Sieve's capabilities truly were.

As easy as walking was for David, he finally realized that walking is not as easy as flying. And soon, David experimented with that as well. And contrary to his experience in the large pool that I described, David was not afraid to fly. For when he was in the pool, he was swimming under his own power, and he felt alone. But when he flew, he did so using the power of the Machine, and as such he felt he was in the secure embrace of a friend. But of course, this was an illusion, because the Machine was not David's friend or any one else's, for it was not alive at all. It was merely a Device – a Machine – that responded to the commands given it.

David's first approach to flying was to create a field around him so that he had only a very small amount of weight. But he found that being largely weightless made it very difficult to travel in any direction except *up*. He found that when he was almost weightless it was a lot easier to push off the ground than it was to flap back down to it.

Recognizing he needed more propulsive ability when airborne, he set a different field around his hands and feet so that the viscosity of the air around them was proportional to the speed at which they moved. In other words, the faster he moved his hands, the thicker the air became around them. The slower they moved, the thinner the air was. Thus, he could move by flapping, but could also cruise.

The practical effect was that David could swim through the air much like a fish swims through the water. The best way to visualize this would be to imagine that the world you live in, instead of being filled with air, was filled with a perfectly clear liquid that you could breathe and swim in.

After he became practiced in this method of flying, David spent many an afternoon, coasting leisurely along the tops of trees, rustling the leaves with his hands as he passed along. Lazily turning over in the air as he flew, he saw sky then ground, they sky again. He liked drifting alongside trees, and gently coasting among their branches, effortlessly nudging himself along from branch to branch.

Kicking himself upward from the ground, he could now float confidently into the air. Several times he flew far upward into the clouds of the worlds to which he traveled, and felt their cool, misty darkness as he lingered inside them.

Then, he would return to the ground once again, drifting slowly along, with an occasional flip of a hand, hanging, hovering in the air, with the Space Sieve standing silently below. It seemed to him like an attentive parent, watching as its child played.

As David began to become more adept at flying and therefore began to fly faster, he found the problem of the wind rushing in his eyes and ears. So he created a bubble of dead air around his body except for his hands and feet, which allowed him to fly rapidly, as birds and insects do.

As he began to fly faster, he found that it was more effective for his arms to act as wings. But this created still another problem. Light as he was, with his arms acting as wings he did not have the strength to keep the back half of his body from swinging behind as dead weight.

He found the solution in the design of the dragonfly. Making both his arms *and* legs act as wings, he found he could fly skillfully, approaching the agility and aerobatic ability of that insect. On one world, he found an aging castle. After climbing to the top of the ancient wall, he looked down to the grassy ground seventy feet below, and he dove off. Keeping his arms and legs outstretched he raced downward with the castle wall racing faster and faster in front of his eyes, and with the ground racing upward toward him. Tilting his hands slightly into the rushing air, his fall became a graceful swoop. He felt the g-forces as his trajectory broke into horizontal flight, and he adjusted his course as he first raced just above the grass, then jumped to cut across the top of a row of trees, blazing in their fall splendor. With another slight adjustment, he rose executing a long, graceful arc, rising into the sky.

It is perhaps difficult for you to imagine – grounded to the Earth as you are – what it feels like to fly – to be simply free in the air. Of course, you have your flying machines, and you even jump out of them and free-fall as the wind tears at you. But it is entirely different to feel only the slightest sense of the air around you and to be able to control your flight at will, like a dragonfly, free in the sky. This is one of the greatest experiences a living creature can ever have, and it is one of the many reasons beings such as I feel a sense of wonder at how primitive your human lives truly are.

Of course, these sorts of experiences did little to stem David's increasing intoxication with the Space Sieve.

But as joyful a thing as flying is, it is also pleasurable to walk. And in the end, David found time and time again that the more interesting things in life are often those that are closer to the ground.

In fact, one of his favorite worlds was one in which he never flew at all. In that lone, largely empty place there was a vast, flat plain with the jagged form of low mountains far in the distance. The colors there were mostly orange and white, and he seemingly endless flatness had a pattern thin lines and squares like an endless checkerboard, with the individual squares measuring five feet across that stretched to the horizon. David loved the splendid isolation, and he called the world, "Parallaxia."

Given David's personality, he could have gone on like this for a long time – traveling from world to world and from reality to reality – alone. For

41

David was what you would call an "introvert": someone who is most happy when alone, or in the company of only one, close friend. Indeed, as time passed David began to think of the Space Sieve more and more as his closest friend. This was not good, as the Device was not a being of any kind but only a machine, having no capacity for love or for any emotion. But as time passed David felt more and more that between himself and the Machine was all that he needed, or all that he would *ever* need.

Part of the reason that people such as David seek, sometimes desperately, to retreat from the world is because of the way people in your world treat beings like David. You would think that for anybody to simply want to be left alone from time to time would be no great request, but this is something that your world views with great disdain and contempt, and sometimes, even anger.

For you see, the vast majority of your kind are what you call "extroverts." (I say the majority of you are extroverts, but it turns out that a majority of the more intelligent of your kind are introverts.) And what the majority – extroverts – seek more than anything else is the clatter and din of constant companionship. You will recall many instances in your own experience where extroverts will sit around talking about absolutely nothing, while an introvert like David will be off, alone or in the company of a single friend, doing something interesting – such as when David was learning how to use the Machine upstairs in his room. Often, extroverts will go on for hours, talking incessantly about subjects noteworthy only for their supreme inanity, while if there were an introvert present, he would have had to leave the room before too long to be able to retain his sanity. And for this, the introvert would be viewed with concern and suspicion, and even hostility.

A more vexing feature of extroverts, and one that is currently unknown to your science, is the fact that extroverts *need* introverts. They need them the way a mosquito needs an animal from which to suck blood. Extroverts take great interest in introverts, and it is from introverts that they draw much of their emotional energy. It is for this reason that extroverts cannot leave introverts alone – they must talk to them, or at least talk *about* them. A room full of extroverts will eventually have to find an introvert to prey upon, in order to be able to feel "recharged."

If you want to do an interesting experiment sometime, fill a room with nothing but extroverts. Let them clatter for an hour or two. Then, as they are nearing the point of exhaustion, send another extrovert into the room. It will make little difference.

Then send in an introvert. The extroverts will descend upon the introvert, as David's grandfather might say, "Like a barnyard full of chickens setting upon a June bug." The extroverts will try desperately to interact with the introvert to the largest degree possible, all the while destroying the object of their attention. Again, as his grandfather would say, "Like a pack of dogs playing with a frog."

Let us not blame extroverts in one sense, for like the chickens and the dogs, they are simply acting upon instinct. They only know that the introvert has something they *need*.

But on the other hand, human extroverts have something that chickens do not, which is the capacity for empathy and reason. Unlike the chickens, extroverts could see the damage they are doing to the introvert, and stop. But in most cases this does not happen. For if one is a chicken, what other purpose is there for a June bug, than to be eaten by a chicken? And if one is an extrovert, what other purpose is there for an introvert than to supply the extrovert with what he needs?

And yet, in spite of their need, extroverts typically feel contempt for introverts, as many of your kind has contempt for things that are different. And perhaps most remarkable of all is that extroverts spend a considerable amount of their time trying to find ways to turn introverts *into* extroverts. You may have noticed that which is common often seeks to turn that which is unusual into that which is also common. (This is what many of your human governments and construction companies seek to do, for instance.)

Failing to affect the change in the introvert (as they must fail, for an introvert cannot be changed into an extrovert) they seek to heap disdain upon the introvert. Indeed, introverts are often among the most mistreated groups in your human societies.

Let me hasten here to observe however, that extroverts are not bad people, per se. On the contrary, they are often very good. But being so dominant, they often overrun introverts, whether deliberately or unwittingly.

Because of all these reason, most of which he was unaware, the danger was that David might have one day left your society never to return, finding entirely within himself, amplified by the inconceivable power of the Device, all that he could ever want or need.

Ultimately however, he felt the characteristic desire of many creatures – that being a yearning to share these experiences – to be able to show them to someone else. (And after all, I am not so different. I wrote this book to share these experiences, didn't I?)

He decided to call his part-cousin and friend, Chip, over for a visit. Indeed, it was David's intent to take Chip to visit one of the more odd and strangely-poignant places that David had ever visited.

In the end, it would have been better had David simply taken Chip to go flying with him. In any case, the place David chose to take Chip was one he had already given a name.

He called it, "The Graveyard of the Gods."

CHAPTER 6

THE GRAVEYARD OF THE GODS

OVER THE COURSE of the preceding weeks, David had himself traveled to the world he called "The Graveyard of the Gods," as well as to many other worlds in addition to those I have described. Indeed, several of the other places he visited had been the graveyards of worlds. Graveyards had a special appeal for David, for reasons he did not understand.

But I, your narrator, *do* understand why he liked those places. First of all, they had a sense of solitude about them. Second, they reduced their occupants to their most simple level, stripped of all pretension. In a graveyard both the lowly and the mighty were all equal. Third, graveyards were interesting because they gave a sense of the culture that had used them. And lastly, David liked to see where societies had been brought to an end. Perceiving human society as often selfish and conceited, and while harboring a simmering resentment for the way his own culture sometimes treated people such as himself (and assuming others were the same) gave David a feeling of satisfaction to see civilizations that had met their deserved end. Or at least that was the way he felt about it, showing a substantial amount of selfishness and conceit himself.

As I mentioned before, many creatures have the interesting characteristic that after they discover something, they long to tell someone else about it. Thankfully, while David had no intention of telling the world about this Device, he *had* developed a desire to tell his part-cousin Chip about it. On the whole this was good, as Chip tended to be more level-headed than was David.

One morning in your month of July, he invited Chip over. This was gratifying to Chip, as he and David had been very frequent playmates in times past. But since the Thanksgiving party Chip had not seen much of David, who had not been interested in the sorts of things he and Chip used to do.

Not that David was always around - David had always been more interested in homework than Chip. But Chip felt it was different now - he really *never* saw David anymore. Chip didn't know whether David had found a new best friend, whether David had lost interest in Chip, or what. But Chip had accepted it and had moved on to other friends. And yet, none of these friends could hold a candle to David, in Chip's mind. So when David called him that day, Chip dropped his other plans and went to see him.

When David greeted Chip at the door he noticed the beaming smile on Chip's face. David realized how long it had been since he'd spent time with Chip, and David smiled broadly too, and he took Chip up to his room.

Chip's happy attitude however, immediately dampened as soon as he entered David's room. For there by the window, he saw the same black shape that had attracted David's attention at the Thanksgiving party. Suddenly Chip had a cold feeling that it was this object that was the cause for him having seen so little of David in the past months. It was bad enough to think that he had lost David to another friend, to schoolwork, or perhaps a job or something else. But Chip began to wonder now whether he had lost David simply to David's continuing obsession with this stupid, black *thing*.

Chip's smile was gone now. His wide eyes looked suspiciously at David, and his voice was formal and unfriendly-sounding as he asked David, "What is that thing doing here?"

Looking at the Device, Chip remembered David's younger sister had told Chip something about the dark object being in David's room. Now that Chip saw it again, the comments of David's sister seemed ominous.

"Close the door," said David.

Chip smiled nervously. But he didn't close the door.

"That's all right," shrugged David. "I'll close it myself in a minute."

Chip feigned calmness, then tried to portray the same playful attitude he had felt when he first saw David at the front door. Chip began to wonder if there was something wrong with David – if his best friend was somehow sick – and if perhaps he'd made a mistake. He asked himself if instead of just wondering about David, if he should have checked on him. He wondered if he should have tried to help David, and whether he'd already waited too long.

Chip walked over to the side of David's room. He ran his finger along one of the shelves. On it were two, small alcohol-powered toys that had been Leland's – an airplane, and a dune buggy.

Chip decided to try to make up for lost time.

"I've always thought these were so cool," Chip said. "Do you want to start them up? My dad has some old equipment and stuff we could use."

Chip took the dune buggy in his hands and walked over to David. "What d'ya think David?"

At this point however, Chip didn't really care about the toy. What he cared about, was David. He was subconsciously trying to diagnose David – to see if David was still the same boy he had known. And he wanted to get him away from the black object.

David did not give Chip any hope for optimism, however. He turned away from Chip, disinterestedly. "Put it down," he said, with an air of condescension. At that moment, Chip seemed strangely childish to David, and he wondered if he should have invited Chip over after all.

But Chip didn't give up. "No," he said. "Hey, I'd *really* like to play with this today."

David walked over to the Space Sieve. He began to rub his hand over the Machine, almost caressing it. A frown crept onto Chip's face.

"Okay. Don't put it down," David told Chip, with an air of superiority, "it doesn't matter anyway."

David placed his hands on the angled surface – the part of the Machine I have called the "keyboard" – and moved his fingers around in a deliberate pattern. Colored buttons protruded from the keyboard, and a stool appeared in front of the Machine.

Chip's frown increased, his brow furrowed. Strangely, his face suddenly looked quite a bit older. "Was, that stool there a minute ago?" Chip asked quickly. "That's funny – I don't remember those colored buttons either."

As David removed his hands from the keys and as the buttons and the stool instantly disappeared Chip involuntarily began to step backward toward the still-open bedroom door. David jumped back in front of the Machine and placed his hands on it. He moved them in a deliberate pattern, the keys and the stool re-appeared, and then David sat down and turned his head toward Chip. As he perched there, motionless he was disconcerting, almost spooky, to behold.

Chip turned toward the bedroom door and as it silently slammed shut in front of him he jumped back, almost hitting the Space Sieve. But catching himself, he landed on the floor beside it. Immediately, he sat up, leaning on

47

one arm. Eyes wide, he glanced at the closed door, then at David, and then at the Machine.

When Chip jumped, he had inadvertently thrown the toy dune buggy that he was holding. It flew across the room and hit the wall, breaking off a wheel. But neither boy noticed that just then.

"I told you it didn't matter whether you closed the door," David said. "But don't worry, nobody's going to come running to find out why it slammed because I made it so it didn't make any sound. Did you notice that when the door slammed it didn't make any sound?"

Chip *had* noticed, actually. It was the primary cause for him jumping, and falling to the floor. His concern for David was beginning to turn to fear. Chip began to wonder something that a lot of you humans have wondered in your lives, namely, at what point does compassion for someone else become a futility, and properly subordinate to your own sense of self-preservation?

In other words, at what point should you stop worrying about the *other* guy, and, figuring he is a lost cause, start worrying about *yourself*?

As David sat at the Device he looked down at Chip imperiously. Chip pitifully looked back into David's face trying to find there some flicker of his trusted friend.

Then, as he looked back into Chip's blinking eyes, David's heart softened as he remembered when the two of them had once found a wild bird caught in a net that a neighbor had placed over some berry plants. David had removed the bird from the netting and held it securely in his hands. The creature had fought to free itself for few moments but quickly realized that escape was impossible, and that its life was literally in David's hands. The bird was in a position where it could neither fight nor flee – all it could do was look at the boys with eyes wide, and hope. David remembered how bad it had made him feel to have terrified that helpless bird to that degree. And it was just a bird. Now, his best friend was looking at him the same way.

For a moment, David realized how fond he was of Chip. He remembered all the campouts, all the bike rides, all the sleep-overs. He remembered his life as it had been before the Machine. He realized he was really scaring Chip. He was arrogantly taking advantage of a power that he had, and that Chip didn't have. He realized it was wrong, and he didn't like himself for doing it.

David took his hands off the Machine and stood up. The stool and the colored keys once again disappeared.

Chip pointed. "There!" he said. "I know there was a stool there – you were just sitting on it! And there were colored buttons too!" He stood up.

"What's going *on* David?" Chip involuntarily wiped a tear from one eye, and then from the other eye. He stood there, breathing hard.

Increasingly, David had been realizing the power of the Machine, and the power that he had while in possession of it. Most humans – when they receive what they think is some power or other advantage – will immediately begin to think of themselves as superior to other humans. To demonstrate that power to themselves – to heap that sense of superiority upon their own lusts – they will begin to hurt other humans, perhaps unwittingly at first. But in any case, they will think little of it. Eventually, they will begin to hurt other humans just because they can. Without realizing it, David's mind had begun to travel down that dark path.

But now, standing there looking at Chip, David became conscious of something that few men or women who obtain power ever realize. David recognized that he too was only human, and he had no right to treat another so carelessly. For David to have gifts, abilities, and opportunities that Chip didn't have gave David no right to look upon him with contempt. Scaring Chip was wrong. David walked over to Chip and put his hand on his shoulder, and then David walked him over to the bed where they both sat down.

"Chip," he said, "I'm going to show you some things that are new today. I'm sorry if I was a little scary to you. I don't want to be. I'll try not to do that anymore."

For a few seconds, the two boys just looked at each other, then Chip glanced back at the Machine, and as he did he also saw the little dune buggy that he had accidentally thrown against the wall when he had seen the door slam by itself. He frowned. "I'm sorry I broke that. I always liked it."

David smiled widely, and impishly. "Don't worry," he said. "It's nothing. Watch *this*," he said.

Once again he stepped over to the Machine and placed his hands onr the keyboard. As he moved his fingers the keys and stool appeared, and he sat down and operated the Machine. After a few seconds, without looking up, David pointed at his shelf and Chip looked. There, next to the airplane, was the little dune buggy, perfect, just as it had been before Chip had picked it up. Chip looked over to where it had been lying on the floor, and of course, it wasn't there anymore.

After a few moments at the keys, David looked at Chip and smiled kindly. "All right?"

Chip, still concerned, nodded with feigned confidence.

Raising a finger, David beckoned Chip to come sit on a second stool that had materialized beside him. Chip sat down.

"Chip, I wanted to show you something today. Are you ready?"

Without smiling, Chip nodded.

"Okay then," said David. "This will be a little strange."

He operated the keys then looked at Chip. "Here we go."

Involuntarily, Chip put his hand on David's thigh near the knee, for support.

"Are you *sure* you're ready?" David asked. "This is going to seem pretty big."

Chip took a breath, and nodded. David smiled, and then looked back at the Machine. He worked the keyboard, and strange images momentarily appeared on the screen, then, the place David called, "The Graveyard of the Gods" appeared on it.

At a point about five feet directly behind the Machine a small circle appeared and grew very rapidly. Inside the circle was a different place from David's room. The circle grew and swept toward them until it was directly overhead, running down and around them from side to side. Imagine you were inside a large hoop that starts above your head, runs down to your left and right, and underneath you. You are suspended inside this hoop at its exact center. As you look to the front you see one scene; behind you, is another.

The hoop swept over them and shrunk to a small circle behind them and disappeared. All of this happened very quickly – in about two-tenths of a second, after your manner of reckoning of time.

David, Chip, and the Machine had traveled 2/3 of the way across their own universe and had penetrated through fifteen dimensions of reality to arrive at this location: The Graveyard of the Gods.

David smiled and relaxed. In your own reality you humans create entertainment that seeks to convince you that you have escaped to another reality. For this reason, what just happened did not seem so strange to Chip even though, of course, he did not comprehend what had just happened at all. He looked up at the blackness overhead then noticed the ground was paved with black, shiny cobblestones.

The boys were in a vast yard, surrounded by huge, sculpted heads. Pathways crisscrossed between the heads, which were arranged in rows. One of these paths lead to a collapsed stone gateway.

Chip noticed one of the heads was made out of white stone. Most of the heads were made of black stone, and a few of red stone. The heads

50

themselves were all polished, each was about eight feet high, and included a neck but no shoulders. Each stone head was on a pedestal, making each about twelve feet high overall. Most of the heads struck a noble pose. One carved head appeared to be laughing. One of the red ones was tilted up, and appeared to be crying in some kind of agony. Chip stood up.

"Wait," David said. "There isn't any air here. We're actually inside a bubble around this Machine. Let me put out an atmosphere so we can walk around." And so, using the Device, he did.

The two boys started walking down one of the paths, leaving the Machine behind.

"Where *is* this?" asked Chip.

They continued to walk. "It's kind of interesting," David said. "This planet was once a great civilization. The men attained levels of wealth, leisure, and power that we humans can only dream of. They became so great they came to think of themselves almost like gods. Because they were all great, they created this place – this final resting place – so their monuments would all be essentially the same – none bigger than the others – although they could all be different, and all would be large.

David enjoyed serving as tour guide.

"How do you know all this?" Chip asked, and seemed satisfied with David's terse answer: "The Machine." David knew all this because he had traveled here before, and had researched it.

Chip stopped. There on the ground in front of him lay a small object of clear amber color. He reached down. David grabbed his arm.

"Don't touch it," David said. "You *can't.*"

Chip trusted David. What choice did he have?

"Why?" Chip asked.

"This planet's air was stripped away," David said. "I put air – an atmosphere – here in this cemetery – but I left a skin on everything – it protects these objects around us from the oxygen in the atmosphere I created."

"Well what about our *feet*?" Chip asked.

"I placed a different skin on the bottom of our shoes. It interacts with the other skin so we can walk on the stones. I could have fixed it so we could have touched things – but I didn't think that you'd . . ."

Chip squatted down. David started to stop him from kneeling on the cobblestones, but Chip wasn't going to – he'd heard what David had said.

The small object lying on the ground in front of them had the shape of a young woman, lying in horizontal pose, carved into clear, reddish-colored glass. Next to her lay a pedestal, and a small white table upon which she had been resting. When the pedestal had fallen over eons ago, her small amber sculpture had broken off.

"They really looked like us," Chip said.

"There were a lot like us," David replied.

In the distance, in the stark light of a dying sun were huge works of marble and stone: the remains of their city.

"Notice that this is only one of a few sculptures of women that you see, and it's small compared to those of the men," David said. "It shows the place women had in this society. They were property, like a dog. Of course, they were valued more than dogs."

"What happened to all of them?" Chip asked.

"Well," David continued his tour guide speech, "they had this great civilization – they had it really good and everything – but one day their scientists noticed that the magnetic field of their planet had shifted a little. After a while *everyone* noticed because it got to where it was about 60 degrees off the poles – the magnetic poles of the planet were closer to the equator than they were to the rotational poles of the planet." He held up his hands and made a ball shape. "So here's the planet like this. Here are the north and south poles." David pointed to the top and bottom of his imaginary planet. Then he pointed to the sides. "And here is magnetic north and south – closer to the equator than the north and south poles. It shifted that way for a long time. And then it weakened – long enough for the planet to lose all of its atmosphere – all of its air."

Chip had a puzzled look. "You mean the air on a planet is held down by *magnetism*?" Chip asked.

"No," David chucked, "the air is held to the planet by *gravity*, but the thing is, there's the solar wind." Chip looked blankly. David struggled to explain. "See, all these particles come streaming off the sun, and the planet's magnetic field directs the solar particles to go up and *over*, or down and *under* the planet. If the magnetic field lines are at north and south, the particles from the sun mostly miss the planet, except some get through at the poles – that's what causes the auroras."

"See," David continued, "If that *changes*, then the solar wind no longer is directed around the planet – it impacts the planet, and especially where it hits the planet at the edges, it knocks the air molecules into space. The planet's air is just slowly blown into space by the solar wind, just like sand blowing away in the wind.

"Their scientists first noticed a drop in the pressure of their air. Then people started to die at a younger age, some plants died out, and then other stuff happened. Eventually practically everything died as their atmosphere became thinner and thinner. This was a long time ago, though."

"So they had no enemy that killed them" Chip said. "Basically the natural – you know – environment on their planet changed and it killed them."

"Yes," said David. "The air being blown off the planet killed everything except a few types of creatures living at the bottom of their oceans. You know, it doesn't take much for a planet to end up like this. People back home worry about having everyone die from wars or from an asteroid impact or something, but there are a million easier ways life on a planet can be wiped out - it's really very natural."

"For another thing," he continued, waxing somewhat philosophical, "most planets have enough trapped underground gas that it could kill everything if it escaped," he shrugged. "Under our own oceans and crust lie enough trapped gasses and stuff that if it escaped, it would poison our atmosphere, if not actually allowing our entire atmosphere to ignite.

"Of course, were our atmosphere to *ignite*, it would kill almost everything on the surface of the planet almost immediately. But since most of the sea creatures also rely on oxygen, they'd die pretty soon too. Really, before too long the only thing left alive would be anaerobic bacteria and worms living at undersea vents that were . . ."

"Okay, okay David." Chip interrupted. It was troubling how casually David was when talking about the ways all life on Earth could end.

But David continued. "Most planets have cycles that if interrupted would kill everything. Like the carbon cycle on our own Earth. Funny, if it weren't for the volcanic activity on our planet, a lot of which is caused by the fracturing forces caused by the gravity from our large moon, before long our planet wouldn't have enough carbon dioxide in the atmosphere to sustain plant life. And well, without plant life . . ."

Chip interrupted again. "David," he said, "I think this is very interesting but I really don't think we need to . . ."

"Take asteroids," David continued. "People worry about a big one hitting the Earth and killing everything and making a lot of dust or whatever. But what they also ought to worry about is a really big one barely *missing* the Earth. See, the gravitational effect that would have on our planet's orbit is the really scary thing. With only a fraction of a degree's worth of change to our planet's orbit, it would become too hot or too cool to sustain life the way it does now. Or, the planet's orbit would become more elliptical – too hot part of the year and too cold the rest of the year – to sustain life.

"Even worse are gamma rays. You could have a sun explode – a supernova – somewhere in our own Milky Way galaxy or even a big sun in nearby galaxy, and it would produce enough radiation to wipe out all life – not just on Earth but all surrounding galaxies. In fact, since the radiation would travel at the speed of light we'd never even know it was coming until we all started becoming fried. Hey you know what? I could just look on the Space Sieve to see whether one has already exploded and when it'll reach Earth!"

"David," Chip replied, "you understand don't you, that we live on Earth, and our families?"

"Well," David continued, "with most of it we could at least see it coming. With the gamma rays there'd be nothing at all we could do . . ."

"David, I don't think I want to – I mean – what good does it do to know any of this if there's nothing we can do . . ."

(But of course in David's case, he could do anything he wanted about any of it. He had, after all, the Space Sieve.)

David sighed and looked around the graveyard. "What's really *not* natural is for there to even be any life on a planet at all. Like this place – all the power, all the glory, all the wonders these people created. Yet one small thing changed, and it is all gone."

"Yeah, okay. Okay." said Chip, trying to move on to something else. He looked up, and gazed at the stars overhead. "Boy, the stars are really clear here."

David nodded and looked too. "Yeah, it's the thin atmosphere,"

"David, why do the stars here move, like those two?" And he pointed.

David thought for a moment then explained, or so he thought. He was the one who was supposed to know everything, after all. "Those aren't stars moving, they're probably asteroids, or maybe rocks that are in orbit. With the thin atmosphere we can see them easier.

But Chip continued, "How come they're getting bigger? And look! Now they've changed directions."

"That's weird – I, I don't know why they would do that." David grew suddenly nervous. "Hey Chip, let's uh – get back to the Space Sieve okay?"

"The *what*?" Chip asked. But David was already running toward the Machine. Chip followed.

When they arrived back at the Space Sieve, it appeared frozen. The buttons, instead of their constantly shifting colors and shapes, were locked

into position. David sat down and motioned for Chip to do the same.
Touching several buttons, David brought the Device to life. Images appeared
on the screen.

"Shoot!" David exclaimed. "Those aren't asteroids – they're *ships*!"

"What? They're *what*?!" Chip asked. "You mean there are *people*
here?"

"Shut up!" David said. Then he looked at Chip, who was looking back,
eyes wide, like that scared little bird again.

"Chip," David said quickly. "I need you tc just be quiet and watch for a
minute, okay? I'm kind of worried and I need to *concentrate*, okay?" David
took Chip's hand and put it back on his knee again. "Here, hold on to me."
They briefly traded nervous glances, and David turned back to the Machine.

As David operated it, the skin flowed off the land and the objects around
them, and for an instant it seemed that the two of them were inside a bubble.
But then the bubble around them could no longer be seen. As David worked
the keys and images flashed across the screen, to Chip it seemed as though
David's operation of the Device was not as smooth as it had been before. He
wondered why David didn't just get the two of them out of there.

But David wasn't trying to leave. Succumbing to his own vanity, more
curious than afraid, he was lingering to study the situation.

"You know what the odds are?" David said, really to himself. "Do you
know how vanishingly rare it is to run into intelligent life in the middle of
nowhere like this? I mean, nobody should be here, and yet, there they are."

"David, one of the lights is still getting bigger. But the other one's
disappeared now."

"I know, I know!" David said, his mood tilting more to concern. "Do
you know what the odds are that if you *do* run into creatures out here that
they would have inter-dimensional capability? Chip I'm sorry. I should
have been more prepared before I brought you out here, before I risked . . ."

At this moment, Chip and David were both seated in front of the
Machine with Chip at one side, and they were facing the Machine. Neither
of them therefore, was looking *behind* them.

But behind them, creeping out of the darkness was one of those two
ships, and the beings inside were far ahead of David in their thinking.
Recognizing that he had begun to scan them, one of the ships had continued
to approach from space as a diversion, while the other had entered an inter-
dimensional seam and had slipped down and re-appeared behind the two
boys.

You may be wondering why the Device didn't warn them of this. Understand please, that this Machine is not these boys' mothers. It is a Device. It didn't warn them for the simple reason that David had not told it to warn them.

In the darkness, the one ship crept closer, behind David and Chip.
It was triangular in shape, pointed at one end, and this pointed end was approaching the two boys. The ship was twelve feet long, and five feet wide at the back end. It was eighteen inches thick. Essentially, it looked like a huge slice of pizza, without the crust, moving toward them, point first. It was largely gray, but was covered with tiny red and black rectangular tiles. Chip continued to look at the Device and at David, who was furiously working the Machine learning what he could about the ship that he knew was approaching overhead.

Then, Chip turned and from the corner of his eye caught a glimpse of the pointed end of the ship that was now about fifteen feet away and approaching slowly. But by this time, the ship had turned, and was coming alongside them.

He turned quickly to face it, and immediately his heart jumped and hammered painfully in his chest. He tried to speak, but could make no sound. He wanted to jog David, to warn him, but his aching body felt rigid as stone.

Once Chip saw it, the triangular ship suddenly illuminated itself in a blaze of blinding lights - largely brilliant white, but also with some red effects. Now David spun toward it and his mouth gaped.

And as he did so, he took his hands off the Machine. The keyboard, and the symbols on its screen, froze.

☼ CHAPTER 7 ☼

PLAYGROUND

YOU MIGHT WONDER WHY, if David took his hands off the Machine and it froze, how was it that the two boys were still alive? Why did the bubble of air that they were inside not vanish? The reason is because early on David had the prescience to set the Machine so that it would never take any action that would injure him, even if he made a mistake. And even when a person is not operating the Machine, it is still operating – it is never turned off.

As David and Chip had swung around to face the triangular vessel behind them, the Space Sieve, in turn, was now behind them.

And behind the Space Sieve, the *other* ship now dropped instantly into view. It was precisely spherical, perfectly reflective, and between the size of a basketball and a beach ball. It hovered, unseen by both boys.

Surely you must wonder that given the only salvation available to these boys was the Space Sieve, then why did they turn their backs to it? This is because often, your kind allows emotion to rule your actions at the expense of reason. This is a good example of that.

A single filament moved out from each ship and connected to the bubble of air around the two boys. As Chip and David watched the filament from the triangular ship (they had not yet seen the spherical ship behind them), the boys saw the filament grew thinner. It became gossamer as a spider's web, and yet continued to shrink, becoming still finer. As Chip watched, he thought it was the most slender strand he had ever seen, and yet it became thinner still. Chip began to wonder how he could still see it, and he began to wonder if there is some limit on how fine something can get. No matter how thin something was, could it not still be half as thin? And then, could it not be half as thin again, and again? The seemingly infinite thinness of the line connecting the triangular ship and the bubble around the boys began to make Chip's mind reel, even as the presence of the triangular ship continued to make his heart hammer inside him.

When Chip turned to David he saw he was now working the Machine again. And then Chip jumped when he saw the spherical ship and the filament that was also connecting it to their bubble of air. David glanced at Chip for a moment, then immediately went back to working the Machine.

Suddenly, both ships shot skyward. Their movement did not involve a period of acceleration as you are used to. One instant the ships were stationary, and the next, they were moving upward at high speed.

Then the bubble around the Space Sieve lurched violently upward, throwing Chip to the floor.

"Don't worry," David said apologetically, "I'll fix it so any other movements will be compensated for so we won't feel them. You won't get thrown around like that again no matter how violently they pull us or no matter how we move. I should have done it before."

As the ground dropped away from them Chip sat on his stool and placed one hand on David and one on the Device. He saw the curvature of the distant horizon increasing, and then he could see the entire planet itself as it dropped away.

And then there was nothing around them but blackness, points of light, and the planet's distant sun falling behind them as it illuminated the two small ships ahead of them in a pale but harsh light. Although once the planet was out of view there was no point of reference, and therefore no sense of movement, they were nonetheless being pulled rapidly into Space.

"Those ships are actually piloted by children," David said, motioning dispassionately toward the two ships, having once again resumed something of the haughty manner that Chip so disliked. "Those ships are actually a lot bigger inside than they look from the outside. That spherical ship over there – it actually has a forest inside of it. They use a dimensional discrepancy to create a bigger space inside their ships than on the outside. That other ship there – the triangular one – can slip into inter-dimensional seams. That's how they travel great distances. The triangular ship tows the spherical one into the seams. The spherical ship is used for lots of other things.

"They're towing us right now." David seemed about as concerned as if he were watching movie that he had seen many times before.

"David," Chip began.

David held up his hand. "Wait a minute. Watch *this*."

Suddenly the two ships in front of the boys lurched together then began to sway from side to side. Chip noticed that something seemed different now.

Looking back, Chip saw that the planet was once again behind them and was rapidly getting bigger.

"Now," said David, "Guess who's pulling *who*." He had retaken control of the situation.

"If we're pulling *them* now they why don't they just let us *go*?" There was a tremble in Chip's voice.

"Because I didn't give them that option," replied David, ominously.

The planet continued to draw closer, and it soon stretched to either side of them.

Momentarily, they had returned to the surface, where they came to a stop.

"It looks like the spider is now the prey," said David, raising an eyebrow. "I wonder what our friends there think *now*." David looked at the two ships. "Who's the boss *now* boys?"

Chip looked at the two ships, then he looked at David, incredulously. "David let's get out of here!""

"Don't worry. I don't plan to hurt them," David said, "I just want to play with them a little."

Chip was urgent. "No I really think we should go home, o*kay*?"

"Just wait," said David, "Just let me show you this one idea I have, okay?"

Chip paused. He knew he couldn't force David, but concluded that right now it would be better to bargain. "Okay, one thing then we go, okay?"

"Okay. Deal." David operated the Machine. "What do you think would happen if they could no longer see us? There, done. Now, suppose they saw a very dangerous looking ship over there." And as David spoke, a frightening new ship appeared on the opposite side of the two ships. It looked like a sea urchin – black, and a mass of spikes. Then suddenly, the spiked ship moved off and the two alien ships followed. David, Chip, and the Space Sieve followed as well.

"I realized that these two ships aren't actually ships per se," said David, "They're toys. The creatures in them are children. They're just playing. Let them chase that ship I just made."

"You mean . . ." Chip started.

David filled in the blanks. "They can no longer see us, I made that happen. Then I created that other thing for them to chase around so we can follow and watch."

When the triangle ship and the sphere tried to apply filaments to the faux urchin ship that David had created it veered and began evasive maneuvering.

"Let's have a look at their weapons," said David. "They have directed energy weapons. Let's sting them a little."

Suddenly, a dazzling white line connected the urchin ship to the spherical ship. The sphere pulled sharply to the side and three intense blue lines appeared, connecting the sphere and the urchin.

"The white line was a beam I sent out from my urchin ship up ahead there. The blue lines came from the sphere ship when it fired back. The beams move at the speed of light so it just looks like lines connecting the ships. You can't really tell which ship is firing, except for the color of the beam. If my information is correct, I think the triangle's weapons are going to look red."

Just then, three fearsome red lines appeared, connecting the triangular ship to the urchin. In moments, the three ships were moving at incredible speed, their weapons firing relentlessly upon each other, with David and Chip trailing behind, watching. As they all sped across the planet's surface, David and Chip matching the spend and movement of the three ships, the ground was beneath them, then overhead, then in front, then under, and then it began to swing wildly around them as the ships maneuvered and fired upon each other to the full extent of their considerable agility and speed. The two alien ships were, in their turn beside, then behind, then over, then under the urchin ship, attacking savagely with their awesome weaponry and being aggressively attacked in return by the urchin ship, all looking for any flaw to exploit in the defenses of their admirably able target. And as David's hands moved upon the glowing keys, Chip's eyes were filled with wonder at the sheer speed and power on display all around them.

Then, intending to glance down only momentarily, Chip's eyes locked upon the screen of the Space Sieve, and euphoria swept over him as he watched the strange, limitless shapes and characters appear and shift with mesmerizing speed, exactness, and intensity upon it. Although he didn't understand it, it was as if there on that screen he could see himself, David, the Machine, and the three ships. He could see inside them all, and he could see their past, present and future movements, as well as the planet and all of space around them, all at the same time. As enthralling as were events taking place all around them, the intensity and totality of what could be seen on the screen of the Space Sieve was far more overwhelming to his mind.

And yet, while it could have all seemed like a wild ride, there was no perception of movement inside the bubble around Chip and David. It was like they were watching a movie going on around them. And in spite of all of the frenzied movement, none of the ships ever missed. The blasts of light always connected their target.

"Darn it," said David, "You know, to really see what's happening – to really see the power of their weapons – we need to be closer to the ground." David operated the Space Sieve. "We have to get them to miss each other. Their ships are too protected. We need to see their weapons hit the ground."

With that, the urchin ship veered toward the planet's surface, and everyone followed. As it neared the ground it pulled up and flew at breathtaking speed only a few feet above it. The urchin ship began to disappear and re-appear in slightly different locations.

"A little phase shifting to stir things up," said David, growing excited.

The triangular ship disappeared, slipping into a dimensional seam, while the spherical ship continued to pursue the urchin ship, trading fire with it.

And, due to the phase shifting of the urchin ship, the spherical ship's beams occasionally did miss the urchin ship. Just as the spherical ship would fire, the urchin ship would phase shift – disappearing and instantly reappearing in a slightly different location resulting in the blue beams of the sphere momentarily missing and swinging aimlessly.

"Good. Yeah. This is what I hoped would happen. Watch for the triangle to appear overhead, as it emerges from inter-space. There!" David pointed, and Chip watched.

The air seemed to peel away as the triangular ship emerged from inter-space like an explosion out the end of a banana, and its three red beams blazed. But the urchin faded and re-appeared in a slightly different place. The scorching rays missed the urchin ship.

"Yes!" cried David, and Chip did too this time.

Rather than hit the urchin ship and have no effect, the beams contacted the ground. Volcanic quantities of rock, dust, and heat blasted into the air as the triangular ship turned to pursue the urchin, beams still aflame, cutting a vast canyon into the planet's surface. The boys' view turned to black as they traveled through the wall of expelled dirt and rock. When they emerged, the three ships had traveled a considerable distance away, weapons still blazing. The boys together with the Space Sieve held back, and they watched the ships speed off into the distance.

"What do you think?" said David.

Chip only nodded.

"Glad you came?" David asked.

Chip nodded again. "Yeah, and it's good to be able to spend time with you again David. It's been a long time."

Chip's wide eyes searched his friend's face, and then David looked at the screen of the Space Sieve. "They've gone back into space," he observed. Then looking at Chip, he asked, "Do you want to keep going, or go home?"

Chip paused, "Well, maybe we can do this a little longer."

David turned back to the keys and instantly they shot upward at such speed that the planet fell away from them and disappeared, and then they were once again deep in space, near the three ships which were still maneuvering wildly with their weapons still firing at each other.

"You know," said Chip, a little puckishly, "what would happen if they caught up with your ship? It isn't real, after all."

"Better yet," said David, smiling impishly, "Maybe our little ship up there is going to have a slight malfunction. Watch *this*."

Suddenly, the two ships – the triangle and the sphere – were cast in a stark light. Vividly in front of them, the urchin ship had detonated in a massive, blue-white fireball. In the silent darkness of space, the brilliant light spread until it seemed there was only the light and the black silhouettes of the two alien ships who, after pausing for a moment, entered the fireball. David and Chip drew closer, so they could see them when the light faded.

As the explosion dissipated, David and Chip saw the two ships fixed in place, motionless. David secured a close-up picture of them on the screen of the Space Sieve. The point of the triangular ship was once again pointing in their direction. David jumped when he saw this.

Chip's hand once again fell upon David's leg. "Okay, let's go home now David."

David was pensive. "Yeah," he said under his breath. "Yeah." and he worked the Machine. "Ready?" he asked.

"Let's get out of here David, wherever 'here' is,"

But it was not to be. A single filament once again emerged from each ship and the two filaments began to sweep around the general location where the boys were. Momentarily one contacted the bubble of air around the boys, and then instantly, so did the other. Then, as the two ships moved very close to the boys their filaments grew thinner once again.

"Shoot!" said David. "I made us invisible! How'd they *do* that?"

"David, you said we were going to leave. Now would be a good time, David."

"Chip I don't know how they saw us. Wait! That's it! Their ships use some kind of gravity drive for low speed maneuvering. They can't see us, but since we have mass, they can sense our gravitational field around our ship! Of course! It's so obvious . . ."

"Well, David the thing is, I really think we should leave, because those stars over there – a whole lot of them – they're moving and they're getting bigger. Actually, almost all the stars around us are moving!"

David looked up then chuckled nervously. "You know, I've got to stop looking when you say to look. I can really see a whole lot more looking right here at this screen."

As David was talking, Chip saw more filaments contacting the bubble around them. But now each time a filament connected the bubble around them, there was a faint rumbling sound.

"There," said David. "I've deleted our gravitational field, eliminated all electromagnetic fields around us, deleted our ability to reflect light (already did that) and our thermal trace. I've also eliminated some forms of sensory characteristics that are currently unknown to our science. We should be completely invisible now."

But Chip was looking around, not paying attention to what David was saying. "I don't think so David."

Appearing around them now were many triangular ships, but these were vastly larger. These were over a mile in length, and their pointed ends were all directed toward the boys. Behind these ships, and all around them, was a constellation of massive spherical ships.

Chip watched as the two smaller ships they had been taunting moved off and entered one of the larger triangular ships, and he spoke in a low tone, as if he really wasn't talking to anybody in particular. "I think those kids we were teasing called for a little help. I know you said we're invisible again, but I think they can still sense us."

Filaments continued to connect to the bubble around them, each time shaking it, and as the full magnitude of the fleet of massive ships became visible around them, Chip's voice drifted off. "I don't think we're going to fool anybody this time."

CHAPTER 8

DESTROYER OF WORLDS

PROGRESSIVELY MORE AND MORE FILAMENTS attached to the bubble around Chip, David, and the Space Sieve.

But David was not perturbed. "Oh, now *this* is interesting, you see all these filaments that are connecting to the bubble around us?"

Chip didn't say anything.

"Well," continued David, ignoring his friend's silence, "It's kind of neat. They're basically a weapon. Sort of like a spider wrapping its prey in silk, except a lot more powerful." He operated the keys on the Space Sieve. "You know what?" he asked rhetorically.

Chip didn't answer. What was he supposed to say?

David continued. "Once they have completed this web of filaments they are placing around us – all those sticky dots that are on the outside of our bubble – this is something they do to an enemy when it sits still long enough – once they complete their ball, well, let's just put it this way. Their enemy will not be going home, ever. See, when this ball is done it's completely impenetrable. It's like . . ."

"Hey!" Chip interrupted, and spoke tones that had clear sarcastic notes. "I know. Why don't we just sit here and find out some more interesting stuff about this? Yeah, let's just sit here while all these powerful ships try to kill us, and study it! That's a really good idea, David. Or maybe here's a better one: How about we get the heck out of here? How about that, David? What do you think? Think that might be another good idea?"

It was getting harder to overlook David's arrogance, particularly since it kept threatening their lives. David was confident he could save them at any time, but Chip now knew he could be wrong.

"Sure," David shrugged, "Yeah, we can go. I just thought it was kind of interesting."

"Let's just go David."

"Yeah well, okay Chip, Ready?"

"Please just do it," said Chip.

As David operated the keys, a spot began to appear behind the Device, just as had happened in David's bedroom, but as the spot grew and swept over and behind them, it did not reveal David's room, but the same place in which they already were. They had gone nowhere.

"Well that was different," Chip said, now feeling more nervous than anything else. "So David . . ."

"Shut up," said David, who was operating the Machine frantically now, and who was beginning to exude fear that Chip picked up on immediately.

After heatedly working the keys for several minutes, David suddenly leaned back and glanced frantically at the ball of filaments that had almost completely formed around them. "It's too late." And then he looked at the glowing symbols on the screen of the Space Sieve. "Oh no," he said.

Now the emotions that Chip had been holding so admirably in check began to take control of him. He put a hand on David's shoulder, then suddenly spun himaround to face him. "*What's* too late?"

But David didn't say anything. He turned back to the Device and slumped, and watched as the ball around them continued to be completed.

"I don't know what to do," he said slowly, "I think we're trapped here. I don't think we will ever leave this place, Chip. I'm sor . . ."

"What?" said Chip, "What do you mean we're never . . . ?"

David shook his head. "I . . . I don't . . . oh my gosh, what have I . . . ."

"What do you *mean*?" said Chip, and his voice had that strange, almost laughing quality that sometimes happens in the face of true horror. And his pitch was rising. "You mean we're going to have to stay here? For how long?"

"No, I don't mean we're going to *stay* for a long time. I mean we can't leave, *ever*."

"What? Can't? What, you mean we're going to stay here until we *die*?"

David sounded distant, if he was in a daydream. "I don't *know*," he said. "I don't know if we *can* die here."

"What?" Chip entreated, and he was almost yelling now.

"It's as I said," David explained. "Nothing can leave this ball from the inside. It's impossible."

As the thought of being trapped there rapidly grew, suddenly a worse thought gripped Chip. He waved his arms at David. "You mean our spirits when we die won't even escape this ball? Our ghosts will just stay here looking at our corpses – and at this black box – forever?"

David didn't directly reply to Chip's question, yet he seemed strangely resigned to it. "No," he replied. "Nothing can leave this ball, according to the laws of physics as I as I have learned them, from this Machine."

Suddenly they felt a lurch, and they were once again moving. "That was weird," said David, still dazed. "We shouldn't have been able to feel that lurch just then."

In the gaps that were still present in the ball that was forming around them, they could still see the stars. But on one side of them, they were growing red and fainter, and on the opposite side they were growing purple and brighter. And all of the stars seemed to be moving toward the red stars, some more than others. When most of the stars were clustered with the red ones, the red ones faded. Then, the few remaining purple stars seemed to tear away and there was only darkness around them.

David glanced at the screen of the Device. "It appears they just now pulled us to the brink of light speed, and thence into an inter-dimensional rift. They're pulling us off to, I would say, their home world."

In contrast to David's calm resignation, Chip was seething. "Well, it didn't take long to run into somebody out here! I thought you said the odds were pretty low for us to run into somebody. And it didn't take long to find out their technology is totally superior to this – this *box*!" And then he kicked the side of the Space Sieve. But he didn't feel sorry. In fact, he almost kicked it again.

David's brow furrowed. "What?" His eyes narrowed.

"I said . . ." Chip started.

But David interrupted, suddenly, seeming to snap out of the lethargic state he had been in. "I heard what you said!" An angry, accusing tone flashed in his voice. "Listen, Chip! Listen to me! I told you that the odds of us running into somebody out here were remote, and they *were* remote. It's math Chip! You can't *argue* with it!"

Chip shot back: "Oh yeah sure! Sure you did the math right!"

But David interrupted again. "The problem wasn't the statistics, I just did them wrong. I figured the odds of running into somebody in any particular place in space. And those odds are vanishingly remote –

vanishingly remote, Chip. But I should have figured the odds of finding somebody around a previously-inhabited planet – a ghost town, basically. The odds of running into somebody in a ghost town are usually a lot higher than the odds of running into somebody in the middle of *nowhere*!"

Chip started to say something again, but David interrupted again. "And as far as *this Device*," he said, pointing a trembling finger at it. "This thing is infinitely – *infinitely* – more powerful than these beings. If I only knew which buttons to push, I could literally . . ."

"What? Get us home?" This time it was Chip who interrupted, and his voice had a dry, snide tone. "Well I suppose when they get us back to their home planet, *they'll* be the ones figuring out which buttons to push on that thing. I'm guessing *your* button pushing days on that thing are about *over*."

David's eyes narrowed. "What did you say?"

Chip leaned forward and spoke again, as if trying to be clear, "I *said . . .*"

But David interrupted him. "Shut up! I heard what you said!"

And he pushed Chip away and whirled back to the Machine.

Then Chip showed an emotional restraint that would serve him well throughout his life, because he wanted to hit David just then, and he almost did. But in the same instant, he realized that it would do no good, and besides, he didn't really want to hurt him anyway.

David was concentrating now, and was regaining his strength again like an old lion defeated by an upstart rival, rousing himself to battle anew. "No," he said in a low voice. And he looked at the ships, still visible in the few remaining holes in the enclosure forming around them. "NO!"

Chip reached for David's shoulder. " Calm down, David. There might not be a whole lot we can . . ."

But David pushed his hand away. "NO!" he shouted. "NO! They *cannot* get this Machine!!" And he started operating the controls again. "There's no telling what they would *do* with it!"

I would like to comment now: Here we see two more interesting examples of human behavior. First, we see that David's handling of the Machine has been hardly what one would call "responsible." And yet, in spite of this he thinks that *he* is far more competent to control it responsibly than anybody *else* is. When in fact the Kex would probably have been much more responsible with the Device than David has been, or that he would yet be. (Incidentally, this is how the beings in the ships to themselves: "The Kex.") Indeed, it would have been better for David had the Kex taken the Machine away from him and returned him and Chip to their home world as they would have done.

The second example we see here – once again – is the power that emotion can have on your kind. But in this case, David's emotion – anger – paradoxically gave him the power to focus himself sufficiently on the task at hand to solve the present problem.

I say "paradoxically," because like most of your emotions, this one – anger – has the power to create as well as destroy. Love, anger, desire: all of these have great creative power – as well as great destructive power in your lives. Whether they are one or the other – whether creative or destructive – is sometimes a function of circumstance. But more often, whether your emotions are creative or destructive is more a function of the ability of the person to control those emotions and to use them appropriately.

In any case, due to his anger, David plied the Machine with skill and focus that he had not applied before. Indeed, in his anger, he operated the machine with a talent and determination at which even *I* must marvel.

In moments, Chip was startled to see that in addition to the screen on the Device itself, another screen had appeared to the right of it, as if floating in mid-air. Then, below this phantom screen materialized a transparent keyboard, and David began to operate it with his fingers. (By the way, have you wondered why, in order to operate this Machine, one must have fingers, and why it has a screen at your eye level?) Soon, another floating screen appeared in mid air, this time to the left, together with another keyboard below it with ethereal, colored buttons. And David was, in turn, operating all three of them.

Soon he looked up, and an angry smile crossed his lips. Several of the filaments tore violently away from the bubble around the boys, and the colossal ships to which they were attached went hurtling off into space. Seeing such massive objects hurled in that way gave Chip a feeling of vertigo, and he grabbed David to steady himself. David looked back at the screens and the keyboards. Chip noticed that David's lip was flinching, and each time it did, it seemed like more filaments were torn off the bubble, and more of the Kex ships were sent careening away.

"Too slow!" said David, his voice angry, and triumphant.

Now, Chip saw an image of a sun, growing larger on the screen of the Space Sieve, together with strange symbols he did not recognize. When he noticed that David and the Device were becoming cast in stark contrast by a bright light behind them, he whirled around and saw a blazing sun, rapidly approaching. An instant later, David, Chip, and the Device plunged into the sun's corona, traveling deeper and deeper into the solar flares and then flashing through the photosphere. Waves of plasma savaged the remaining

Kex ships and ripped their filaments away, forcing the ships to veer away in panicked retreat.

In moments, it became totally black around the boys. Although the temperature inside the bubble they were in had not changed, it felt hot to Chip.

David was breathing hard (so was Chip), and David was smiling now, wickedly. David gently slid a button on the machine, and Chip, David and the Machine were illuminated with a dull light.

"Does it seem a little hot?" David asked. "We're at the center of that sun we dove into." He waved his hand. "Our 'mighty' friends out there can't seem to come after us in here."

Chip wondered why it should be that it was completely dark in the center of a sun, but he didn't ask David about it. There was something of greater importance in Chip's mind.

Then, suddenly, David swung around and faced Chip. For an instant, Chip felt relieved that David appeared to have saved them from the Kex. But now the look on David's face was beginning to scare him as well.

David clenched his teeth as he spoke, and Chip noticed his fists were clenched too. "Those ships are all hanging around the outside of this sun that we're inside of right now, with others joining them."

He turned back to the Machine, and then pointed to each of the three screens in turn, but did so without looking at them.

"This screen," he pointed angrily at one of the ghost screens, "will destroy all of the ships in space around us. This one," he pointed to the other ghost screen, "will destroy those creatures' home planet – they call themselves 'Kex" – and it will destroy all of them wherever they are – all of them, throughout their entire galaxy."

Then David pointed at the main screen – the one of the Device itself. "And this one will now take us wherever we want to go, right now."

David was angry, yet excited, but Chip was horrified. He looked at David, eyes wide. "David, are you crazy?"

David looked back. His eyes were also wide, and frenzied. He replied, "What . . . you mean because we're inside the core of a sun? It's not a problem, we . . ."

"David, why would you do that?" Chip didn't touch David. It was a though he had realized something terrible about his friend. This was more important to Chip than anything else that was happening. "Why would you even think about that – about killing them – David, about killing *all* of them? What have they done?" He shook his head. "What is the matter with you?"

Interesting, isn't it? With all the power of David's intuitive mind, Chip was right. Now was the time for David not to feel, not to act, but rather, to think. Let there be no misunderstanding. While your kind has an intuitive mind that has great (and I would say, unappreciated) capability, you also have the ability to think, and you could use both of these abilities far more than you do. It was time for David not to act, but rather, to first think about what he was intending to do.

Chip continued. "David, for all you know these people thought we were going to harm some of their children. All they may have been trying to do is stop us. Maybe they just buttoned us up to where we couldn't do that anymore. So now, what, you're going to kill all of them for *that*?"

David looked at Chip with a shocked expression, then his brow furrowed. And then he turned back to the Machine. The two ghost screens disappeared. Then, a spot appeared behind the Space Sieve. It instantly grew larger as the boundaries of it swept over and under, then behind them, and then they were in another place. Once again, it was dark.

Chip looked around. They had traveled. They were someplace else. He smiled for a moment, relieved. Then he shook his head. "Why do you always take us to places that are dark?" he asked.

Running along to their right was a range of black cliffs over a mile high, and vast craters stretched before them. Everything appeared to be knife-edge sharp, and had a shininess to it, to the extent that it could be seen in the faint light. A white sun blazed far in the distance, and set the features in stark relief.

"This is where I like to go to think," David said quietly.

As Chip swung around, he could see something was different. The horizon was closer than it was at home – this planet was smaller than the Earth. Also, everything looked very hard, as if the entire planet was made of metal or glass. A tiny spot of light passed overhead. As Chip looked up, he saw a jagged, tiny moon.

"Don't worry," David said. "That really *is* an inert object. It's not a ship this time. I've already looked. There's nobody here – nobody for light years around at least – nobody in inter-space either."

Chip's expression was blank. He didn't know when to trust David anymore.

"Nobody's going to pop in on us through an interdimensional rift," David clarified. "There will be no unexpected visitors this time. If any of that changes, we'll immediately leave."

Still breathing hard, Chip had forgotten all about the fact that he and David had already been gone a long time, and should be getting back home. In the over-stimulated and somewhat dazed excitement of the moment, his fear became curiosity as he looked around the strange world. In terms of curiosity, Chip was not that different from David. "Let's just take a break here for a minute" he said.

"Yeah," said David. "I'll just put a skin . . ."

"Wait," said Chip. "This time could you just put air all over on this planet so we can walk around and, you know, touch things this time."

"Yeah," David shrugged. "I guess so." And without thinking, he operated the Machine.

Suddenly the surface of the planet turned white like a giant flash bulb, and in the same instant the bubble around them turned a brilliant white. It appeared as if they were once again inside the outer layers of a sun. Fearing they had again made a major mistake, the mood switched once more from excitement to trepidation. Chip bowed his head and looked at David. The unspoken thought was: "Here we go again, another problem."

But David was already operating the Machine. As he did, the light collected to one side of the bubble, and then like a wall it moved away. Then the light formed into a ball, and then the shining ball moved off to their left. David looked unhappily at the shining ball in the blackness of space.

Then he said, "That's the planet we were just on," and it appeared they were looking at a small sun. "Look," he pointed, "there's the little moon." And Chip saw the same, small, jagged moon still in orbit. Chip looked to the side and saw the planet's distant sun was still there too.

David leaned back and took a deep breath. He closed his eyes then after a pause said, "I wrecked it. Now I've wrecked my favorite thinking place. I never walked around here. I never tried to put out at atmosphere here before. But I should have known."

This time, in the interest of economy, *I* will explain what happened: They were in an antimatter universe. When David placed an atmosphere – air – on the planet's surface, that air – consisting of matter – immediately reacted with the antimatter of the planet's surface, destroying both the matter and the antimatter, and releasing a vast amount of energy that turned the planet's surface temporarily white hot. As David and Chip moved off to a suitable distance in space to see it, it looked like a small sun burning where the planet had been. It is not a tribute to David that he did not anticipate that this would happen.

Unlike David, while Chip found this world interesting, its destruction caused no sentimental feelings in him. Nonetheless, in making his next comment, Chip had the answer to the problem. "You know," he said, "it's too bad we didn't go home when we said we would. How many times don't we wish we could go back and do something over – to do something different the second time? But I guess that's just something we can never do."

David looked at Chip, thought for a moment, and then he operated the Machine.

"Why not?" he asked.

Moments later, the blazing orb beneath them had become a black ball once again – the planet was restored – together with the little moon, and the distant sun. Everything had been returned to the way it had been.

Then, a brown spot appeared behind the Space Sieve and it rapidly grew, sweeping over and under, then behind them, and Chip instantly recognized David's bedroom. The brown spot had been the front of David's dresser. They were home.

"Thank goodness!" thought Chip.

"Look," David said, pointing out the window, and then he pointed at the clock.

As Chip looked, to his surprise he could see it was not afternoon, but was still morning – the same time it had been when they left.

"Everything looks like it was when we were here," Chip said. "We were gone a long time but it looks like we came back at the same time as it was when we left. What, is it a whole day later?"

David paused, and then he spoke quietly, expressing a just-found realization. "I know when I've been gone to some places I can come back here at about the same time. But I think this Device can actually move things *back* through time, including *us*." And then, while studying Chip, David raised one of his eyebrows, and he said, nodding, "not just back, *forward* too."

"You mean . . . that black planet . . .?" Chip asked.

"I just reset the time index to prior to the time we arrived there. In effect, we had not been there yet. So we never destroyed it."

Chip pondered, then said, "Well great, so you mean this thing can change the past? So I can go back and undo all the bad things I ever did? I can do everything different – the way I would have wanted to do them if I did it over?"

"Well," replied David and he continued rather incoherently, "it could, I mean I could change *that* much of it – enough to fix my thinking place – the planet we destroyed. But it was in a non-time-constrained antimatter universe. I don't know if . . ." his voice trailed off. "But the thing is Chip, we did move it back through time. I mean, I'm not sure how it does it, but *I* come back here close to the time I've left, even when I've been gone awhile. That much we can do – I do it all the time. But I never thought I could actually go backward or . . ."

"So, doesn't that mean we could . . ." Chip began.

"Yeah," David continued, "I mean, I think you could be right. Maybe we *can* go backward and forward in our own time, ourselves."

They looked at each other for a moment. Now back in David's bedroom, it seemed they were safe once again. Everything was back to normal; all was well. In their minds emerged a fanciful notion that perhaps while frightening, all that had happened had been entirely safe and unreal after all, like a thrill ride.

As the thought of being able to travel through time began to distill on them, the boys' eyes aimlessly searched the room. Then faint smiles slowly appeared on their faces.

☼ CHAPTER 9 ☼

ALL OUR YESTERDAYS;
ALL OUR TOMORROWS

OVER THE WEEKS THAT FOLLOWED, David used the Machine to travel into the past as well as the future, many times.

David would set the Machine to take him into the past or future and then, after a specified time there, return him to his bedroom in the present once again. So for instance, he would set the Machine to take him 20 years into the past or the future in your world, to leave him there for exactly one hour, and then return him to his bedroom in the present at the same time as when he left, no matter what.

Each time however, he found himself simply sitting in front of the Machine. It would indicate that it had performed the requested function – that indeed it *had* sent him backward or forward in time. And yet, to David, it always seemed like nothing had happened.

Smart as he was, David never did figure out what had been happening. *I* on the other hand not only understand what happened, I will illustrate it with one example. In this particular instance, it was *Leland* who traveled back in time.

One day in the summertime, David set the Device to take him roughly 23 years back in time. He wanted to see what the world was like when his own father was a boy, and indeed, what his own father had been like then.

But just as he was getting ready to go, his mother called for him to come down for lunch, which he did. Being distracted as humans often are, he left the Machine "live" so to speak. As it sat there, it was ready to take David

75

back in time 23 years whenever David told it to. It was also set so that one hour after arriving, it would return David to the present.

What happened next was this: Leland had come home from work to take care of some matters, and he had also planned to have lunch there, but as he passed David's room he saw the Machine sitting there at the foot of David's bed.

"That's strange," said Leland under his breath, and the hair on his neck stood up as he first noticed a stool attached to the front of the Device, and then a single, small red button on the keyboard. The stool looked to be of solid construction – much better than what one would have expected that his son could have constructed. After running his hand along the stool and then testing it for strength, Leland sat down on it, and faced the Machine. A cold feeling came over him as his gaze fell upon the strange, red button. Then he reached over and touched it.

Leland was standing in the high school classroom, and he smelled the wetness in the air as the cool breeze from the evaporative cooler blew across him. Sitting down at his desk he took out his algebra book and his pencil and placed them in front of him. He glanced around the room. Yes, Jane was there. He had always greatly admired her, and the memory flashed through his mind of how once, when he and she had been alone in the school hallway, she had walked by and had started wiggling her hips noticeably as she went. But at the time, he had not greeted her or acknowledged her at all. Now, here in the classroom he dreamed that he would perhaps ask her out, or perhaps even take her to the Prom.

As the soft chalk clicked against the hard green surface of the blackboard, Leland's teacher was at the front of the class, drawing figures. He told the class that today they would be moving from pre-college algebra to something different. It was called "permutations" and "combinations" and was part of the subject of "probability."

"So you mean we finally get to learn something we can actually *use*?" Jim asked. "Will this stuff help me in *Vegas*?" Jim was the class clown, but the truth was, he was also one of the smartest kids in the High School.

Leland smiled as Mr. Day replied: "Maybe, who knows? But be sure before you go searching for the big time Jim, that you ask your parents." And the class laughed.

As Mr. Day described the subject matter on the blackboard, Leland wasn't listening. He dreamed first about taking Jane to the Prom, then thought about how he saw another girl he liked, Polly, kissing a boy he didn't like. He saw her outside the school, and she was kissing him for a very long time. And then, he was thinking about how he and his friend in years past used to play with Hot Wheels after school. They'd take the orange plastic track and string it down the stairs in his friend's basement, then back up against the far wall. They would let a car go down the track, and up the other side, and then as it came back, they would roll marbles down the track, bashing the car off. They did the same thing using other cars instead of marbles to bash the cars on the track. They would also take his friend's large slot cars, build cities on the slot car tracks, and then crash the cars into the cities directly, or using ramps so the cars would fly before crashing. Suffice it to say they were not too kind with the toys of Leland's friend.

Suddenly, Leland realized he wasn't paying attention in the algebra class. "Why is Mr. Day writing numbers with exclamation points behind them?" he thought. It didn't make sense, and he realized that he'd better start paying attention.

Leland had always been smart. He mused over the fact that all through elementary school and junior high, he had always been the smartest one in the class. But working his way up into harder and harder classes in high school left him realizing he was no longer the smartest kid in class – he found that now he actually had to *work* to get good grades. Now that he was a senior in high school, he determined that he would have to start buckling down.

But soon, he was daydreaming again.

He remembered how once his friend and that friend's two brothers had all been given new bicycles by their father. They had soon discovered that the bicycles, if they were brought up to speed and then jumped off of, would continue to travel a considerable distance all by themselves before they would crash. Soon, the three brothers had the idea of getting at opposite ends of the street and riding towards each other, jumping off, and letting the bikes crash, similarly to the way they'd played with their slot cars years before.

Drifting from reverie to reverie as the sun streamed through the windows of the classroom, he thought about how years ago he'd hurt his foot when he had jumped off his friend's roof, and about how as little boys they'd snuck around the side of his friend's house late one Friday night so they could listen to his friend's older sister and her boyfriend talking as they sat on the grass in front of the house, hoping to hear something embarrassing.

Leland chuckled at this memory as Mr. Day's chalk slid across the blackboard, and he had an indistinct awareness of his teacher's voice as it reverberated throughout the classroom. He really did need to start paying attention. As he looked around, it made him feel all the worse when he saw that even Jim was paying attention. Even Jane was. They seemed to be following what Mr. Day was saying. Leland on the other hand, had no idea.

It came as a surprise when the bell rang. Had the whole 50-minute class session already passed? He looked at the blackboard. "Thank goodness there's no homework," he thought.

He placed his pre-calculus book into his backpack and got up to leave the classroom. He remembered that today was the day he had committed to himself that we would stop Jane to see if she would go to the Prom with him. As he walked toward the door, Jane was nearing the door too. Leland could see from the corner of his eye that Jane was looking at him. "This is great!" he thought, "She's noticing me!" Then he made a distracted expression on his face like he was thinking about something important, and he hurried out of the room. As he headed down the hall, he thought about how good it had been that Jane had been looking at him, and that he would definitely ask her to the Prom tomorrow, which of course, he never did.

Leland headed out the door at the end of the school wing. His locker was in the next wing over. He had wanted for his locker to be in the same area as the one in which his algebra class was, as this was where most of the people he knew had their lockers. But as it happened, Leland's locker was in a wing where he didn't know most of the kids – who to him were just a bunch of odd balls who came from some strange, cross-town school.

As Leland walked along the sidewalk between the wings, he noticed the dry Bermuda grass. It was early spring, and as such, the grass was brown. Along the edges of the sidewalk was bare dirt, where the students would step off the sidewalk and wear out the grass with their walking. Even though it was still the cooler part of the year, there was already the faint sense in the air of the intense summer heat that was to come.

Opening the door of the wing wherein his locker was located, he felt the refreshing blast of the evaporative coolers in his face. As he walked toward his locker, Leland looked forward to the coming summer. Whether it was the swimming, the running around with little clothing on, the endless heat, or the days that seemed to go on forever, Leland really liked the summers. Turning the dial on his lock, he slid it out of his locker handle and opened the door. Lingering, he looked at the other kids walking up and down the hallway.

Then, after trading his math book for a book of English literature (which was his next class), Leland slammed the locker door shut, returned the lock, and clicked it shut.

Leland fell back onto the floor in front of Space Sieve, which was sitting there black and inert, as he had always seen it before. He immediately jumped up. "Wasn't there a red switch on the front of the Device? Where's the stool?" he wondered, and, "Why was I on the floor?"

He got up, shook his head, walked to the bedroom door, and with a last suspicious glance at the Machine he headed out the bedroom door and down the stairs into the kitchen, where he found his son David sitting eating his lunch.

You see, like David himself had done so many times before, Leland *had* gone back in time – back to his math class roughly 23 years before. Naturally, when he was there, he didn't *notice* it. Nor did he remember it once he returned to his own "present." And indeed, while Leland had spent a full hour in the past, when he returned to what you call the "present," no time had passed there at all.

Oddly, the purveyors of imagination in your world seem to think that people can go back in time without really doing so *themselves*. It usually goes like this: A man goes back in time – say, to what you call "the 15th Century." Strangely, although everything around him at that point is as it was in the 15th Century, the person who traveled back in time is not any different himself. He is still wearing the same clothes, still thinking the same thoughts, and still in possession of the same memories, even though in the 15th century the clothes he is wearing had not been made yet, and none of the things he remembers had happened yet. Indeed, the man himself had not even been born yet! Odd, don't you think, that the man went back to before he was even born, and yet somehow, there he is – not having changed himself at all?

The concern is then that, "Let's hope he doesn't change history." We hope, for instance, that the person who has gone back in time will not accidentally kill his own great-grandfather or something like that. If so, then the person who traveled back in time would never have been born, would he? Having not been born, how could he then have gone back in time and killed his own great-grandfather? This then, is called the "time travel paradox."

Silly isn't it? Somebody comes up with some foolish idea like traveling back in time while actually not traveling back in time, and then they anguish over the fact that their foolish idea contains a paradox. In other words, you cannot travel back in time and kill your own great-grandfather, because were you to travel back in time when your great-grandfather existed, you yourself would not exist in that time!

Take your theory of evolution. You come up with the theory then anguish over the fact that it can't explain how something like an *eye* can come to be. How can something like that *evolve*? You see, the problem is that an eye is largely useless unless all the parts are there working perfectly, right at the start. There is no reason to have an eye unless it completely works as soon as it appears in the species. So for an eye to happen by evolution, it would have to exist fully formed at the time it was created by the very first mutation that made it. It doesn't seem likely, does it, that a mutation would form a completely-developed, functioning useful eye? Indeed, given that even a one-celled organism cannot exist without its full, vast complexity, all operating perfectly at the very beginning, how can even a single-celled organism therefore *evolve*? How does a cell evolve what you call mitochondria over millions of years, if it needs the mitochondria to be able to live in the first place? Do you see that were an organism to form from the primordial ooze it would have to do so fully complete, and fully functioning, for the first one of it to be able to survive? It all has to be there in the first place, or that first cell will not live to evolve into anything. Do you know what the odds are of a single-celled organism spontaneously forming?

Suffice it to say, it doesn't work that way. But, having come up with the theory of evolution and finding it very much lacking, rather than just come up with a new theory, you torture your explanation of reality and of that which is so obvious to try to make it *fit* your *theory*.

Let me explain to you how time travel really works for you, and for your reality. Remember, you live in a reality that is time-constrained. You can go back or forward in time all you want, but if you do – as happened with David's Father – you will look, feel, act, think, etc, as you did when you did it the first time, or as you will do it in the future. Nothing will be different. In other words, if you go back in time, your body and all that you are, must regress as well. Were you to go back to when you were a baby, you would become a baby. Were you to go forward to when you were old, you would become old. Nothing would change by your having traveled in time. Of course, were you to travel to before you were born, you would never arrive there, because you would not yet exist.

Of course, this is all providing that you as a time-constrained being traveled backward or forward in a time-constrained reality, such as the one in which you are living.

Naturally, creatures such as *I* can travel back or forward in our own reality all we want. Indeed, there *is* no "back" and "forward" time in our reality. Past, present, and future are all the same to me. Moreover, were *you* to travel to a reality that was not time-constrained, *you* could do whatever you wanted to do as well, as far as time goes, because in those realities, time does not exist. This is what happened when David "fixed" his "thinking place."

And so, even though David never figured out what was happening when he would travel backward and forward in time in your world, after a while he found some worlds that were not time-constrained to which he traveled, and then he started taking Chip with him again.

They first went to a place David called "Pathia." Chip didn't ask David why he called it that, and David never said.

They arrived inside a disheveled house. One side of the house was gone, as if it had been torn away, and as they stood there in the great room they could see a valley sweeping away in the distance. "This is one of my houses," said David.

He stepped away from the Machine, and it went black. The stools disappeared. "Let me show it to you."

"What do you mean it's *your* house?" asked Chip.

"Well, I guess it's not really *my* house," David replied. "Actually, I just found this place." He motioned to the large room around them. "Nobody's ever here, so I just fixed up a few things. But most of it's the way it was when I found it."

As they walked through the house, Chip could see it was vast, with many rooms. One room was a great, tiled hall, and there was a large, empty pool in the middle of it. One wall was entirely made of large glass blocks and the light glinted in through it.

Another room was a large theater, complete with rows of seats. The walls were blue, and they had images of fish, shells, seaweed, and so forth, as well as castings on the walls of various ocean features – rocks, waves, etc.

As they walked through the hallways Chip noticed that everywhere they went the house was in disrepair, as if it had been cluttered and unattended for years.

Opening the front door of the house and stepping outside, Chip looked down the street and was shocked to see there a forest of towering pines, and they were burning. It was totally dark, except for the light from the flames and embers which cast a ghastly orange light on the house fronts.

"This is a forest fire," David said. "I made this happen. I think they're kind of neat." The pines were huge columns 100 feet high. As the trunk of one tree exploded, another came crashing down. The two boys went back inside. While the forest fire was some distance away and appeared to pose no imminent threat to them, Chip gave David a concerned look anyway. "I don't think you should do things like that, David."

David looked back at Chip, paused, then nodded his acceptance. In a sense, David had begun to see Chip as his moral compass – as an augmentation to his own sense of right and wrong, which in the case of David, had seemed to be getting more and more out of whack lately.

They returned to the Space Sieve, and then suddenly they traveled to another world – a huge indoor space that was very tidy. Rows and rows of room fronts – an apartment complex, dormitory, or such place – rose up all around them. They were in a huge, interior atrium. The apartment blocks and their common balconies stretched far above.

And what struck Chip as strange and for a moment disconcerting, was that there were also other people all around. While there were the obvious works of people in many worlds to which they traveled, and while David had seen other people when he'd traveled alone, this was the first time Chip had.

David got up from the Machine, casually as before, and walked off. Chip followed. While everyone else appeared to be about 20-25 years old, David and Chip drew some attention since they were younger, but it was not a disconcerting amount.

It did not occur to either of them that their appearance in the middle of this atrium with the Space Sieve should have seemed far stranger to the other people, but didn't seem as though it did so.

As they went into a doorway of one of the rooms, they found eight of the young men and women there, lying about on the floor and sitting upon the furniture. All were dressed in bright, casual clothes. One side of the room was completely covered with windows which were open, as well as a large glass doorway that was also open, with a pleasant breeze blowing through. One of the people in the room smiled at the two boys, and pointed out the window. Just then, a formation of sleek but strange-looking aircraft streaked over.

Through the window, Chip saw another large dormitory building with many windows in the distance, set on a grassy hill. As Chip stepped outside and looked, he could see another large building at an even greater distance – that one located in a bleak desert.

The people all seemed so nice and friendly it never occurred to either boy that they might be in any kind of peril as they traveled within the facility. After crossing a small field they came to yet another dormitory. This one was much different. Its appearance was grim. The hallways inside were

82

littered and unkempt, and the walls were harsh and rough – made entirely of concrete and wood – and were covered with painted symbols. The rooms were very small – little more than enough space for a bed and a tight workspace – and the people in them were rude, self-absorbed and frightening. They stared at David and Chip, and they took a disturbing amount of interest in them as they walked along the dirty hallways.

About this time, it occurred to Chip that he had basically let David "do it" to him again. He had let David take him somewhere, and in the interest of the moment they had not taken sufficient thought about what they were doing. They had let their curiosity carry them. A cold chill swept over Chip as he realized that they had walked away from the Machine and had left it in plain sight surrounded by other people. Not only was he not sure how to re-trace his steps back to it – how could he even be sure it would still be there when they returned?

He mentioned this to David and they both quickly returned to the large, interior space where they had left the Space Sieve. It was still there, but it had attracted a lot of attention by now. A crowd had gathered around it, and in the balconies and rows sweeping many stories above there were people looking down, talking, smiling, and pointing.

As the boys approached the Device, Chip brushed against one of the people there who looked at him with a curious longing as he passed – as if he wished Chip would stay with them for awhile.

As they regained the Machine and David began to operate it, the people smiled and applauded as the keys emerged and flashed. Then the hoop instantly swept over David and Chip, and they left.

They materialized in a nondescript city, and it was nighttime there. This time, rather than leave it in the open and unattended, David made the Device move into a wall where it would be both hidden and inaccessible.

The avenue was a dark, grimy place cluttered with storefronts in one- or two-story buildings. There was little traffic, and it was almost entirely all foot traffic and a few bicycles. As the boys went in one store after another, they found little of interest. There were also a few eating places, but the food looked greasy and unappealing. The people themselves appeared dull and idle.

Returning again to the place David had left the Space Sieve, they were swept away, this time appearing inside a large mall. David found a locked closet which he unlocked using the Device and which he then placed inside, as he and Chip set off to explore. The mall was immaculate - the floor was tiled and the walls and storefronts all around were clean. Three appealing young women approached them.

"We heard you talk," one of the girls said, beginning the conversation. "Is this right?" she asked. "Am I talking after your way?"

The girls told the boys that in this place all the people's needs were taken care of for them. They were provided with food, clothing, entertainment and all of the other necessities and luxuries of life, by those who ran the place. When David asked what the people do in return for all these gifts, the question seemed odd to the girls. They shrugged and one of them laughed. They all shook their heads. They didn't understand the question.

Momentarily distracted, Chip turned back and looked out the huge glass wall nearby. Outside the mall and immediately around it stretched a lawn, that was impeccably kept. The sky overhead was dark, almost black, but the grass was brightly lit. At the edge of the grass and light was a boundary, beyond which was bare dirt, with black and gray soot scattered upon it.

It was apparent that the mall complex was inside a zone. Inside this zone all was beautiful; outside, beyond the light, all was dark and forbidding. Chip called David's attention to it then Chip took one of the girls over to the window and asked her about it.

The girl then took Chip back to the others, and one of them pointed out that their people were at war – for all she knew they were at war with David and Chip.

David turned to Chip. "You know," he said, "if they think we might be at war with them perhaps we should be leaving." Agreeing, David asked, "Did you think my house was a little junky? I can show you a nice one."

Retrieving the Device from where they'd left it, in an instant they were hovering in the air in a reality David called "Skylia" Based on previous experience with the Kex, it didn't come as a complete shock to Chip to be hovering several hundred feet off the ground, seemingly in mid air, with only his stool beneath him. But while no longer terrifying, it was still disconcerting.

Below them was a wall around a vast, beautiful building. The wall was hundreds of feet high, 75 feet thick, and made of gray granite finished with impeccable workmanship, encompassing a vast, wooded area. As the wall stretched into the distance, the boys could not see the ends of it. Inside this area stood a massive building, also of gray granite, that was roughly the shape of a stepped pyramid. The bottom was a large rectangular shape, and on top of it another, smaller rectangular shape. The free space around the smaller rectangle was a balcony. The next level was a smaller rectangle, and so forth. At the fourth level, the walls rose vertically to a height of two rectangles, and there was a cavernous entry, with massive pillars. As they and the Device drew closer they could see two people on one of the balconies.

"This is a guy's house," David said, "one guy's house." He nodded. "Wait until you see the inside."

And then they were inside. The immense room or "hall" they were in was two thousand feet wide, and two thousand feet long. The ceiling was twelve hundred feet above the floor. The boys and the Device floated near this ceiling, looking down. The interior of the hall consisted of white marble walls with green accents. Along the top of these walls was an intricate mosaic of green and white tiles – although it appeared to be an intricate mosaic at a distance, the stones of the mosaic were actually ten feet wide. Near the four corners of this vast hall were four huge columns of white stone – two-hundred feet in diameter – also with green marbling. Comprising the top 100 feet of each column, was a cylinder of translucent, glowing jade, followed by a 100-foot-tall round capital. The last 100 feet of the column below was an ornate, round base.

People on the floor of the hall were visible, and one could occasionally hear their voices and footsteps as they rose upward, echoing.

"Let's go," said David, as though growing tired of the sightseeing.

Appearing back in David's bedroom now, Chip asked, "So that was the future or the past?"

"It's the future." said David. "The thing is – some of the places we went – I'm not supposed to go there. They're, I guess you'd say, prohibited."

"What are you talking about?" Chip asked, his suspicion rising.

"The Machine makes it clear," David replied, "that we're not supposed to go into them – there are some realities I've been physically stopped from entering – but the places we've been going today are only *prohibited*, not *blocked*.

"What do you mean we've been going to places that are prohibited?" Chip demanded.

"Well," David shrugged, "If we weren't supposed to go there then whoever didn't want us to should have made it so I *couldn't*, instead of just posting a *warning*. If it's just a warning, and I can get past it, then whose business is it?"

As he listened to David's, Chip began to realize how cavalier and arrogant his friend was becoming. Chip by contrast, grew concerned. For, while David was more intelligent, Chip was wiser. And yet, Chip's wisdom fought with his human craving for the experiences David could provide him with.

In response to all this, Chip's next statement was illogical. "Hey, you know what might be neat - what if we took our cousin Diane and, you know, my sister, with us sometime?"

I say his response was "illogical," but perhaps it is understandable for one who is familiar with humans. How often it is when beings such as you – when faced with a choice between reason and stimulation, choose the latter, such as having one's thoughts turn from logic, to desire.

In any case, the two boys resolved that next time, they would invite Diane and Sally to go with them, which they did the following week.

Ordinarily it could have been an innocent-enough idea. But it would prove to be the beginning of the most unfortunate event that would ever happen to Diane and Sally and to David and Chip in all their lives, as well as in the lives of numerous other innocent creatures.

☼ CHAPTER 10 ☼

NO MORE GOODBYES, FOREVER

YOU MAY BE INTERESTED in what happened when David and Chip first explained the Space Sieve to Sally and to Diane and when they first showed them how it worked, and how surprised, scared, and then intrigued the girls were. And you might want to know all about what was said and so forth. But it holds little interest for me.

Suffice it to say that after a few hours of explanation, demonstration, shock, fear, surprise, excitement, and delight, the girls had become familiar with the Device, and soon all four of them, atop their stools, headed off to the world that David had chosen. It was another cemetery.

As David announced proudly the place to which he had taken them all, Chip winced. "Another *cemetery* David?" he said quietly. But David was committed to showing them around.

This world was much different than the one that David called "The Graveyard of the Gods." Here they were in clear sunlight under a blue sky, on a sloping field of well-tended, green grass. All around were small flags measuring about 2 inches square, each on its own little mast, so that the flags were flying about six inches off the ground. Almost all the flags were red or yellow, but a few were blue.

As they walked along, David explained that each flag represented a person who had "passed on."

"Interesting isn't it?" David asked. "That other cemetery with all its colossal monuments and this one is so simple – no puffery – all the flags the same size, just different colors."

Diane stooped and pointed. "Look!" she said.

Moving down the hill was an apparition that looked like amber glass, half-visible, half-invisible. As it moved, it faded completely from view then re-appeared as its ghostly, glassy form seemed to come in and out of existence. The four children soon realized there were numerous such shapes appearing, moving, and disappearing on the hillside around them. On the whole, it looked like the apparitions were moving in and among the little flags, stopping to look at them.

"Those are the creatures who live here," said David, almost casually, motioning toward the transparent, reddish-brown creatures. "I don't know for sure what they are, but they're harmless."

And so the children spent much of the day exploring this place, as the fading, glassy beings moved among the little flags.

As they eventually came back to the Space Sieve, Sally asked, "What time is it? I'm supposed to be home by 5:00."

David and Chip smiled knowingly. Chip said, "Don't worry – we have time – as much as we need – as much as we could ever need." Chip smiled and looked at Diane, hoping to get some kind of response out of her. But he didn't get any.

"Well," continued Sally, "I wonder if next we could go someplace with animals. You know – animals that we can see or maybe even play with – like little dogs and cats or something."

It is interesting how various humans will have such divergent interests. Sally's request seemed pedestrian to David. David smiled weakly at Sally. He *did* know of such a place however, and after giving Chip a look of resignation, he plotted a course for such a reality.

You will recall that while Chip and Sally are brother and sister, that Chip is not related to Diane by blood, nor is David to Sally. So in that look of resignation that David gave Chip, the two boys communicated more than words would, or could. The last thing either boy wanted to do was to take the girls to a place where they would have something they would be able to play with, independent of the boys. Although neither boy said it, they had both been hoping this outing would lead the girls to being interested in *them*, and in doing things with them, not with a bunch of animals. But such was their luck, both in terms of the girls' expressed wish, and in terms of the two boys acceding to it so quickly.

A spot appeared, and a hoop swept around them, taking them to yet another world.

But this particular transit across vast tracts of time, space and reality using the Space Sieve was unique, inasmuch as it was the last one that the two girls would ever experience. This was the last time either girl would ever travel again using the Space Sieve. And because of this, it would be one of the last journeys using the Device that the boys themselves would ever take.

Now inside a forest of thin, tall trees, a canopy spread overhead as though they were inside a vast, dark cathedral. A trail led away from them over a large log and into the distance, where it exited the forest and went out into the light.

"There are a lot of animals here," said David. "And all of them are harmless. They're pretty interesting and some are fairly cuddly too." He smiled, gratuitously.

The girls joined hands and looked at David. "Where *are* they?" Sally asked. David pointed in the direction of the light. The two girls began to run off, then stopped, turned back to the boys, and asked, "Well, aren't you coming?"

But both boys at this point could tell that the girls really had little interest in either of them. Here they had taken the girls past multiple universes and through multiple dimensions of reality. The boys' hope was that this would awe and impress the girls into having a great deal of interest in them. But here they all were, and all the girls seemed interested in was playing with animals. "Couldn't they have done that at home?" Chip thought, and as he and David looked at each other they both knew what they would do. Let the girls stay here and have their girl fun. They would go have their boy fun someplace else.

And they both decided too that the next time they went somewhere they would leave the girls home. But of course, they never got the chance to make that decision, ever again.

"No," said Chip politely, with a wave. "Go ahead – we'll go do something else. See you in what – say an hour?" And with that, the two girls nodded, and ran off down the trail.

Strange isn't it? Here are these four, in possession of a Space Sieve – in possession of power and capacity that your species cannot begin to comprehend – and all the girls wanted was to see playful animals. And all the boys wanted was for the girls to pay attention to *them*. It is also strange that the girls (as well as Chip) trusted David's assertion that this world was completely safe – which indeed it was – at least at that time. Having traveled so far, and in such a remarkable manner, the girls nonetheless felt at home here in this strange world. It's just as well that they did. And David had no doubt they could return and retrieve them at will.

And so, while David operated the Machine Chip watched as Sally and Diane ran off, climbed over the log then scurried into the distance. And as they bounced away through the forest, silhouetted by the light in front of them, their hair flinging back and forth and the sound of their voices and their laughter echoing among the silent trees, David paused and looked too, and he and Chip thought that those two girls just then were the prettiest image that they had ever seen.

And then as the hoop formed behind the Device and swept over them taking David and Chip away, Chip had a strange and terrible feeling, and appropriately so. For this would be the last time either he or David would see Diane and Sally for the rest of any of their lives. But none of them knew that yet.

With a few strokes of the keys the boys materialized inside a spacious structure. David had taken himself and Chip once again to the reality he called "Skylia." From the ground floor the two looked up at the interior space that stretched upward for several hundred feet and was entirely empty except for numerous escalators that rose to various interior platforms that stretched out from the walls. All of the surfaces they could see were made out of glass, except the various floors, which were made of red felt – at least this was what the boys thought when they saw them. Some of the escalators began at the ground floor and traveled up several to stories overhead, while some began at upper floors and traveled to still higher levels. There was a great deal of chrome ornamentation on the walls of the ground floor - some walls were almost entirely vertical bands of the gleaming metal. And while neither boy was cognitively aware of it, each somehow realized that this was like nothing they'd seen before, in the sense that all the shining metal was perfect, without smudge or blemish of any kind.

At this point you may be wondering why I am going to the trouble of describing some of the places that the boys are visiting to such a degree as I am. The reason for this is because my sense is that these worlds are unusual and are not anything like your kind has ever experienced. You may recall earlier in this account that at times I declined to give details of the surroundings in which the boys found themselves, such as when they were in a home or when they were visiting family members and so forth. In these cases there was nothing unique or worth mentioning, unlike the place in which they currently are. Therefore in some cases, such as this one, I take some effort to describe the surroundings for documentary purposes.

At this point David operated the Space Sieve and as Chip watched, the Device lowered itself into a spot on the floor and disappeared. This is similar to what David had done previously when he had seemed to place the Device within a wall where it would presumably be safe. He then immediately strode across the plaza and stepped on one of the escalators, Chip at his side. As the two boys traveled up the escalator they noticed something unusual: The escalators, which were several hundred feet long with glass sides had no support under them, except at their two end points. As the boys began to reach the floor to which they were traveling they noticed that the floor itself seemed to have no support either, except at the outer edges where it connected to the external walls of the building. Indeed, the various floors extended out from walls, hanging out into the open space as it were, without any support, except at the outer edges. Even more strangely, these higher floors did not have any barricading walls around them to prevent anyone from falling off. As David and Chip walked around on the floor to which they had just traveled, all this gave them a very uneasy feeling.

The people who were on the various floors walked calmly and assuredly around on the floors, embarking and disembarking the escalators, without any care of falling at all. Then the boys noticed something even more strange. Where an individual wished to travel down only one or two floors, rather than use an escalator, he would use *slides*. The slides traveled down and sometimes curved, to take the person to platforms below. Like the floors themselves, these curving surfaces had no sides on them to keep anyone from falling off of *them* either. And yet no one ever fell.

Something else that struck the boys as very unusual was that the slides and the floors all were very *thin* – almost paper thin. In spite of this, an escalator would start from the edge of a platform and travel up to another platform. In other words, slight as they seemed, the various floors nonetheless had the integrity and rigidity to hold not only their own weight and the weight of the people standing (or sliding) on them, they also had the strength to hold the weight of the escalators that were connecting the various floors and platforms to each other.

Chip and David did not spend much time traveling the escalators from floor to floor before they found the entire experience frightening without being particularly interesting. Soon, they walked to the back of one of the platforms and through a doorway, stepping into a spacious area. Standing at the back of a wide hallway that curved away from them as it stretched to the left and right, they looked across the open space to a transparent wall. It appeared that the entire structure they were in was circular, for the glass wall had a curvature, such that it curved away from the boys while the middle bulged toward the boys like a gigantic fishbowl. And like a fishbowl, large as it was it appeared this transparent wall – about two stories high, and a hundred feet wide as far as what the boys could see – was made from a single piece of transparent and optically perfect glass. Behind it the boys could see a large classroom comprising chairs for one hundred attendees, and people entered and exited the classroom as well as mingling around hall. At some distance the two boys noticed an elevator door and concluded it might be a more interesting way to explore the building, as well as being far less frightening than the escalators that they had just been on.

As David and Chip entered the elevator, two people watched them and turned to each other with questioning looks – not seeming malevolent in any way, just curious.

Scanning the complex elevator control panel, David moved his hand higher and higher. Then his hand moved down and touched an odd-shaped form near the center of the panel. The doors closed and the elevator began to move upward, and after a few moments the elevator stopped and the doors opened. Two young men stepped on the elevator at this point. They traveled up a few more floors and the elevator stopped again. But this time, there was something unusual. When the doors opened, it was clear the elevator had stopped between two floors. There in front of them was the floor above and the floor below, with the flooring between them. Rather than expressing any surprise, the two men glanced at the boys, and then simply climbed out of the elevator onto the upper floor. The doors of the elevator closed again.

This time, David's hand moved higher and higher on the control panel until it pressed the highest button. The doors closed and once again the boys traveled upward. But this time they could feel their speed increasing – faster and faster – and they noticed the walls of the elevator began shaking gently, as though they were only marginally held to the elevator box itself.

"I'm starting to feel like this thing's not all that well put-together," said Chip.

Nervously, David too noticed that the walls were becoming increasingly loose. Suddenly, the left wall of the elevator – as a single piece of sheet metal – simply slid off with a slicing sound; then so did the right side. At this point only the front and back of the elevator had walls. Then, the back wall slid off too. Traveling upward inside the shaft, the elevator now had only a floor, ceiling, front doors and control panel. Crouching near the floor, the boys could see the dark walls of the elevator shaft rushing past as the elevator continued to travel upward.

Even more frightening than this feeling of exposure was the fact that it was clear the speed of the elevator was continuing to increase, as they now felt themselves pressed against its floor.

Fear quickly turned to terror as the elevator suddenly shot out of the finished part of the building into an upper section of building that looked as though it was nothing but steel girders with an open frame elevator shaft in the middle of it. (I say "steel" here, but as you will see this material was not steel, but something much stronger. Nonetheless, I will refer to it as "steel" for the sake of your reference.) As the air roared around them, the girders most near the shaft whipped passed faster and faster with a rapid, tapping sound. The more distant girders passed more slowly than the blurred near ones, and yet their speed was increasing too.

Although neither of them said a word, the question that began to cross the boys' minds was this: What was going to ultimately happen? Would they suddenly shoot out the top of the building? Or would they somehow come crashing to a halt as they reached the top of the elevator shaft in this unfinished section of the building?

What did happen was this: just as moments before the elevator had suddenly exited the finished part of the building and plunged into an upper unfinished section of the building, with a sudden change of air, it now left the unfinished section of the building as well.

Now, they were inside an elevator without walls, roaring upwards into the sky itself, inside a lone, framework elevator shaft, teetering in the wind.

But the elevator car was not accelerating anymore. The upward speed, while still intense, was constant now. This was noticeable only because the boys did not feel themselves pressed to the floor any longer. As frightening as it had been, there had been a benefit to the acceleration in that it had kept them pressed to the floor. But now even that was gone. Hands flailing for something to hold on to, both boys realized that an elevator cannot travel upward forever inside a single, spindly shaft. Like a fishing rod with a heavy lure on the end of it, the elevator shaft must begin to bend as the weight of the elevator car traveling upward made the shaft increasingly top-heavy. And if the shaft bent over on itself, what would the boys hold on to then?

Then it began to happen. With the wind roaring and the girders of the elevator shaft flashing by in a continuous blur, there was the noticeable feeling of tipping from side to side. Lying flat on the floor, fingers spread wide, the boys tried to hold on as the car began to gently drift and tilt as they continued higher and higher into the sky.

Then, just when their fright began to turn to a blank, hopeless resignation, the situation changed again. Together with the tremendous roaring of the air there was suddenly a high, whirring sound, falling in pitch, and the boys, rigid with fear, floated to the top of the elevator car. With a chillingly smooth precision, the elevator was decelerating now and the boys were once again pressed safely but frighteningly against a surface – this time, the ceiling. From this new vantage point, it was very easy to see downward, and to see just how high the car had traveled. Below, the thin elevator shaft writhed gently as it stretched far below, like a snake that was casually reaching from branch to branch. A final whirring brought the car to a full stop, and the boys were thrown back to the floor.

Lying numb there, eyes pressed shut, it occurred to both of them to crawl to the edge of the elevator car and peer down at the remarkable view, but racked with fear this was far beyond either's capability. Nonetheless Chip opened a single eye intending to find the control panel with it, but instead was struck with nauseating terror at the pure field of blue all around. Mustering his fortitude he forced his view to the controls, and raising a strangely rigid finger pressed the lowest button he could find. He wasn't going to wait for David to decide this time. All he knew was that he wanted to go *down* – and *down* as far as he possibly could.

The lights on the control panel shifted, but for several seconds the elevator did not move. The terrifying thought occurred to the boys that they were suspended there thousands of feet above the ground with no way to go back into the building except to somehow slide themselves down the spindly elevator shaft.

Momentarily however, and to their great relief, the elevator began to move smoothly downward inside the shaft. Even more gratifying, this downward speed increased as they went, taking them ever more quickly back to the safety of the ground. The boys felt light, but were not floating up inside the car as they had done when the car stopped before. And as they traveled downward, the shaft began to seem more rigid – there was less of the tipping, leaning feeling. Pushing themselves up slightly, they could see they were approaching the unfinished section of the building. And happily to the boys, the speed of the elevator continued to increase.

With a change of sound, they plunged downward into the unfinished part of the building. They watched the steel framework flying past, from the framework near them to the distant framework at the building's edges.

It sounded like the crack of a whip as they crossed now into the finished part of the building. Although the inside of the now dark elevator shaft was rushing past at frightening speed only inches away from them, relief swept over the boys as they knew that they were back inside the building, instead of looking down at it.

However at approximately the same instant for both boys, emotions once again turned to concern as they realized that while the elevator was traveling downward, this downward pace was still *accelerating* – so much so, that they once again found themselves floating up to the ceiling of the elevator, and then pressed against it.

Then suddenly, instead of the metal framework of the blurred shaft around them there was smooth concrete – they had passed the ground floor and were now rushing rapidly into the basement section of the building, still accelerating, still pressed against the ceiling.

When the elevator had been traveling upward, the boys had anguished to think how an upward journey in an elevator at high speed might end. But now, traveling downward at accelerating speed they had no need to wonder what the worst outcome might be.

As fast as the air had been rushing around them, now it suddenly increased. They began to feel as if they would drift back to the floor, but just as they did, a panel opened on the floor of the elevator. Blasting through this hole was a gale of air so strong it felt more like a wall of water and it kept them pinned to the ceiling. Then the panel closed and the boys were rapidly, but not painfully, thrown once again to the floor. There was a loud roar with a falling pitch followed by multiple whirring sounds also falling in pitch, as they were pressed harder and harder to the floor.

And then, with a noticeable precision, the elevator stopped. Heads bowed, eyes closed, neither boy moved. Then the doors slid open. With only a momentary glance, two young men, who apparently had been waiting for the elevator to arrive, stepped into it, and with difficulty, trembling as they were, David and Chip drug themselves out. As one of the men leaned over and pushed one of the buttons, the other gave they boys a curious glance. Then the doors closed and the elevator left.

This floor had none of the opulence the boys had seen on the upper floors. The minimal lighting made the bare concrete around them appear cold and lonely.

As they looked around in the dim light they saw no stairs, and so having little other choice, they resolved they must board the elevator once again.

Chip silently walked over to the elevator control panel and pressed the "UP" button, and he noticed there was no "DOWN" button – they were at the absolute basement of the building.

95

After standing silently in front of the elevator doors for several minutes, a small stream of air began whistling out of the crack between the elevator doors. Ordinarily, such a tickling flow of air might have caused the boys to wince and move away, but after what they had just been through, neither boy bothered to move. Soon, they heard the same roaring and whirring, and then the doors snapped open to reveal the familiar elevator with the ceiling and floor, but no walls except the front.

Neither boy looked at the other, and they paused only briefly before stepping inside.

Chip reached for the panel of glowing buttons. He paused, turned to David and for the first time in this dark place, their eyes met. "Which floor do we need?"

There was no answer.

"David?" he asked, with a strange, calm formality in his voice.

David stared into nowhere, thinking and distant, then reached over and pointed at a button. "This one," he said. "It's the one that was lit when we started." Chip numbly raised his eyebrows, nodded, and pressed the button. The doors slid together.

A stiff acceleration of the elevator car followed, but not nearly as extreme as before. Both boys wondered whether this acceleration was less, or whether it simply seemed less because they were getting used to it, but it *was* less. As they neared their selected floor, both braced themselves for the expected deceleration, which came, but only mildly. The doors opened and they staggered torpidly out.

As they did, there were a number of people waiting to board the elevator. Looking at David and Chip, the people (all appearing to be in age of about their mid-twenties) seemed amused – the way experienced people would look when watching two frightened children disembark from a thrill ride for the first time.

And actually, some people in this world use elevators for that purpose, in buildings that are under construction. It just so happens that in this world, when they build a tall building, the elevator and its shaft are the first structures they build. And every once in awhile, somebody rides to the top or the bottom, for a little fun. Of course, it's fast. The boys never knew, but they had never been in any real danger.

Without speaking, they instinctively returned to the Space Sieve, and retrieved it from its location in the floor where David had left it. As a crowd began to collect around them, David operated the Device, and the two boys – with the Machine – disappeared.

☼ CHAPTER 11 ☼

AS THE DEW IN THE SUN

DAVID AND CHIP MATERIALIZED inside a dark warehouse. Startled by their sudden arrival, pigeons fluttered in the steel framework overhead. Except for some large wooden boxes, the building's cavernous interior was largely empty. The Space Sieve was dark, and David began to manually push it behind a crate.

"Were back on Earth," he said. "There's nobody here. This is an empty building near the docks. We can rest here without any more excitement." He stood there silently for a moment. Chip felt relieved at the stillness and at the familiar surroundings.

But David was not being entirely honest. He too wanted a change of pace to distract him from the experience with the elevator. But David's mind had begun a process of descending further and further into an increasing separation from reality, brought on by extreme vanity. In other words, so many things about his life had changed so fast and seemingly so greatly in his favor that his ability to be responsible or even rational was failing. (This is a common trait among your kind.) As evidence of this, I observe that at this particular moment he not only wanted a change of pace, he wanted something newly exciting and dangerous to watch from a distance, to entertain as well as distract him. He had the sense that after some time to rest had passed there would be some new excitement to watch. But his timing was off.

He exhaled heavily. "Here, help me with this," he said, and he and Chip lifted the Device into the side of an open crate.

Just as they were finishing, the door at one end of the warehouse began to open. It was a huge, rollup door that clanked and screeched as it opened. Two black limousines came though the door, careened recklessly to the middle of the warehouse, then came to a stop.

With David unwisely expecting a welcome distraction for his mind and Chip too dazed to think much about what was happening around them, the two boys watched.

Momentarily however, it became clear to Chip that they were witnessing two groups of organized criminals preparing to undertake some kind of business between themselves. At that moment, Chip looked to the Space Sieve and then turned back plaintively to David as if to say, "David, let's get out of here." But David, in spite of the excesses that they had already experienced that day, was becoming excited once again.

"After all," he thought, "we can leave whenever we want, or do anything else we want to, for that matter." And at the same time David remembered how the two girls had run off into the forest in the world where the boys had left them. By contrast, here he and Chip found themselves in a dark warehouse ready to witness something frightening before their very eyes. In a way, he felt this was an odd form of payback to the two girls for not seeming interested in them. If the girls had wanted to go with the boys after all, they could have had the same sorts of fun the boys were having.

David leaned over and whispered to Chip. "How's this for some fun – a little danger? Who needs those two girls for *this*?" Looking in the direction of the limousines, where men were still piling out he said, "See those guys? They're organized criminals. This is a deal they are going to do here. We get to watch. I looked it all up before we came." He smiled and his eyebrows twitched slightly.

Chip grimaced and then he shook his head and stared sternly at David. "How could you do something like this, after our near-death experiences with the Kex?" he thought. "Don't you know by now that beings aren't just playthings – that they can *hurt* us?" But he kept still, saying nothing.

And so what we have here are two examples of what happens with your kind when you escape imminent peril. In one case, such as with Chip, you respond by becoming more cautious – less willing to take risks as a result of a near-miss. In another case, such as with David – your kind sees an escape from peril as proof of your own invincibility – and you become *more* willing to take risks. You assume that because random fate operates once in your favor, that you are somehow "lucky," and can therefore "dodge a bullet"

98

every time. Of course, this is irrational. And yet, this was David's reaction to the frightening experiences that they had already had.

Unfortunately, as is the case with random events, they do not always operate in your favor, and they would not operate in the boys' favor this time. David's increasing tendency to act as though he was invincible would this time prove to be entirely ruinous, as well as tragic.

As the men talked, their voices rose as if they were all becoming more and more angry and soon, they were shouting. Then, events turned very much to the bad. What happened next is what is sometimes referred to as a "fire fight." Perhaps this is because the weapons used depend on the combustion of powders that are confined inside small, metal cases, which have a relatively high-mass insert on one end. You call the weapons, "guns." These weapons – your guns – are easily dealt with by any one of a number of superior technologies, yet they are very harmful to your kind when your bodies are unprotected, as in this case.

What happened next, as the two groups of men fired their weapons at each other, was a scene consisting of a vast amount of noise, men standing, kneeling, falling, and leaning into their weapons as they fired them, with their arms shaking from the concussion and the recoil. Other men were trying to dodge, dive, and so forth, as their bodies jumped and shook from the bullets hammering into them. In moments, many of the men had fallen dead, and the side with the largest quantity of remaining, living men began the task of "finishing off" the remainder of their opponents, both the living and the wounded, until only a few remaining men were left alive, some standing, some kneeling, wounded, and some lying on the ground, dying.

The leader of the victorious side, as it happened, immediately took cover inside one of the limousines when the fighting started. This is typical of such societies. The leader is effectually the only person of importance, while the other men, his foot soldiers, have lives that are meaningless to their leader. And, if they follow his wishes appropriately, the leader would prefer that his men's lives should be meaningless to *themselves* as well.

During all this time Chip had confined himself completely behind the crate, while David had watched the spectacle. But as David now drew himself back behind the crate he saw Chip with his head pressed against the rough wood, teeth clenched. And then David saw why. There was a hole in the crate where a bullet had come though next to Chip's head – he had survived literally, by inches. David's excitement immediately turned to regret. He exhaled suddenly, then said quietly, but definitely audibly, "Chip, I'm so sorry."

He said it so softly that in most settings it would not have been heard. But in the vacant warehouse, with the boys standing beside the metal exterior of the building, David's voice carried. The leader of the men – his name was "Ernesto" – heard it and immediately motioned for one of his men to investigate. The man ran over, found and caught the boys, and dragged them back to Ernesto, where they stood amidst the blood and the bodies, and where they were surrounded by the living remnants of Ernesto's men.

At this point I will observe that the lesser sorts of your species have a peculiar characteristic. As crude and difficult as your language is, these low persons insist on inserting into their already coarse speech words which have little functional value. Rather than repeat these words here (and since they perform no useful purpose) I will simply insert the word "ding" in place of those words.

"Hey, ding, what were you doing over there, ding?" Ernesto said demandingly. The adrenaline in his voice was apparent. "What the ding is going on – two little ding boys in this ding warehouse?" He motioned to one of his men. "Hey ding, what's the matter with you ding? How'd these little dings get in here? Go see, ding! They got their little ding bicycles over there or something? Ding!"

The man quickly darted behind the crate, then found and drug out the Space Sieve. "Ding!" he said. "There ain't no ding bicycles. Just this piece of ding." He pushed the Space Sieve over on its back, and it slapped against the floor with a crack that echoed in the building. He looked back at Ernesto.

"Ding!" said Ernesto, and he walked over to the Device. "This is why you dings all work for me and not the other way around! You're all a bunch of ding ding!"

He kneeled down and looked at the Device, and ran his hand over it. After pausing to think for a moment, he stood up and walked back toward the boys, and while acting nonchalant fixed his gaze on them. He waved his hand dismissively and said, referring to the Device: "Take the ding piece of ding outside and throw it in the ding bay."

As he spoke David's eyes flashed, and Chip shot a glance at him.

Without saying a word, they had confirmed Ernesto's suspicion. He had never intended to throw the strange object away, but was interested in how valuable the boy's thought it was. And with their facial expressions they had told him. It was clear now to Ernesto that the seemingly nondescript object was something very valuable to the boys. He smiled.

"Well, well boys!" he said. "It looks like maybe this little black boxy thing is yours huh? Hey, you know what?" Using his foot he rolled over a dead body that was next to him. "Maybe I won't throw that thing in the bay after all, huh?" He gave a big smile.

Looking at Ernesto, Chip thought that in smiling Ernesto actually looked far worse than he did when he frowned. Chip had not seen anything like that before. It may be worth noting, if you haven't noticed, that for the moment Ernesto is not saying "ding" when he speaks, thus showing that people who use that sort of language understand that for the most part, it is unnecessary, even counterproductive.

"Hey, two cute little boys, huh?" He walked over and bumped David with a finger. This reminded David of something his father would do – give David a little bump or a pat. But in the case of his father, David sensed it as a mark of affection. In this case, it was more like intimidation. Then Ernesto ruffled Chip's hair. "Hey Skippy, what we got in the car for these nice little boys? Don't we have some ding soda . . . I mean, don't we have some soda pop for these nice boys? Hey, you like ginger ale? Sure, all boys like soda pop. Hey Skippy, get my friends here some ginger ale. Hey Skippy – a couple of glasses and a little ice too, huh?"

And so, stepping across the bodies, Skippy got two glasses of ginger ale and ice from the bar in the back of the limo, and he lumbered back to the boys. Chip noticed that under Skippy's coat his white shirt was bloody. "Here, here you go." He handed David his drink. "Yeah, and here *you* go, yeah. Yeah, *nice* boys."

Ernesto paused for a moment, still smiling. Then he walked back to the Device. He stood it up, looked at it, rubbed his hands over it, and ran his fingernails along the edge as if looking for a seam. He clenched his teeth with frustration. Then he looked toward the boys. He smiled again, and walked back near them. Standing about 10 feet away, he crouched, looked at both of them, and he held out his hands.

"Well okay boys, let's have it. What *is* it?" He stared for a moment, and then his face grew grim.

"I SAID WHAT THE DING IS IT, DING!" he screamed, and as he did, his men shifted nervously. Then he smiled again and came very close to David. He brought his face right up to David. Once again, he spoke calmly.

"So, tell me you little ding. What the ding is that ding?" Then he smiled again and he closed his eyes.

"WHAT THE DING IS IT, DING?!!" But David said nothing.

Then, Chip spoke quietly. "Ahem. Umm, David?"

Ernesto smiled. "Oh, it's *David?*" said Ernesto as he moved toward Chip. "Oh, where the ding are my manners? *David* is it? Ding. And what's *your* name, boy?"

"Chip," he said.

"Oh, *Chip* is it?" replied Ernesto. "Hey Skippy, this little guy's name is Chip. Hey Skippy, look at Bernard over there. See what Carlos did to him? Hey, maybe we should call him Chip too huh?" Chip looked over at the body of Bernard. Suffice it to say, it was clear to him what Ernesto meant when referring to the body of Bernard as "Chip."

"So," Ernesto continued, "I guess your name is 'Charles' huh? Hey, calling you Chip – it's better than calling you 'Charlie', huh? Yeah. Yeah. Hey *Chip*, so tell me, tell your nice uncle here – yeah, that's me, think of me as your uncle. Hey, does your real uncle give you a nice ginger ale huh? Hey boys," he said to his men, "do you think this nice boy has an uncle that gives him ginger ale?"

The men smiled nervously and looked at each other. Then, turning back to Chip he said in a soft voice, "So tell me. Tell me Chip. Tell me what that ding thing over there is huh?"

And he waited for a moment. And then Ernesto took out a pistol.

"David," said Chip, "Why don't you just *show* him?" Chip tried to be brave, but his voice cracked when he said it. When Ernesto heard Chip's voice crack, he rubbed Chip's head again.

"There, yeah," he said, and he waved his pistol at his men. "You see what your mama always said, huh? The way to get what you want out of people in life is to be nice to them right? Yeah." And he walked over to David while giving another of his sickening smiles.

This was what Chip had hoped for. He had bet that Ernesto would not imagine that the black box could possibly be a weapon, and Chip believed that he had just won that bet.

"It's all yours," said Ernesto, motioning for David to go to the Machine. But as David walked over to the Machine, Ernesto stayed nearby him. "Hey, mind if I watch?" he asked.

David kneeled in front of the Machine. He began to rub his hands over it as he had done the first time in his bedroom. The texture appeared on the surface of the Machine, and yellow and black parallelograms began to sweep across the screen as a set of buttons rose and flickered on the previously flat keyboard.

Ernesto stepped back. "Ding," he said under his breath. Then quickly, he was back at David's side, resting his hand heavily on David's shoulder with his fingernails digging into it. As David glanced nervously at Ernesto and winced at the pain, the yellow parallelograms diminished. The screen of the Device became darker, and the colored buttons dimmed and became more nondescript. All in all, the Device at this point looked more like the sorts of machines your kind makes, than the sorts of Machines beings such as I are accustomed to.

"Why doesn't he just *do* it?" Chip thought, wondering why David didn't just whisk them away as he had done so many times before. But nothing happened.

"DING!" A man was looking up, his bloodshot eyes bulging, and then everyone looked. Hovering in the space overhead was a duffle-bag shaped object covered with colored lights. It was the Tic. Although neither the men nor Chip knew what the Tic was or what its appearance meant, you should.

It meant David wasn't operating the Machine correctly and so it had spawned the Tic. David's attempts to operate it were so inadequate the Machine believed it was in the hands of a novice. And in appearing, the Tic had neutralized all of the Space Sieve's external functions. The Machine was powerless.

Ernesto looked up too, his eyes widening with fear. "Ding it! Ding that ding thing! Ding it you bunch of ding!" And his men opened fire. Bullets ricocheted in the rafters, but nobody could seem to hit the object.

Ernesto barked: "Johnny! Ding! Go ding up there! Go *get* it you ding!"

Johnny froze for a moment, then reluctantly ran over to the wall and began to climb a facility ladder that was bolted to the wall and that ran up to the roof. But as all eyes turned back to David, the Machine had returned to completely black. David was rubbing his hands frantically over its surface. But the keyboard was dark. The screen was black. And when they all looked back to Johnny, the object – the Tic – was now gone too.

Without realizing it, Chip had sunk to the floor. "This is really bad," he thought.

It had never occurred to Chip that a time might come when David could not operate the Device. But it had come. David was so overwrought that he had lost his intuitive sense about it. He was *thinking* about it too much. And in doing so, he had lost his intuition of how to use it. His mind was nothing but a sea of fear and regret for what he had done – for the foolhardiness to which he had once again succumbed. Now, even the Machine would not save them. No matter how hard he tried, he could not regenerate the former thoughts and feelings he used to have when he would operate it. He was trying desperately. But somehow, he could not connect with it. He could not work it.

In his hands this Device of so much wonder and power now felt like nothing more than an old, useless piece of equipment, or even, a block of wood.

Where it had seemed before to be connected to him – responding to his every command – now it was only an obtuse, unknowably-complex Mechanism. Where it had seemed before like his closest friend, now it seemed as though it couldn't care less.

Yet, it had not changed. It was still just a Machine. It could still do the same things as before. It still worked exactly the same way.

What had changed was David's frame of mind.

Now, *he* could not operate it.

"Ding!" said Ernesto. "Where'd that thing up there go?" Then pointing to the Machine, "And what happened to all the ding lights on that ding! What's going on? Make the ding lights go ding on again! Hey! What's your ding problem you little ding?"

At this point David looked at Ernesto, and then he looked at Chip, and then David shook his head. "I'm sorry Chip," he mouthed silently. And then tears filled his eyes.

Ernesto winced. "What? What the ding?" He pointed the gun at David. "Hey ding. Hey lookie here you little ding! Hey look around! You see all the dead dings lying around here? Huh? Hey ding! You want to join 'em? Huh ding?" And he cocked his gun.

"Hey Ernesto!" It was Skippy who spoke, and he gestured toward David. "Hey Ernesto that ding over *there's* the one who knows how to make it do the lights and ding." And then he motioned toward Chip. "But *this* piece of ding over here's about as much use as a pair of ding on a ding."

Ernesto looked over at Chip, then smiled. "Yeah," he chucked. "Yeah." And he walked over to Chip. Always respectful to adults, Chip stood back up.

Now at this point while I will cease to describe the events in detail, suffice it to say that Ernesto took his gun and pointed it at Chip at a place where it would not kill him but where it would do great harm and cause great pain, and he pulled the trigger.

At which point it would have been safe to say that Chip would never be truly the same again. And indeed, as he watched, David would never be the same again either.

As Chip fell, David saw his face. There Chip was, innocent, paying for David's vain foolhardiness. But as Chip collapsed to the floor, even then in his face was the same trust that he had always had in David. Even as Chip fell to the ground, he looked confidently to David to save him. And what really wrenched David was that in Chip's eyes it seemed he believed somehow that all of this was something David had anticipated, that it was all according to David's plans and that David *would* save him. Even now, he still trusted David. And as Chip looked toward him, David could see in Chip's eyes there was no hate, no anger, only friendship, only trust. And as David watched the full, horrible consequences of his own careless actions fall upon his innocent friend, it's worth mentioning that in that moment, in that situation, a lot of men when faced with the realization of what they had done would have sunk into an abyss of horror, remorse and a self-destructive form of guilt from which they would have never returned.

But none of that happened with David. For suddenly in that moment, David felt no more fear, no more dread. He had no hate, no anger. He felt nothing at all. Having seen what he had just seen and realizing it was all because of his careless selfishness had been an overload, erasing all human sentiment from him. His emotional gears were stripped. Now he was as unfeeling, as uncaring, as the Machine itself. His face was expressionless as flint. Now, he didn't care about Ernesto, about Ernesto's men, or about the dead bodies around them. He had forgotten about the girls, about his mother and his father, and about everything he had ever known or cared about. He didn't even care about his own life anymore. Now, in this moment, the only thing he cared about was *Chip*. And in that same moment, the only things that *existed* for him in all the world, in all of creation, were only himself, Chip, and the Device.

With no interest in what anybody would do, say, or think, he turned toward the Machine. He touched it. The screen flashed to life. The keyboard blazed. His stool snapped into view.

He and Chip were instantly at a distance of exactly 396 miles from the surface of your Earth. The stars in your part of Space glittered in the darkness, and your Milky Way traced its magnificent course across the sky. Your moon was silhouetted by your sun directly behind it.

David was sitting on the stool.

Chip was standing beside the Device. He had no sign of the injury he had just received.

But while he looked whole, Chip was trembling terribly. Leaning against the Machine, he sank to his knees while looking at David, and as he tried to smile his face began to shake from side to side. Chip reached over and put his hand on David's leg to steady himself and it appeared to David that within moments, Chip would faint. Chip had a pleading expression on his face that even with all that he had been through, David had not seen anything like it before.

David knew that he had repaired the damage done to Chip's body – that was relatively easy - but what about Chip's *mind*? Chip's mind clearly could not endure the memory of what had just happened, and perhaps, neither could David's.

Chip's body had been repaired. But repairing his mind – repairing *both* their minds – this was much harder.

But David was committed, and his mind was yet a pure vessel of singleness and purpose, together still with all his innate talent. And so, he operated the Machine once more.

Momentarily Chip jumped back to his feet, made an expression of confusion, and chucked, as if to say, "What was I doing on my knees just then?"

What David had done, is he had erased the memories of everything that had happened from the time they left the girls, until the time right now. He had erased *both* his and Chip's memory of those events. Therefore, both of them believed they left the girls and had gone directly into space around the Earth.

But he was not done yet. David now operated the Machine with a fervor and fluidity that even he had never before expressed. Numerous lighted screens and keyboards appeared to the left and right of the Space Sieve, with strange shapes moving across them. The screens and keyboards under them bounced forward to David and back again as he operated them. The best way I can describe it to you is to say that the screens and keyboards looked like a group of pets that were being fed by their master, jumping in and out as they each received a piece of food.

David was fixated, and moved with chilling precision.

Chip had never seen him like this – so purposeful, in such concentration – so robotic and at the same time, so human. Chip stood silently and watched.

And in those next few seconds, David did what no living creature using this Machine had ever done before. In a moment, the auxiliary screens and keyboards of the Space Sieve disappeared, and the single remaining screen faded to a pale, glowing blue. David swung around, and as he did so, he tipped to one side momentarily, as if he had been mildly drugged.

"I deleted everything," he said.

Chip raised his eyebrows, questioningly.

"Something just happened a few minutes ago," David explained. "I deleted it from your memory, from my memory, and from the memory of this Device. The hardest was deleting it from the memory of this Device." David motioned toward the Machine.

"What did you delete?" asked Chip.

"That's the thing," said David. "I don't remember *either*."

Chip paused. "Why did you delete it from the memory of the Machine?" he asked.

"Because I needed to have it be gone," David replied. "All I know is it was very, very bad."

You may be wondering then, exactly what it was David deleted. I will tell you. What David deleted was the entire memory of the Space Sieve. This is a remarkable feat that up until this time no one had ever done before. And in his desire to purge the events fully from their minds, David erased his and Chip's memories of the events in the warehouse. Or at least, that was his intent. But your minds, and your memories, are complicated things with many interconnections. And David was not sufficiently knowledgeable regarding the workings of the human mind to have been skilled enough to remove only those memories he had intended to remove.

Suddenly, Chip had that familiar feeling again. He didn't remember the deleted memories, but he did still remember something important.

"David, the girls?" he asked.

And then David's eyes twitched and grew very wide, and in an instant he had a feeling that he would remember for the rest of his life.

It was a feeling far worse than he had ever felt before. It was worse than how he had felt when he caused them to be trapped in the hands of the Kex. It was worse than how he had felt when he had almost destroyed all of the Kex. It was worse than how he had felt when he had destroyed his thinking place, and although he no longer remembered it, it was worse than he had felt when he had seen Chip fall inside the warehouse. David felt worse than he would ever feel again – worse than any human should ever have to feel.

In fact, this was the strongest feeling David would ever feel in his lifetime.

David swung around and faced the Space Sieve. He operated it slowly, haltingly. As he did, Chip watched the lights on the keyboard, and the strange moving objects on the its screen. But then, he began to feel sick as he saw the expression on David's face.

Then, David bowed his head.

Chip looked at him pleadingly. Somehow, Chip's mind immediately went to the absolute worst possibility. "Oh, David. No. No." Tears were filling Chip's eyes.

David's voice now somehow, sounded not like the voice of a young boy, but like the quaking, quavering, oddly-pitched voice of an old man. "I didn't just delete the part of the Machine's memory about what just happened. He paused.

"I deleted the *entire* memory." David was trembling.

"Wait. David, you don't mean. David, you can't . . ."

David's voice was weak. "There is no record of where they are. I have no record for where we left the girls. And the thing is Chip, I don't remem . . . Chip, my own memory – I, I don't remember."

Chip paused and thought for a moment. But as he did, he began to feel a little dizzy. His mind was beginning to reel.

Then he started pacing back and forth around the Machine "No, no, no . . ." he repeated, "NO, NO, NO, NO. NO!"

David shook his head, then bowed it. Chip saw this and he involuntarily grabbed David, and he shouted at him.

"David! Take us back! Take us *back*!"

Then Chip smiled sickly, and he plaintively entreated, "Yeah. Yeah – take us back – back to the beginning. David – take us – we can go all the way back. David, like you always do. David, just take us *back*!"

David was still trembling, his eyes were filled with tears and there were drops of sweat on his face. He bowed his head. "Chip," he said, "what have I done? Chip, what I have I done?"

"David? David?" Chip asked plaintively, and he too seemed far older now.

"They're *gone*. The girls are *gone*, Chip. There is no way to tell where they . . ."

And then Chip begged David. Using his most precious remaining memories, he entreated David from the heart.

"David, remember how we used to play on the swings when we were little kids? Remember the backyard pools and the barbeques? You remember when we'd run down the alleys at night in our swimming suits and jump in the neighbors' pools? They'd turn on the lights and come running out, and we'd run away and laugh?

"David, remember the blue skies and the dust storms and how it would turn all dark and there would be a cloudburst? Remember riding our bicycles through the rain and coming indoors and changing our clothes and playing inside with it all thundering and pouring outside? Remember the ball games and the sleepovers and the birthdays and the candles on the cakes? Remember the summers and playing in the wheat fields in all those vacant lots? Remember sneaking back to the school and getting inside and running down all the empty corridors with nobody there? Remember getting up early in the mornings to go fishing – we'd make bait out of cheese, but bread dough worked the best - and the marble games we played with our friends in the Bermuda grass at recess when we were little kids and all those happy, happy days?

"David, remember the first days of school and the new books and new teachers and being in a new classroom and seeing everyone again?"

Chip knelt next to David, who was slumped on his stool, one hand on the Machine.

"Remember all those days?" Chip continued. "Remember your mother and father and my Dad, and our brothers and sisters and all our friends? Remember the Cub Scouts and the Boy Scouts and the campouts? Remember the firecrackers and the bottle rockets and all the fourths of July? Remember your old mini bike and our slingshots and the butterflies and the TV shows and the snow cones after school and all those great, great days? David, remember all our yesterdays?

"Oh David just take us back. Take us back to the Thanksgiving party where you found the Space Sieve. David, we won't go play that game. We won't try to hide in that closet. David, we won't ever, ever go into that closet.

"Just take us back, David. Just make everything go back the way it was. And then we'll all just go on like we would have. David we'll all just go on without ever having *seen* that Machine. That's really all we have to do. Just take us all back to the way we all were."

Chip was looking fondly at David, but now, at last, it was without confidence.

David shuddered. No one spoke for a few moments. Then David bowed his head and a tear dripped off his cheek.

"Chip," he said faintly. "It's impossible."

"No," Chip assured. "No David, you did it before! Remember, that planet you destroyed? You fixed it! You just went back in time a little way! You can do it David. You can! Remember?" Chip stood and placed his hands on the shoulders of his friend.

But David only leaned back, closed his eyes, and cried, "Oh if somehow I could be *saved* Chip. I've lost my very soul. They're gone. There's no way, Chip. Oh, if only I could trade places with those two girls!"

David turned away, and his voice was low and hoarse. "Oh, if only I could never have been born."

Chip shook him. "No," continued Chip. "No. Don't say that. No. Listen. Now that's not right. Come on." Chip chuckled a miserable, forced chuckle. "Come on now, be confident!"

Chip looked around at the stars. They were beautiful.

"Come on David," he said. "Look at the stars. Remember: always reach for the stars, David. You can *do* it!"

David shook his head now, becoming a little angry. "Look!" he said. "This isn't some stupid thing where you can change the world if you have enough confidence. This isn't 'reach for the sky – you can do anything' garbage. Listen to me, Chip. When I went back in time, and when we went forward, all I did was move back or forward along the time index of this Machine. It was like moving forward or backward along a string. But the memory is *gone*. There is no *string*, Chip. It's *gone*."

Chip trembled as he looked at David. Then he said, sternly. "Well, if we can't go back, then we'll just have to *find* them."

David smiled and shook his head, and closed his eyes. "There are billions of stars in our galaxy," he said. "And there are uncounted trillions of galaxies. And that's just in *our* universe. And the thing is, where we took the girls, it wasn't even in *our* universe. Do you know how many universes there are?"

For a few minutes, they both just sat there and looked out at the stars. They were sharp, clear, and bright – and strikingly beautiful.

For a moment, both felt everything would some how be all right – that somehow none of this had happened – that somehow, none of it *could* have happened – that perhaps it had all been a dream, even as below them stretched the brilliant expanse of your planet.

But then they both saw the Space Sieve, its screen dimly glowing with a blue light. And as they looked, they both knew.

There before them, waiting obediently, the unavoidable proof of reality, indeed as if embodying all of reality itself, the Space Sieve stood, silently.

It was real. All of it had really happened.

And yet, real as it was, the Space Sieve didn't care. It took no interest in any of it at all. For it was only a Machine. All it had done was exactly what it had been instructed to do.

The realization slowly sunk in. The girls were beyond their ability to retrieve. They had lost them, and there would be no surprise "fix" this time. Their parents would never know what happened to their daughters. The boys had lost a cousin. And they had lost Chip's sister.

After awhile, David spoke, and his weak voice had a strange, tuneful quality to it.

"You know what the worst of it is?" said David. "The place where I took them isn't even a real universe like this one. It exists in an almost-timeless reality. Our world – our solar system – will end before either of those girls will ever even be able to die. They will have to live there, as girls, forever."

Chip thought for a moment, but didn't fully appreciate what David said. Then Chip said, somewhat inexplicably, "Well, given what that Machine can do at least I guess it's a good thing we didn't destroy our entire Earth."

And at this point, Chip did something that humans do when they are extremely upset. He expelled the contents of his stomach. David immediately whisked it away, using the Machine.

Now, you are probably wondering, "So how do the girls then become reunited to their families? How does this all end well?"

But I would remind you that this is not a story. It is not make believe. This is real life. And sometimes real life does not turn out the way we want it to.

And I would remind you moreover, as I have already pointed out many times: That as far as your concept of reality can assimilate, when Chip and David watched the two girls run off through the forest, this would be the last time either of them would see those girls in their lifetimes.

However, a little later on I *will* tell you what happened to the two girls. That will comprise the second part of this book.

And while that next part of this account is the most important part, you might be surprised to know that the Space Sieve itself will hereafter no longer be a major part of this story. The part of this account that concerns the Space Sieve is now largely over, and the part that concerns David and Chip is now largely over as well. But before we move on, there is one more event having to do with the Space Sieve that I will relate.

"It's too bad that thing doesn't have an 'emergency button', said Chip, trying to offer resignation or humor, he didn't really know which.

"You mean like – an elevator?" replied David, and David's ears perked a little.

Chip looked at David with sad eyes and smiled. "Yeah."

David leaned back on the little stool in front of the Space Sieve and looked out at the stars. Then, he appeared to become very animated once again.

"I have an *idea*," he said.

And then David began to operate the Space Sieve with renewed fervor. Once again, auxiliary keyboards and screens materialized to either side the Space Sieve and David began to operate them as well. Soon, the stars around the two boys began to grow and merge, and soon the boys found themselves in a place that was entirely white, or perhaps more accurately, entirely *bright*.

Then, David released the keys of the Space Sieve and leaned back. But unlike other times, the Space Sieve did not go dark, nor did it freeze. The screen flickered and the colored buttons on the keyboard were still fully illuminated and animated.

"I did it," David said. "You could say I pressed the 'emergency button'."

Chip, still reeling from the experiences that they had just had, looked at David blankly and shook his head.

"I did what you said, Chip," David continued. "I pressed – well, not the 'emergency' button – you might say what I did was I pressed the 'home' button. I've returned the Space Sieve to its place of origin. This is the place where it was created," David looked around, "the place where it was made – the place where it began."

Chip looked back at David incredulously, and his brow furrowed. "I, I don't understand," he said.

David motioned toward the Space Sieve. "This is a Device," he said. "Every Device has a maker, and every maker works in a workshop of some kind. This is simply the workshop where the Space Sieve was made."

Chip shook his head. "But how do you ... how did you know where ... have you been here before?"

David frowned dismissively and shook his head. "No, I haven't been here before. I simply found a way to command the Space Sieve to return to its point of origin. Somehow, even though its memory was lost it still retained the information needed to return to its point of origin. I just had the idea that the best place to have something fixed is in the place where it was originally made."

"But," asked Chip nervously, "you said something about the 'maker.' What did you mean the 'maker'?" Chip just stared at David. Somehow the thought of meeting the maker of this Device had only just occurred to Chip, and it was not a comforting one.

And at that moment, the thought of meeting the maker of the Device did not seem so comforting to David either. David smiled and his eyes blinked nervously. "I know Chip, and maybe I didn't think enough about that. But the thing is, we have to do *something*. We have to somehow find out where I left the girls. This is the only thing I could think of. But now that you mention it, maybe it wasn't such a good idea ..."

At that moment David saw in Chip's face that something had just happened. Chip's eyes grew wide and his head bowed. With is own eyes widening, David began to turn to see what it was that Chip was looking at. But while still focusing on Chip's expression it occurred to David for a split second that it might be better if he *didn't* turn to look. As he hesitated, he heard a voice that was powerful, yet pleasant and gentle.

"Hello, my name is 'Actio'."

CHAPTER 12

TO MEET THE MAKER

DAVID WHEELED AROUND, and saw standing near them the figure of a young man. The creature, Actio (pronounced <u>AK</u>-tee-o), although fully mature, had a face and features that were very mild - his skin very smooth, with boyish qualities to his appearance. He wore a simple, white robe that while very sheer was completely opaque. As the two boys looked at him, Chip, for one, found him strangely compelling, even beautiful perhaps, although Chip had never associated that word with anyone but a girl before.

They also noticed that Actio glowed with a pure, white light that seemed to radiate from his person. And then they noticed that they, and the Space Sieve, seemed to be glowing too. In spite of the fact that most of what they could see around them emanated this whiteness, it was in fact not so much "white," as simply "bright." And in spite of the fact that this radiance was essentially monochromatic, it was nonetheless, a strikingly beautiful light.

And now in the interest of time, I will stop referring to the perceptions that the boys had of their situation, and I will instead for the sake of efficiency simply describe to you some things that you have no doubt begun to wonder about, to the extent that your minds have the capacity to assimilate it.

You may perhaps wonder why it is that almost all of the worlds to which David and Chip have traveled have been occupied by beings such as yourselves and why virtually all of these beings have appeared to be, in affect, young adults of your kind. The reason for this it is twofold. First of all, most of the beings within the sphere of existence that are similar to your kind have an appearance of being young adults of your kind. And is this really so surprising to you? Ask yourself: Had you great enough power to take any form you could choose, what would it be? The second reason is simply that those are the sorts of worlds to which David chose to travel. As far as Actio is concerned, and the question of who he is and the reason he bears such a striking resemblance to your kind, is because he is indeed a being after your kind. However, he simply exists in a different reality than the one in which you presently do.

Chip looked around and marveled, but David got straight to business.

"You're the one who built this Device?" David asked. "If you *are*, I need your help."

"Indeed, I am the one who created this Device," Actio said, with a smile in his voice. "And I have been observing you David, from time to time. Your ability with my Machine is remarkable."

Chip looked at Actio then at David, and then Chip smiled. David was his friend, after all.

But David continued, "If you've been watching us, have you been watching us in the last few minutes? It's the last few minutes that we need your help with."

Chip joined in, "We've lost our cousin and my sister."

"We took two of our cousins to another world, another dimension, and we don't know where it is," said David a little incompletely. "We need you to help us find them."

Actio smiled knowingly. Then he said, kindly, "No, I haven't been watching you recently but as far as helping you find someone you've misplaced using the Device, yes, I can certainly help you with that. You can put your fears to rest regarding it."

A great sense of relief swept over Chip. "At *last*," he thought, "we can find them. If this being can't find them, then no one can." (But of course, his last sentiment would prove to be the correct one.)

David, for his part, was not so sanguine about being able to find the girls, at least, not yet.   At this moment it was only David after all, who knew the full extent of the problem.

But Actio was as confident as he was radiant and charming. He motioned toward the Machine and David stood up from his stool.

Actio smiled. "A stool?" he asked. "It's a good idea. It's a lot better than standing up while you operate my Machine, isn't it?" Actio walked over to the Space Sieve and sat down on David's stool. "But I prefer," he continued, "something a little more ... shall we say ... elaborate."

And at that moment Chip and David both saw someone operate the Space Sieve with more dexterity and skill then even David himself had shown. The Device leapt to life as it responded to the touch of its master and creator. Instantly, the small black stool that David had created turned into an elaborate chair, almost throne-like. It was clear, as if made entirely of glass. It resembled what you would call a "recliner" in the sense that it had a high backrest with armrests to either side in addition to a small slope upon which Actio rested his feet. As it formed under Actio, it tilted back, and the Space Sieve rose off the floor and tilted in the air over Actio, in precisely the most comfortable position.

And then the boys noticed something else. It was music - a kind that was fantastic and ethereal, unlike anything human ears had ever heard. Indeed, a sound both blissfully comforting yet exciting – a sound that your kind could never independently imagine, much less create – flowed from the Device. And here, in Actio's presence, in spite of the fact that this was clearly a being of great intelligence and power, Chip felt very comfortable. So much so, that he reached out his hand and felt the material out of which Actio's chair was made. Although it appeared to be made of glass, its surface was soft and smooth, and it had an exciting, energetic quality to it as well. In fact, it reminded Chip of something. The only time Chip had ever felt something that interesting was when he had momentarily brushed against Diane at the Thanksgiving party, when they had first found the Space Sieve.

Within moments, several auxiliary keyboards and screens appeared to then left and right of the Space Sieve. As they did so, Actio turned to the boys. "I bet you've never seen anything like that before have you?" he said as he gestured to the auxiliary panels.

"Oh yes," replied Chip immediately, "David's done that."

Actio looked a little taken aback by Chip's comment. "Oh," he said, "I guess I missed that." And then he turned back and continued to operate the Device.

As Actio continued to operate the various keyboards of the Device, his gaze passing across the various screens as he did so, the music continued to rise.

David's eyes drifted to Chip, and he saw Chip's gaze had once again fixed on something off to the side. David spun around and he and Chip saw another being.

While Actio's features and been very fair – his eyes were blue and his hair blond – and while Actio had been wearing a simple robe that was entirely white, *this* being had hair and eyebrows that were brown, and *this* being's robe was an intense blue color.

And although Actio was appealing and even beautiful to both boys, now both were looking at a being whose beauty and appeal far exceeded even that of Actio's.

For this being, was *female*.

Actio turned around for a moment, smiled, and then returned to his work on the Device.

"Oh ," he said, "I see you've met my wife. Introduce yourself to the boys, Sapentia." (Sapentia is pronounced, "suh-PEN-shuh")

As the two boys stood transfixed, both with their mouths a little open, Sapentia spoke.

"How are you boys?" she asked kindly. She turned to Actio. "Are these the ones you told me about?"

Actio turned his head briefly for moment, and the two boys looked at him, noticing that Actio's formerly blithe, cherubic face was slightly less so now. In fact, he seemed a little worried. He smiled briefly – with what to the boys seemed a somewhat feigned assurance – then turned back to his work, and said, "Yes ... yes. Why don't you get to know them?" He waved his youthful hand and then continued to work on his Device.

"Well then," said Sapentia, and to the boys it was as though her voice was the softest, most evocative, and most dreamy sound that either of them had ever heard. And when she smiled, without knowing it both boys beamed glowingly back.

Feeling strangely confident, Chip spoke first. "I ... I didn't know *God* had a *wife*."

David glanced at Chip, somewhat surprised, then, with a sense of realization on his face, he glanced back at Sapentia.

But Sapentia seemed taken aback by the question. She turned to Actio. "Did you hear what he just said?" Actio didn't respond, being too engrossed in his work on the Space Sieve. "*Actio*," she said more clearly, "Did you hear what he just said to me? He said that he didn't know God had a wife. Actio, did you tell him . . . ?"

Actio spoke this time without turning his head. "I didn't ever tell either of them that I was *God*. I don't even know where they would have *gotten* that idea."

Sapentia turned back to the Boys. There was a note of sarcasm in her voice. "Well," she said, "I just can't imagine why, faced with the presence of a powerful, glowing – and if I may say, attractive – being such as yourself

Actio, that they would think they were in the presence of God. No," she continued, now growing concerned at Actio's distracted manner, "I can't even imagine that at *all*." And she turned back to the boys.

But it went over both of their heads. Somehow, whether or not they were standing at the feet of deity was not what was most on their minds. (And obviously they were not in the presence of divinity. Neither Actio nor Sapentia are God, and of course, neither am I.)

Rather, the only thing on the boys' minds, was their sensation of Sapentia's beauty, and the feeling they had at the sound of her voice.

Actio was still energetically operating the Machine. When Sapentia asked him when he would finish, she received no response. So she decided to take a few minutes to explain who she and Actio were.

"Actio," she called, and then she spoke in her own language to Actio. To the boys, the sound of her true language more evoked a feeling than a mere listening to words – like a calm, summer evening when suddenly you hear the comforting song of a mourning dove. She had asked Actio to give her and the boys something to sit on.

With an only partially-interested glance from Actio, three soft objects materialized behind Sapentia and the two boys. The objects then pushed gently forward and up while slipping their feet from under them.

The three were seated. But as Sapentia spoke, she could see that neither boy was listening. Each was sitting in his chair, looking upward, seemingly stunned, mouth open. For Chip and David the sensation was not so much sitting in a chair as something much more compelling – perhaps the feeling of a baby has when in its mother's arms on a calm, cold evening. It is difficult to describe such feelings and events as these using your words and your limited experiences. I must be content simply to say that it is difficult to describe the comfort, the security, and the scintillating pleasure the boys felt when sitting in these chairs.

"Actio, not these sorts of chairs for these boys," she said affectionately. "It's too much for them. Give them something more like they're accustomed to. I wanted to talk to them, not enrapture them."

And then under the boys, in the place of the chairs they had been on, appeared two large, very overstuffed recliners of the sort your kind has developed and which you find comfortable. And yet, compared to what they had been sitting on, these two chairs seemed more like they were sitting on burlap bags filled with pumpkins.

But now indeed, Sapentia once again had their attention. And so, she briefly described who she and Actio were, where they came from, where they lived, and so forth. This information would no doubt be interesting to the reader of this document, but it will serve little purpose in my relating it, as it is not pertinent to the narrative. Perhaps you will forgive me if I say only that these two beings come from a reality very different from you own. And yet, there was a time when they were much like you are now.

Once Sapentia had finished her brief account, the three noticed that Actio had also completed his work, and the Space Sieve was resting on the floor once again, its single screen and keyboard flickering eagerly. Actio's chair had become a small ottoman, and he was sitting on it and had been listening to Sapentia as well.

"So," she said to him, "Are you all done? Are you ready to reunite these little boys with their little playmates – their relatives? Where are they?"

Chip looked at Actio very expectantly. But David didn't. David looked off into the distance, and his teeth were clenched. For David didn't eagerly await the answer. He dreaded it. He already knew what it had to be.

"I . . ." Actio paused. "I . . ." and he didn't say any more. His face was grim and his youthful visage somehow was considerably dimmed.

Sapentia's face grew a little stern. "What's the matter?"

Actio then began to speak in his language. The sound cannot be described to you, but it made the boys feel like the first sound of rustling leaves in the fall, when the joys of summer are gone, and a definite chill is in the air.

Sapentia shook her head, and she spoke in English. "I don't understand, Actio. And I know it's unpleasant, but please speak in their language. They deserve to hear what you have to say."

"Sapentia, listen to me," he said, in a low, quiet voice. "Somehow – I don't know how – it's virtually impossible – somehow they . . ." he looked over at David, who continued to stare off into the distance. "Somehow he cleared the memory nexus. He erased the Machine's memory." He looked at her. "Sapentia, I don't know if even *I* could have done that."

Sapentia's face puzzled for a moment, then began to grow grim with realization.

"Without knowing where the girls are," Actio continued slowly, "and without the central memory nexus that tracks all activities of this Device, we cannot – there is no possible way to – know where they are. Dead or alive, they are lost. They are truly, and irretrievably, lost." Then he spoke to her in their own language again. It made one feel like the sunset on the last day before you were leaving your own home, never to return.

As he spoke, Sapentia held her perfect hands to her mouth, and a sparkling tear quickly formed in the corner of each of her ethereal eyes. "Oh Actio!" she said, "but you assured me. You said that if I let you make something like this Device that it would never irreparably harm anything – that if it did, you would always be able to change things back. Oh, Actio," Sapentia did not know as much about the Device as Actio did, but she knew enough. "How could this have happened? What have you done? And her glance fell to the boys. Chip's face now had changed to a state of disbelief. David was breathing heavily.

"You see," Actio began a relatively useless explanation, "It's not that they no longer exist, but that they're *lost*. Imagine if you took a grain of sand. Imagine if this tiny particle had certain distinctive features that you could recognize – it was unique and valuable to you. Now imagine that you put this tiny grain of sand into one of your flying craft – one of your airplanes – and you flew around your world."

As Actio spoke, Chip listened, still clinging to hope. But David's head felt like a watermelon. And he was getting dizzy. He was hardly listening. He already knew everything Actio was saying anyway.

"Now," continued Actio, "suppose that when you got home, you found that your precious sand particle had fallen out of the airplane, but you had no idea where."

"Do you see why you could never find it again?" he asked, now turning to Chip, who seemed to be the only one still listening to him. "Of course, if you looked at every grain of sand on your planet, you could find it. But do you see that to do that – to look at every particle of dust – would take so long that essentially it's out of the question to ever find it? It would take what you call, 'forever.' Do you see why it would be impossible to find the little grain of sand?"

"But," asked Chip with his usual optimism, "even though *I* don't remember anything about it, *David* does. You remember where we were, don't you David?" He looked over to David with his trusting face. They all looked at David.

Chip continued, "You're the smartest person I have ever known, David. You remember *something* about where they are, *don't* you? We can use that, can't we?"

David straightened himself up. He sniffed, and wiped a tear from his eye.

Actio shook his head. "While it might help to remember which ocean you were over when you dropped the grain of sand, still, there is no possible way . . ."

"Actio, be quiet." Sapentia interjected. "Let David speak. Darling, do you remember which universe or galaxy you were in? Do you remember the planet?" But even as she heard herself ask the question, Sapentia began to realize the futility of it too.

"I *do* remember," said David, suddenly a little confident and hopeful. "But it wasn't a planet or a universe," he continued. "It was what I called an extra-dimensional realm." He looked at Actio, and back at Sapentia, plaintively. "It had no planets, suns, or any of that kind of thing. It just existed in and of itself. Another thing I called it was 'boundless reality.'"

Sapentia quickly took a breath and began talking rapidly to Actio in her own language. The sound made one feel the way one does when looking out over the rolling waters of a cold, dark sea.

When she had finished, Actio appeared to have been seriously chastised. "You said to speak in their language," he reminded her.

Sapentia looked at the boys with her head bowed, and briefly repeated what she had said as she motioned toward the Device: "Actio, you created this Device such that beings like them could go into the upper realms – into the *alter*-worlds?"

"Sapentia," Actio said plaintively. "It was protected. Yes, *I* used it to go into the alter-worlds."

Chip interrupted. "They were different from our world. A lot of things about them were different. David called one of them 'Pathia,' and the other, 'Skylia.'"

Actio nodded, a little condescendingly. "Yes, well, *I* used the Machine to go there – into the alter-worlds. But it was prohibited to beings like them, and it was protected by codes. How could he have gotten past the codes?" He shook his head in disbelief.

Almost interrupting, Sapentia followed up. "I thought this Device was intuitive for their kind? How can you predict what he could do, if it was intuitive?"

And then Sapentia spoke to Actio again in their language. When she spoke, the sound of her voice made the boys feel the way one feels at the end of a crucial battle lost, when a lone bugle slowly plays out the defeated army's anthem for the last time.

You see, Actio and Sapentia have the ability to look backward and forward in time where time exists, to see events that have, and will, happen.

She asked Actio why he could not simply look back and watch David operate the machine when he took the girls to that world – why he could not simply watch the strokes of David's fingers and the images on the screen and repeat them. When Actio replied to her, it made the boys feel the way they felt at scout camp, when they stood at the gate of the camp surrounded mostly by strangers, and watched their parents drive away. Actio told her that he had already tried to do that, but the operation of the machine is so intuitive that simply watching David perform a function was of no use. For you to understand this, imagine watching someone execute an expert water skiing trick, then going and doing it yourself. Even if you knew how to ski yourself, it is unlikely you could execute the trick precisely the same way, no matter how many times you tried. You are after all, a different individual than the one who did the trick. And the operation of the Device is far more varied and complex than any sport. Actio could never have duplicated David's keystrokes no matter how exactly he observed them. And unable to duplicate them, he could not have followed David to the correct location, among the countless possibilities.

Then, for awhile they all just sat there. As the moments passed Chip looked around and thought. As his hopes slowly faded, his eyes filled with tears, and he cried.

Then, for a moment, they all did. David and Chip cried for the loss of Sally and Diane. Actio cried for his errors that had led to their terrible loss. And Sapentia cried because of her empathy for them all.

After awhile, she spoke. "Actio, I want you to tell these boys that you will fix this." "But," he pleaded, "I *can't*, you see, it's just imposs . . ."

"Actio," she reiterated quickly, "I want you to tell them you will try – you will do all you can. Actio, you must." She looked at him, sternly.

He looked back at her, then at the boys. "I will," he said. "I will try to find a way to recover the girls." He paused. "You have my assurance." Then he looked at Sapentia, and back to the boys, took a deep breath, and nodded authoritatively. "And I am a being of some abilities. There is a lot I can do that you haven't seen. You can trust me."

Chip smiled at this assurance, but when he saw David his smile faded. David didn't smile at all. He knew so much more than Chip, and as such he believed Actio's assurances were empty. He was confident that they were made for the same reason people in your world sometimes make assurances – simply to make people feel better for a while. (And for what it is worth, as we will see, Sapentia was just as convinced that Actio's assurances were insincere as well. But she too felt that at this point that even a false assurance would be better for the boys than the alternative, which was complete and utter hopelessness.)

And at this point I will reiterate that both David and Sapentia were correct in thier estimation. Actio had no idea of what to do. In agreeing to make all things right again, he was essentially doing only what Sapentia had told him to do, in spite of the fact that he felt certain he was just giving empty words to the boys to spare their feelings.

Without going into any further detail, David and Chip returned to David's bedroom with the Device. And after that, David, for the rest of his life, never operated the Space Sieve again.

And, for the most part, this outing was the last one the two boys, Chip and David, would ever have together again. Other than for a few brief interactions that would occur from time to time, it was also essentially the end of their friendship.

As an aside, you may be wondering how it can be that nobody could find out where the two girls were, given the fact that *I* must surely know, and since indeed, I have produced this document. The reason is that while I happened to be present when David took them all to the place where he left the girls and I could therefore follow, and thankfully could also follow him when he returned to what were familiar surroundings to me, I did not have any way to track or re-trace our course through so great an expanse either. While you may think I am a being of infinite power, I am not. That is something relatively few beings attain.

But of course, you cannot be in any suspense at this point. For, as I have said, Sally and Diane never traveled interdimensionally again, and neither Chip nor David ever saw either of those two girls again, for the rest of their lives. I have said this many times already. If it is difficult for you to understand, what more can I do?

Naturally, Chip, his brother, and especially his father were horribly distraught over the loss of Sally, as were the parents of Diane. Strangely, for your kind, the burial of a person's remains gives you some kind of comfort – in the case of Sally and Diane, their loved ones did not even get this opportunity. Their two beloved girls had simply vanished. Chip for his part, had tried to explain to his father and brother what had happened. But this had resulted only in an abundance of tears with no one believing a word of it anyway. Chip's father, having previously lost his wife in years past, had now lost his only daughter. Suffice it to say that this final blow was sufficiently disabling to Chip's father that after this, of necessity, Chip had

124

had to take over a somewhat larger portion of the family responsibilities than one of his age should have to do. Yet, he bore it ably, and it made him a stronger man in his later years.

David never tried to explain what happened, to anyone. He never even brought up the subject of the Space Sieve again. And while David's parents somehow suspected the strange Device had something to do with all of it, they never asked him about it again, either.

David and Chip saw each other only rarely after that, even though Chip's family had moved into David's neighborhood years later. It wasn't that they avoided each other; their lives just took different paths.

The last time David ever saw Chip in their youth was many years later, when each boy was nineteen.

David was working on his father's car. It was parked in the street, and he was leaning in under the hood. It was a clear, late summer afternoon.

In recent years, Chip had taken to going around much of the time wearing only a pair of shorts, and nothing else, and that is what he was wearing on this occasion. In that time and part of your world, for someone to dress in that way was not considered unusual. Naturally, he was very tan.

He and Chip talked politely for awhile as David worked, and the substance of their conversation is unimportant. After a few minutes, the conversation ended somewhat abruptly, if politely.

Then Chip walked off down the street to the west, with the sun in the position of late afternoon. As David looked up from his work, he watched Chip as he walked away. As he did, Chip jumped onto a low, brick wall and padded along the top of it with his bare feet. Chip outstretched his arms and fingers to balance himself, and he tipped slightly from side to side as he went.

David's gaze fell back to his work, but suddenly realized how much he had missed seeing Chip over the years, and he thought how evocative it had just been seeing his onetime friend, Chip, walking along that brick wall like a child, with his arms out and balancing himself as he went. While Chip and David both were almost men on the outside, there was still much of two little boys on the inside.

And so David looked back down the street again to catch a last glimpse of his boyhood friend. But as David looked first down the street, and then scanning from side to side, to his surprise he found that Chip was already gone. And in that moment, David realized that something else had perhaps vanished as well.

As David looked back to his work, he realized that time had passed without him really noticing, and in the process, his childhood had disappeared – like Chip had just disappeared – suddenly, and unexpectedly. Chip was gone for good when David looked back up, and David's boyhood was probably already gone for good too, now that he had noticed. And in the same fleeting moment that he wished Chip would come back, David wished his own boyhood could somehow come back too.

The decades passed, and both Chip and David lived out the rest of their lives as your kind does, largely apart from each other, except for a final meeting between the two of them that happened late in their lives. Or, perhaps I should say, after your manner of reckoning, they *will* live out the rest of their lives, and they *will* have a final meeting at some point in their *future*. It is difficult for me to get used to your language and in particular, to get used to how constrained you are by time. For you see: your past, your present, your future – it is all the same thing to me.

And yet, while past, present and future are all the same to me, it is not the same as knowing all things. That is something few beings attain.

This final meeting between David and Chip happened fifty-seven years later. Both Chip and David had married and divorced. At this point in their lives, each had lost virtually everyone they had known and loved (other than their own children) to old age. David was living in a small room of a complex of dwellings that looked out over the China Sea.

Chip had arranged to visit his boyhood friend and part-cousin, for what he assumed would likely be the last time.

We take up the conversation at this point: David and Chip were sitting on David's porch, looking out over the ocean. They had already gone through the typical pleasantries. When Chip had arrived it had been late afternoon. Now, it was twilight.

"You know I remember," Chip said wistfully, "that we used to be pretty good friends. What ever happened to that?" And his lined, pallid face still had an impish quality that sparkled beneath his bald head

David looked back at Chip. His face too, was aged; his skin was lined, spotted, and gray. His hair was white, and lifeless. But unlike Chip, there was no sparkle in David's face. "What do you mean, Chip?"

Chip smiled and his eyes twinkled. "You know, nobody's called me that for years. Everybody calls me 'Charles'. Well, my business associates call me that. My friends call me 'Chuck'. It's kind of nice to hear you call me 'Chip,' David."

David looked at him witheringly. "Well, in that case *Charles*, just what the devil are you talking about?" (That last time just then, would be the last time David would ever call him "Chip.")

Chip was taken aback, but then he smiled again. He looked up. Colored characters and figures were being drawn on the dome of the sky overhead. I say "dome" here to refer to the fact that while it appeared the lasers being shined up from the ground were writing on a dome overhead, in reality there was no such dome. Beside the figures being drawn in the sky overhead were the stars, which were very bright on this particular night.

"Look at that – kids shooting their lasers up, drawing up there in the sky." Chip shook his head. "It's amazing the talent kids have – no training at all." Then he looked back at David. "I remember a boy once who I thought had a lot of talent. When we were kids, I always thought you were the smartest person I had ever known. And I still do David."

David looked back at Chip and clenched his teeth. Then he looked back toward the horizon. In the twilight could be seen two large creatures, flying over the sea. They were about the size of a man, with large, fleshy arms, tipped with feathers. Strips of loose skin hung behind them and flapped in the breeze. Small, colored feathers dotted the strips. Flaps of skin like a chicken's comb but red, blue and green, protruded garishly from their heads and also flapped as they flew.

"Sickening creatures," David said, changing the subject, motioning toward the flying creatures, "genetic mutants. Never should have existed. They should have killed them all. Now we have to look at the disgusting things."

"Well," countered Chip, "I guess the thinking was that whatever we may think of them and however they may look to us, to themselves those creatures matter a great deal, and however they came to *be*, they're *alive*. And I guess to most folks it just seemed wrong to wipe them all out, although I suppose some have tried to, before it was illegal to kill them. I guess some still do try to kill them. Of course they go to jail for it now."

As the mutants flew into the distance, the sound of the surf dominated the evening once again.

There was a long pause.

"Well . . ." said Chip. And the two sat there for a few moments.

Then David broke the silence, taking up the question Chip had asked him previously.

"What *happened* to our *friendship*?! What happened to our *lives*?!" David looked at Chip with eyes that looked like they were ready to hurl hot embers at Chip. "What happened was that Infernal Contraption *ruined* them. Or maybe I should say *I* ruined all our lives with it!"

But Chip looked back at David with only affection and concern. "Oh David, come on. You don't blame *yourself* for that, do you – for Diane and Sally – *do* you?"

David's sour expression – it was engrained into his face – turned even more so. "Well then just whose fault did you think it *was*? *Yours*?" His voice became more hoarse, and his words sounded like he was trying to fire them out of a cannon at Chip.

Chip looked back calmly, with a feigned cheerfulness, and he studied David's face. As he began to realize the extent of David's psychological problems and the vexation and trauma that had plagued him through the many years, Chip tried to shift from mere conversation to an attempt to help. He became more firm. "David, you're not serious. You haven't blamed yourself for that for all these years, have you?"

David didn't say anything. He just blew some air between his aged teeth.

Then, with the realization, Chip slumped back in his chair. "Oh David," he said dolefully. "I had no idea – no idea you blamed yourself for it all these years. If I had known . . ." and his voice trailed off.

David turned and looked at Chip. "What the devil are you talking about, Chuck?" he commanded accusingly.

Chip looked out over the ocean, a sad expression creasing his face. "David, you blamed yourself for it? You were only . . . and it's been so many . . . Listen, you know in a way it *is* my fault. Here I've left you for all these years wrestling with guilt and remorse. I never knew. I should have visited, David. I should have tried to help you with it. I should have tried to have been there for you. But I didn't know. I'd never imagined you'd been blaming yourself for losing them, all these years."

David shot back, "*Been* there? You should have been there - for *what*?" "What the devil are you talking about, Charles? It was *my* fault. *I'm* the one who did it. *I'm* the one who should have suffered for it: not *you*, not *Sally*, not *Diane*, not your *family*, and not *Diane's* family, and not any of the other people who lost those two girls."

Chip looked away, then back at David, and then he said, a little harshly, "You were a little boy. You were what, fourteen, fifteen? David, do you realize that had most people gotten into possession of that Machine they could have turned themselves into dictators over our entire planet – they could have destroyed out entire *world!* David, all you did was take two little girls someplace you thought that they would enjoy. And when something bad happened that you thought was best forgotten, you did what you thought you had to do to make everything all right. There was no meanness in you, no selfishness, no greed, no avarice. All you did was make some mistakes. David, we *all* make them."

David bowed his head. He closed his wrinkled eyes, and after a few moments it was clear to Chip that his old friend was crying. At that moment, Chip remembered that the last time he had seen David cry was when he himself had been crying in the presence of Actio and Sapentia.

Chip put his hand on David's shoulder and they sat there in the quiet for a moment. "You know," Chip said. "It almost seems like it was all just a dream. And David, I suppose it's all been like a dream to me for at least the last 50 years. Things have changed a lot since then. It was a long time ago."

David pulled away, turned and looked at Chip, and when he did, he looked to Chip like some kind of red-eyed animal. "Well let me tell you something," said David fiercely, "It hasn't been like a dream to *me*. It's been *reality* to me every day of every year since it happened. They were my *cousins*. Sally was your *sister*, Charles. I took them away from the people they loved and who loved them. I took their lives away. And the worst of it is . . ."

Chip looked at him but said nothing as they sat there in the gathering darkness.

"Let me tell you something," said Chip. "I'm going to tell you something. You know they say you never forget your first love? Well, I know we were all just kids, but I've wondered if that could have been one of the reasons for my divorce – heaven knows there were *enough* of them. But you know I could never forget Diane. She meant something to me too. Not just my sister – Diane did too. It's kind of funny, really. I know we were all just little kids then, but I always remembered her running off into that forest with the light in the distance. It seemed so simple, so pure. I didn't know what it was about it. I knew I liked her but I didn't really have a crush on her. There was just something about that that I always . . ."

David interrupted. "Same for me," he said. "I liked Diane too. And I liked your sister. When they ran off with their hair all flinging back and forth . . . I always remembered that too." He snorted. "It's stupid. When my ex-wife's lawyer heard me talking about Sally once – he used it in court against me in my divorce. He said I'd never really loved my wife – that I pined for Sally and that I never showed affection for my wife. He said that was the reason she wanted to divorce me. What a load of nonsense – that I was pining for a girl from when I was fourteen. Jeez. Shows you how many girls I've known – the divorce lawyer had to go all the way back to when I was fourteen. But he said I never loved my wife. He said that was good enough reason for *any* woman to divorce a man." His voice trailed off. "Who knows? Maybe it *is*."

"But it's stupid," he continued. "She was just a little girl."

They both slowly shook their heads. A few moments passed.

Then Chip looked up and cocked his head toward David. There was a harshness in his voice. "What in the world ever *happened* to that . . . crazy *Machine* anyway?" he said.

David's head tilted back, and he became distant. Then he turned to Chip and for a moment he was his old, lively, energetic, intelligent self. "You know," he said, "after we left those two – Actio and Sapentia – I never worked the Machine again after that, and it's funny I ended up with it. You'd thought that Actio would have wanted it back. And to tell you the truth, I lost track of the thing. My parents put it in the attic for awhile, and after that I went away to college. After they moved I never asked about it – to tell you the truth I have no idea what happened to it. Maybe it's still in that attic; maybe it got thrown away. Who knows?"

(For your information, when David's parents moved, they threw the Space Sieve away and it was hauled off and buried under tons of garbage in a landfill.)

Then David looked over at Chip, smiled wryly, and said, "But I guess it all turned out pretty good for you, didn't it, Mr. Millionaire?"

"Yeah, it did." Chip replied. "When I was a boy, I never would have imagined I would've gotten into the furniture business. You know it took me 20 years to figure out how to make those chairs. But once I had the secret recipe for how make them, it was a goldmine."

"You know," said David, vigorously, "I still remember when we sat on those chairs when we started talking to Sapentia. I'd never felt anything like that in my life. I have to admit, your chairs – the chairs your company makes – they're not quite as good, but they're pretty darn close."

Chip chucked. "Yeah, the chairs felt so good the government even thought about making them illegal. The politicians and corporate types thought that if people had chairs like that to sit on they would never do any work. The tax revenues would fall off. The whole economy might collapse with everyone just sitting around in the chairs. But then, in the end, the government bought a *ton* of them.

"Now, it seems like they're everywhere. It turns out having a comfortable chair to sit in isn't really such a bad thing after all," Chip quipped.

They sat there for a couple more hours watching the children draw their art work in the sky with their lasers, and listening to the sound of the sea in the distance.

And that was the last time David and Chip ever saw each other. A few years after this meeting David came to the end of his life and died, and five years after that, he was followed by Chip.

And so, my account of David, of Chip, and of the Space Sieve – for all practical purposes – ends here.

But when the two men died, neither Sally nor Diane had died yet. Indeed, neither girl had even aged from the time they first entered their new world. But during the interim, a great deal had happened to them there.

And you may recall that I mentioned that my desire to document David's experience with the Device was my *secondary* reason for writing this document, and that there was another, *primary*, reason. The events surrounding the experience of Sally and Diane in their new world comprise that primary reason. Within their experience in their new world was an event of such importance that it is something that is spoken of and remembered not only by my kind, but by all creatures in existence that know about it.

☼ CHAPTER 13 ☼

THE LAST OF THEIR KIND

IT HAD NO NAME when the two girls arrived there with David and Chip, at least, nobody had given it one. Sally and Diane decided to call it, "New California," because they liked the sound of it.

At this point I have a difficulty: this world – New California – was a time-constrained reality – such as the one in which you live, and yet, it was very different. It was not a planet orbiting a sun, and so there was no day and night, nor were there seasons. It was always light there; it was always day, and it was always the *same* day. And yet, as I will describe, time did pass there, in a sense. Events took place, and there was a sense of past, present, and future. But to the extent that time passed in New California, it passed much more slowly than on Earth.

Another difference was that this place was for all intents non-*spatially* constrained. In your world, if you travel in one direction, you will eventually travel around your Earth and come once again to the place where you started. But New California was not a planet. If you were to set off in any given direction – including up – you could go on in that direction forever – the reality would simply expand accordingly.

And indeed, since beings there do not need to eat, drink, or breathe, you literally *could* head off in a direction and keep going for a very long time, after your manner of reckoning of time. In that sense, this reality could not ever become over-populated; its resources could never be exhausted. The world was infinite, in the sense that your minds can understand that word.

Having said that, it was many days, after your manner of reckoning of time, before either of these two girls even noticed that the day in which they

133

arrived had not *ended*. It was many more days before it occurred to either of them that it had been a very long "time" since they had first come to that place.

Part of the reason for this lack of awareness was that they were very happy. There was no need to eat, or to sleep, or to wash their clothes or their bodies, or to seek shelter, or to take care of any of the other needs that so preoccupy your existences, although they could do any of these things had they wanted to. They simply went – and did – whatever struck their fancy.

And what a great deal there was to do! For this world was filled with creatures of all shapes and sizes. And while many of these animals were powerful, they were all harmless both to the girls and to each other. Using this base form of communication – your language – with which I producing this account, it is impossible to convey even a minute fraction of the diversity and wonder of the life forms in this place. Therefore, for the most part I will refrain from doing so except where necessary.

One case where I need to describe a particular creature is in the case of the ones that Diane named the "communication beetles." These were insects that looked like large "June Bugs," except they were a dull brown color. That is, they were brown except when facilitating *communication* between the other creatures, as required. Whenever a creature in this world wished to speak to another creature, it would emit sounds, or pulsating colors, or in some cases, odors.

So for instance, when the "chameleons" would speak, the communication beetles would fly and flash green. When a "pterodactyl" would fly overhead and speak, the beetles would flash alternating green and grey. When the "minnows" would speak, the beetles would flash silver. And as the beetles did so, all the other creatures could understand what the creature speaking was saying. This included the two girls. When the girls would speak, the beetles would not flash a color, as the girls did not emit color when speaking. However, the beetles would make sounds, translating the girls' speech into sounds the other creatures could understand.

Some time after Sally and Diane arrived in this world – it would be about 300 years after your manner of reckoning – they succeeded in organizing various animals and gathering various materials of construction, and had built a great castle in the valley of what they named "Shenandoah," although neither of them had ever been to the Shenandoah Valley on your world – again, they just picked a name they both liked. Framing this valley were two high peaks, that the girls named "The Two Alps."

The fact that the girls built this castle 300 years from the time they arrived would seem to you to mean that this event will happen in the future. I suppose that would be true based on the way you understand the past, present, and future. But past, present, and future are all the same to me.

They named their castle "England Castle." Thus this castle was rimmed on the sides by the great "Two Alps of New California" standing in the distance to the rear of their great building.

All of the creatures were welcome in the castle. Indeed, a number of them lived there. The girls' lives – and those of the creatures – seemed an endless time of discovery and joy.

One favorite activity for Sally and Diane was flying the "cherubs." (Diane had initially called them alternatively the "cherubims" or the "seraphims," inaccurately using a double plural terminology. Later, they used the simplified term "cherub" to refer to one of them, but the still inaccurate term, "cherubs" to refer to both.) The cherubs – or so the girls named them – were two large, blue, feathered creatures considerably larger than the size of your elephants – more along the size of a whale. And yet, the shape of their bodies differed from elephants or whales, as their bodies included large, bird-like chests, tails, and vast, powerful wings.

The first time the girls saw the cherubs flying overhead, Sally, the more impetuous of the two, had begun to wonder how to saddle the creatures so she could fly on them. Several decades after they arrived, she had succeeded in making a harness and saddle that both she and Diane could use to fly on the female Cherub, which they named "Asherah" (pronounced ASH-er-uh), after a name Diane had heard and remembered from a Bible class. They named the male "El," which is pronounced the same as the letter, "L."

The first time they ever flew on Asherah was a time they both remembered ever after. It is an interesting aspect of this place, that while El and Asherah were perhaps the two most noteworthy animals there – and by far the most intelligent – even more so than the human girls – they were nonetheless very humble and kind. They willingly allowed the girls to hatch their scheme to saddle and fly upon Asherah – indeed their main concern was for the two girls' safety. The cherubs had agreed to this, and the stronger male cherub had decided he would fly alongside Asherah and the two girls, ready to snatch one or both of the girls in his large jaws in the event that either fell off.

So the time came for the first attempt to ride Asherah. Tucking a communication beetle into her belt, Sally saddled Asherah, and both girls climbed onto the saddle and strapped themselves down. As the two girls sat on the back of Asherah, holding on to the saddle, Asherah extended her wings. At that moment, Diane realized that she had not noticed before just how long Asherah's wings were. Asherah paused for a moment with her wings extended, and then she began to gently flap them. As she moved them harder and harder, they thrust the air downward against the grass below. Soon, Asherah began to generate enough down draft that it felt as if she would soon become airborne.

But then Asherah flashed blue. The cherubs were the only creatures in New California that were an iridescent blue. They were the only creature of any kind for which the communication beetles flashed blue.

In response to Asherah's wish to speak to the girls, the communication beetle under Sally's belt flashed blue, and spoke.

"I can't lift off just flapping my wings. I'll have to jump."

Sally, in the front, looked back at Diane, whose eyes were wide.

A communication beetle conveyed Sally's affirmative nod to Asherah who tucked her wings to her side and crouched. Both girls screamed, bent low, and held on. Then, Asherah jumped into the air.

Her wings drove down, and up, down, and up. Just as Diane had not noticed before how *long* Asherah's wings were, she had not imagined how *powerful* they were. Like you sometimes feel when you are on one of your "thrill rides," Diane felt the fear that comes with finding oneself in a situation where one's body is being moved strongly in a way that is completely beyond the person's expectation or control. Both girls felt the powerful lunges forward, the brief pause, and then the powerful lunge again with each wing stroke. It was exhilarating for both girls, feeling Asherah's strength as she drove them further and further into the sky with her magnificent wings.

In a few moments, her strokes diminished in intensity and Asherah's wings became more extended, as they began to soar. About this time both girls realized something else about flying. It was something that David had realized when he first flew: Flying is very *windy*. In fact, it was so windy that almost all either girl could do was hold on and listen to the rushing of air. If you have ever ridden on of your motorcycles without glasses, a helmet, or a windshield, you know what I am talking about.

You may remember that in David's case – when he had the Space Sieve – he took steps to alleviate the problem of the wind in his eyes and ears by creating various energy fields around himself so that the rushing air could not contact him. Thus, his experience with flying was much more pleasant – much more along the lines of what your kind imagines flying would be like. (In other words, when you imagine what flying would be like, you always forget just how much rushing of air there would be if you were to fly.) But since neither of these girls had the means to remove the effects of the rushing air, they just had to put up with it.

Sally and Diane both put their heads down. The air was whipping by so fast neither one could look forward into the gale. As they looked to the side, they could see the massive and powerful El, attentively flying alongside, watching for any difficulties.

Suddenly, Asherah banked. It was actually a very gentle bank, but it seemed hard and sudden to the girls who felt their insides turning as their bodies were forced into the curve, and they momentarily felt themselves being pressed hard into their seats by the forces of flight. Diane bent over and closed her eyes. But based on a great many other experiences with the two cherubs, Sally had decided that she trusted Asherah and El more that she trusted anyone she had ever known, and she had concluded to try to soak up the experience without fear. Looking to the side and down, she could see their England Castle below. And indeed, this was Asherah's reason for banking – she had wanted to show them their castle from the sky – from the vantage point she herself had seen so often.

Struggling against both the wind and the g-forces, Sally looked back to Diane, who had her face down and was merely trying to hold on.

"Look!" she said, pointing at the castle, but Diane didn't move.

She caught a glimpse of El who was now circling below, watching for any possible contingency.

Sally was Chip's sister, so she too had lost her mother as a child, and had to come to terms with it. But now, with El and Asherah, she felt she had found new parents. Sometimes – when a child has the peace and security that comes with having thoughtful, caring parents – the child seeks more. And Sally wanted more now. She wanted *excitement*.

Deciding that what she was doing now wasn't really flying, Sally decided she would put her new guardians to the test. She didn't know how it would all work out – she knew she couldn't fly – but she was confident that no harm could come to her with El, her powerful surrogate father, flying watchfully below.

And so, while firmly grasping the handle of the saddle she had made, she undid the straps that held her. She raised her legs, and crouched. She hesitated. And then, she let go of the saddle and jumped off Asherah's back.

As soon as she came off, she felt the shock of the air in her face pummeling her far worse than it had been before. Unbeknownst to Sally,

Asherah had been using some of her forward feathers to act as a wind break for the two girls.

As Sally felt the full force of the wind, she was thrown backward violently, with Asherah appearing to race away from her. Something else Sally had not appreciated was the skill with which Asherah had been flying. For it is often the case that when creatures that are unskilled in something see a skilled creature performing an action with great ease, the unskilled creature thinks the function is therefore easy. Asherah had made flying look easy. Sally began to tumble in the air like a leaf in a waterfall. She had no control at all now. She closed her eyes, tucked herself into a ball, and plunged downward. Far from experiencing the joy of flying free, what she had instead achieved was only danger and intense fear.

Then, only a few seconds later, she felt warm all around her, and it became dark.

Sally realized that she was inside El. He had swallowed her.

I mentioned earlier that the girls in this place had no need to eat. Naturally, they could eat, but they didn't have to. In the same manner, they could breathe while in this place if they wanted to, but they didn't have to do that either.

Sally felt only a sense of weightlessness, and could hear the sound of the air outside rushing faster and faster. Momentarily, she felt herself pressed hard against the inside of El's belly, and the sound of rushing stopped. El had landed. He pushed Sally back out.

For the next few minutes, several other communication beetles hovered around, facilitating communication between Sally and El. Sally told El that everything was all right and El asked Sally what had happened and then chastised her for being so careless. Asherah soon landed as well, and the conversation continued along these same lines with Diane joining El and Asherah in chastising Sally.

Sally was still trembling, but her fear had turned to excitement, admiration, and affection. What an experience it was to be saved by the might and devotion of El!

And so the first flying experience ended. There would be many, many other flying experiences. But in these future cases, Sally always obeyed El and Asherah, who made her agree to a list of rules that Sally would rigorously follow. For Diane's part, she was level headed enough that the two cherubs saw no need for any rules with her when they went flying together. And indeed, there was generally no need for any rules with Diane at all.

138

As time passed, their flights often included a host of the other creatures of New California. In some cases they flew under their own power, and in some cases El and Asherah and other flying creatures carried those creatures that could not fly.

And so, time – all consisting of a single day – passed, filled with the pleasures of exploring this world, discovering its creatures, and concocting all sorts of adventures. The possibilities for excitement, joy, and peace, seemed endless. Indeed, they almost were.

None of this however, is central to the purpose of this account, and therefore, I will not relate more of those experiences.

Rather, there are a few other comments about New California that I should make. First, there is something important to mention about the two cherubs, who have an unusual function in this place. While there were many of each type of creature, there were only *two* cherubs. For reasons that I cannot explain here (it's hard enough to explain what little I do using your language) the creatures of New California live for a great time, after your manner of reckoning, but they do eventually reproduce during their time, and die. As they do reproduce and multiply, the limits of their reality expands to accommodate the new creatures that are born.

In the case of the cherubs however, the cycle is different. In their case, *all* the cherubs die at once, except for *two*. These two cherubs then live for a time, then conceive and bear all the young that will allow the cherub kind to continue. It was therefore vital that this life cycle be allowed to complete, or there would never be any more cherubs once Asherah and El grew old and died.

The second point worth mentioning is that while this place appeared very idyllic, it was not by accident. In a previous time in this place, all of the Evil had been identified, captured, and then securely locked in a material I will call "hematite" because of its color and appearance. This hematite was placed in the walls of a vast cave at what was then in the furthest limits of this reality. While most of the creatures didn't know about this hematite, the cherubs did. Thus, inside the walls of a certain cave in this reality Sally named "New California," *all* of the Evil that had once been, lay, locked perfectly in hematite.

One day, the cherubs mentioned to the girls the story of how the Evil had been locked away, and how the hematite had been placed in the cave. They also told the girls that the only way to break the hematite was with the warm breath of a creature that no longer lived in New California, but which had lived there when the Evil had been totally defeated. These creatures, having paid a very high price to defeat the Evil, then left this world forever to prevent any possibility of the Evil ever being released again.

Without my having to describe all the details as to why, Sally became obsessed with the possibility that the creatures who had defeated the Evil, and had then left, were *humans*. She became obsessed with a curiosity of whether *her* breath could release the Evil that was locked in the hematite.

What a truly odd characteristic this is – to be in a place of such bliss, and yet to be obsessed with the only thing that could destroy it all. How odd it is that Diane had the capacity to live and be happy in a state of endless joy, but Sally did not. Instead, Sally had to focus on the one thing that could take it all away.

Yet, isn't this characteristic of Sally's common for your kind? Is this feature not the one that destroys and suppresses you more than all other things? Is not your curiosity of evil the final, irrefutable proof of the abject imperfection of your kind?

☼ CHAPTER 14 ☼

LITTLE THINGS

THERE WAS A TIME THEN, once, when Diane busied herself in a part of the castle, that Sally set off for the cave. The time she was gone would have seemed long to you, but did not seem so in this place. Having come to it, she went inside the cavern where she saw the horrible, twisted shapes of the hematite, just as it had been described.

She told herself that Evil was not something she sought. She did not want it, nor did she want to release it. But rather, she told herself, it was simply her *curiosity* about whether her own breath could affect it which had called her here. Her actions therefore, were not about *Evil*, but only about *curiosity*, or so she told herself. But of course this was all nonsense. Anyone can understand that if one jumps into a cesspool because of *curiosity*, she will get just as dirty as if she jumps in for any other reason. Why do you need to be told these obvious truths? And yet, you do need to be told, it seems. Your ability to deceive yourselves is truly remarkable, if regrettable.

"This little corner," she thought. She looked at a tiny peak of hematite in one part of the cave "Just this little bit should make no difference."

As she breathed on it, it seemed to melt. Then, it disappeared. She heard a faint sound, like the sound of air leaking from a tire with the sound of fingers scratching on a blackboard. She felt a cold chill.

"This is enough," she thought. She had seen what she had come for. Her breath *had* melted the hematite after all. And importantly, when she left, the rest of it remained intact. She reasoned that she had satisfied her curiosity and at the same time, had done no harm. She left the cave and returned to the castle.

141

For a long time after, Sally thought only occasionally about what she had done. She had melted the one little bit of hematite with her breath – nothing more. And yet, whenever she thought about it a cold sense of foreboding came over her.

Many years passed, as you would count them. Then, something odd happened. When the two girls were sitting in the great hall of the castle, with the flying creatures flying in the space overhead, Sally was looking at the vast paintings on the walls when she thought she saw a shadow pass in front of one of the murals. As it did, she thought she heard a sound like air leaking from a tire together with the sound of fingers scratching on a blackboard. It gave her a strange chill.

As this happened, one of the creatures they called "butterflies" paused briefly as if it had noticed too. But nobody else heard or saw it. That was all that happened. But Sally began to feel more and more concerned. Some time later, it happened again, and this time several creatures noticed it.

As more time passed this strange occurrence happened more and more, and each time more would notice it, in addition to Sally. Sally didn't know what it was, but she did remember where she had heard the strange, leaking, screeching sound the first time.

The last time this happened, Diane noticed it too.

"What was that?" she asked, turning to Sally.

But she didn't have to wait long for an answer.

El came rushing into the great hall. Although the animals had no leader – having no conflict they had no need for one – as the strongest, most intelligent, and most selfless of the animals, the cherubs had always been the creatures the others looked up to.

As El rushed in, the animals and the girls involuntarily felt their hearts jump. For El's normal, tranquil appearance was replaced with an expression of great urgency. His iridescent feathers flashed a wild blue and the communication beetles flashed blue too.

"The hematite is melting," he said. "The cave is almost empty. The Evil once trapped there has been released! It has already been among us in incorporeal form. But now it is becoming corporeal as well."

And as he spoke, the vague shadows that had been flying overhead inside the great hall appeared far darker and seemed to shriek, or laugh – which it was no one could tell – and then the shadows all disappeared.

The other animals were frightened. While the shadows were disturbing by themselves the animals all well knew their great, beloved El, and none had seen him this concerned before. As the animals cried out, the communications beetles flew and flashed, rising in the great hall like fireworks.

Many didn't even comprehend what El could be talking about. But El was older than the others. He was the last male of his kind, and he remembered.

El continued. "The Evil is assembling at the far end of our world – in the place near what we once called (you can't pronounce this), but that we have come to call the "Plains of Wyoming."

Before anyone could assimilate the magnitude of what he was saying, El looked around the great hall at his friends. "We must all once again learn to practice the ancient art of war. Many of us will die. But we must fight, for we will all wish we *had* died if the Evil triumphs. Time is short."

As the communication beetles glittered over and under and all around them, Diane remembered – somewhere in the distant parts of her mind – what it meant to have conflict, and to fight. While she was still a girl here in this place, and although it had been very long ago for her now, somehow she could still recall how in another place, and another part of her life, she had also known what it meant to die. But as Diane looked around she became concerned, for it was apparent that few of the animals understood any of this. Indeed it was clear many of these animals did not know what conflict was, much less, war.

She looked at Sally, who was kneeling, and crying, and in time, Sally would confess to everyone as to why. She would say she was sorry. She would say she didn't mean for any of this to happen. She would describe what she had actually been doing, and what her intentions were when she went into the cave.

"It was just curiosity," she would say, "It was just a little thing." Indeed, in describing what she had done she would make a great use of the word: "just."

But it was of no consequence. The situation had changed. New California would never be the same. They had all lost paradise.

And if you want to know, once lost, Paradise can only be regained by the shedding of blood, by the willingness of many to sacrifice themselves for the common good, and only by many actually making that great and final sacrifice.

Indeed, it is to document this great and final sacrifice that is the primary reason for my producing this account.

And so to make a long story short, the animals of New California learned the art of war once again, as they had done in eons past. They fitted themselves with those works that are made to cut, and break, and stab, and kill, and they protected their bodies with materials and objects that they could find and make that were strong and light.

The animals prepared as did the Evil, and a time finally came when the attack of the Evil seemed imminent.

El's battle plan had been well rehearsed. They would draw the enemy into an attack on the main plain of Wyoming. After the first action, the animals' forces would appear to retreat, so the Evil would be drawn forward into a breach between forest and foothill on either side. There were two groups of animals hidden there – one on each side – that would then sweep to the rear of the Evil and flank them, so the Evil would be surrounded. This would strike terror into the corps of the Evil, leaving them disorganized and easier to subdue.

It was a decent plan and indeed, is a fairly commonly known maneuver among those who practice warfare. But the "Achilles' heel" of such a plan as you would say, is if the enemy keeps a sizable force in reserve to counterattack. This has the effect of basically, capturing the spider in his own web.

In other words, the Evil's plan was: In anticipation of such a "pincer" maneuver or any other type of maneuver, the Evil would simply appear to play into the animals' trap while keeping a large force in reserve to counterattack, whatever the outcome of the initial skirmishes.

In any case, this was the original planning and the thinking on both sides. As is often the case in war, what actually happened was somewhat different.

The number of animals was greater than the number of the Evil, but the Evil was more determined. Oddly, this is often the case in many worlds with many sorts of beings – the forces of Evil often, for whatever reason, are more determined in battle than are the forces of the good. Only when the good becomes at least as determined, can they win.

The time for the fighting came.

(Note here that for the sake of brevity, I will use names for various animals that were given to them by Sally and Diane, without actually describing the animals themselves. Suffice it to say, each creature so named bore some resemblance in some cases to animals on your world, while many were completely different. In the case of the Evil, their form was humanoid or hominid as your words would describe them. It is interesting that while this form – the one that looks most like you – is one of the most beautiful and

144

functional forms in all creation – and one capable of true greatness – it is also one that is capable of some of the greatest depravities. The human form is also one that often exists in a state more savage, primitive and brutal than that found in almost any other form of life. And in these cases, leaders are usually self-selected on the basis of their abilities in dominating others through power and fear. Thus, they were the Evil.)

The Evil began their attack with high-speed, sweeping movements from their flying forces that were largely repulsed by the eagles. As the flying forces of the Evil plunged and retreated, the eagles destroyed them in considerable numbers. But as the Evil hoped would happen, some of their forces survived contact with the animals and were able to return to the Evil's central command, where they recounted valuable information about the locations and deployments of the animals.

In this way, the Evil sacrificed some of their troops in order to obtain valuable information. Indeed, this is a common strength of corrupt organizations – since the Evil did not value their own lives, they could spend them freely and remorselessly when needed.

Having thus ascertained the deployment of the animals, the Evil set out their attack in four groups. The first would comprise their aerial forces that would once again fly ahead and engage the animals. But this time, after the initial skirmish the Evil's flying forces would pull away from the battlefield. The hope was that this would draw away the more numerous and superior aerial forces of the animals, in pursuit. In other words, realizing their flying forces could not defeat the aerial forces of the animals, the Evil's plan was instead to lure them from the battlefield, rendering them essentially useless. The second group of the Evil would comprise their heavy battle groups, set out in front. This force of heavy troops would race forward and plunge into the animals' lines, wreaking havoc. Third, the lighter ground forces of the Evil would attack where needed, while a fourth, hidden group of Evil was held in reserve.

Initially, the first part of the Evil's plan of attack was successful. The Evil's flying forces were met by the aerial forces of the animals, including El. As the animals warred with the Evil in the air and began to defeat them, the Evil broke to one side and flew away. Still engaged, the animals pursued them and as such, the animal's aerial forces were drawn away from the battle. El, however, remained at the main battle.

This clever action on the part of the Evil had alerted El and a few of the other animals that their enemy was more cunning than they had imagined.

The animals quickly regrouped, anticipating the next wave of attack. As the heavy forces of the Evil began to mass and move forward, the animals' battle lines quickly formed into tight, heavily protected rows that ran parallel to the path of the Evil's advance. The heavy battle groups of the Evil had been commanded to plunge through the animals, wreaking terror and havoc. Finding the animals in rows, the Evil's heavy forces quickly swept through them as they had been commanded to do. But instead of doing any damage, the rapid advance of the Evil down the animal's rows was more like water running down the furrows of a field – doing little damage to the furrows themselves. The Evil's heavy forces therefore found themselves suddenly at the rear of the battle, and having inflicted little damage to the animals' forces. Nonetheless, these heavy forces began to attack. But at this point the aerial forces of the animals returned from chasing the flying forces of the Evil, and they began to attack the increasingly bewildered heavy forces of the Evil to great effect.

Thus, at this point, the animals' efforts had been very successful.

Sadly however, this moment proved to be the high point of the animals' efforts. For as the Evil saw themselves in the jaws of defeat they began to fight as you say, like dragons. They fought with ferocious abandon. And indeed, as the animals began to fall, the animals' love for life, and their love for each other, proved to be their greatest weakness. For as the animals saw their cherished loved ones fall, their hearts shrank, even as the Evil gained new strength for their cause. While the images of death all around shocked and weakened the animals, it strengthened the Evil. The Evil knew that its strength lay not in numbers, but rather, in determination, in cunning, and in remorselessness even toward *themselves*. They knew they could sacrifice their forces if need be, as merely a tactic. Indeed, while the animals valued the lives of every one of themselves, the Evil could afford to dispense their lives as casually as one would spend any other military materiel.

And indeed, strange as it may seem, at the point early on when the battle had at first turned so much in favor of the animals, some of the animals actually began to feel *pity* for the Evil. The animals' odd compassion also caused them to fight far less vigorously than they could have done, which too played into their enemy's hands.

And lastly, the Evil knew that whatever the outcome of this battle, they had troops hidden in reserve with which to attack. The animals' forces appeared to be concentrated in the primary battle as the Evil had hoped they would be.

The Evil hoped that when their reserve forces eventually attacked, it would shock and surprise the animals. With luck, the animals having been so surprised would see all their plans ruined and would become disorganized and struck with fear, whereupon they could be defeated, and enslaved.

The battle having at first proceeded largely according to the animals' plan, now proceeded largely according to the Evil's. The animals and the main ground forces of the Evil clashed in the Plains of Wyoming in a terrible battle. On the whole, while the animals were strong and quick and had larger numbers, the sheer heedless determination of the Evil began to push them back. Indeed, ironically, while it had been the plan of the animals to retreat at this point all along, they ended up doing so anyway – the Evil pressed the battle so fiercely.

As the Evil pushed the animals back, two forces of animals waited on either side to sweep and attack at the Evil's flank.

El, the mighty flying Cherub, had been in the main force, and he retreated with the other animals while anticipating their friends' counterattack at the rear of the Evil.

But while he had insisted on being part of the battle himself and fought valiantly, El had also insisted that the precious Asherah would not be part of this war, as the tiny, priceless baby cherubs she was now carrying within her were the only hope for the continuation of the cherub species – because if Asherah died – her babies – and therefore the entire cherub species – would die with her.

And so she had to be saved at any cost. Indeed, the two girls and all the animals had agreed. Asherah would not be part of this war but would be hidden in a safe place.

For their part, the girls were each in one of the two pincer groups where they waited for the word to attack at the rear of the Evil forces.

At the same time, the reserve forces of the Evil lay hidden in the valley the girls had once named "The Grand Canyon." This canyon was the place the Evil had viewed as being the most secure place to conceal themselves. (And it was, in fact, not actually a canyon, but a wide valley between high mountain ranges where there was much vegetation and small features wherein to hide. It lay at some distance from the Plains of Wyoming, around a mountain prominence.) It was on the marching path between the hematite caves and the location of the main group of animals. When they had passed through, the Evil had left some forces there, well hidden.

Indeed, almost one-third of the Evil's initial aerial forces were operating in the Grand Canyon, their sole purpose to destroy any animals that might venture toward them. This remaining aerial corps of the Evil would sacrifice all of themselves, if necessary, to protect the secret of the existence of their reserve forces. This, they believed, was crucial to their plan for their terrible victory.

But it turned out, it may not have been so crucial after all. What actually happened was that the main force of the Evil that was attacking the animals was having more success than they had thought possible in their wildest hopes, for as the Evil swept forward, they left a swath of dead and dying animals. Indeed, when the animals' pincer forces were finally called upon to attack at the rear of the battle, the scene of devastation that they saw not only among the Evil, but among their own forces as well, was entirely dispiriting and even shocking to them. Nonetheless, the animals' pincer groups pressed their attack upon the Evil's rear according to the animals' plan.

Finally, by sheer force of numbers, the animals began to prevail. Yet all this while, and unknown to the animals, a powerful force of fresh Evil was secluded in the Grand Canyon, prepared to imminently enter the battle.

But as it happened, it was not only the Evil who had concluded the Grand Canyon would be the best place to hide something valuable.

For, this was also the place where El had chosen to hide Asherah. This he had done, leaving her there long after the Evil had passed by – or so he thought. As she hid there deep inside a cave, she had heard the forces of the Evil, as they emerged from their hiding places and began to mass. But rather than emerge and fly away, which she could have done in the beginning, she stayed hidden, according to the plan.

Thus we see two mistakes were made – of hiding her there in the first place, and of her not leaving when she could have. It is not enough to be good, or even wise. It is important that one's actions are also the most correct ones possible, taken at the most correct times.

Quickly though, and imperceptibly, a communication beetle left her side. Flying extremely low and fast, it skirted the surveillance forces of the Evil and arrived at El's side, where it informed him that his dear friend and love – and the future mother of their entire cherub race – was now in imminent danger, completely surrounded by the reserve forces of the Evil.

And then, a most demoralizing event happened to the animals in their fearsome battle against the Evil. Upon hearing the danger that Asherah was in, El instinctively, without thinking, spread his mighty wings and jumped into the air. As a cheer went up from among the Evil, El beat his wings and rose high into the sky, and left the scene of battle. Once again, the Evil's spirits rose, and they began to prevail against the animals.

Diane and Sally too fought bravely, if ineffectively. For the two young girls, though they may have had heart and willingness, lacked strength. And whatever you may have imagined, lacking strength is an overwhelming disadvantage in battle. And whatever other qualities they may have, when it comes to physical strength, human women usually have very little of it, and especially human girls.

Seeing this early on, the animals had rushed to protect the girls. And just as they had been willing to sacrifice so much to protect Asherah, the animals assumed that since the girls also were unique, they must be protected too. And so the animals spent far too may resources in this effort – for while the girls attempted to make themselves useful, the truth is, it would have been of far more use if they had left the battle altogether.

As El crossed over the edge of the mountain range and swept over the valley, his heart sank as he saw the extent of the Evil's forces there. El had never imagined that the Evil had held any forces in reserve. Indeed, the Evil's reserve forces even had left a number of heavy, mobile weapons groups there. You will recall that early in the battle on the Plains of Wyoming, the Evil had begun to use some of their heavy weapons against the animals before the animals had destroyed them, and it had been through the animals' stratagems that these heavy weapons groups had been eliminated. This time, the element of surprise, as well as the weapons themselves, would be in favor of the Evil.

El remained at a relatively high altitude, looking down. While he assumed that the Evil had seen him, he did not want his looking for Asherah to give her hiding place away. And since the cherubs could fly higher than any other creature while still being able to see the ground, at this altitude the aerial forces of the Evil could not reach him.

But it didn't matter. El shuddered. As he looked down, he saw a bright blue creature in the midst of the Evil's forces.

It was Asherah. They had already found her.

✿ CHAPTER 15 ✿

EVER YOURS

THERE ARE TIMES when even the most intelligent of creatures will abandon all thought, all reason, and will simply *act*.

As El pulled both his wings tight against his sides and plunged downward, his speed increased as though he were a falling blue meteor. A hush went up from the Evil as they saw the distant, blue object overhead streaking faster and faster toward them. Asherah saw him too. For a brief moment, her heart rose to see her beloved, but it soon turned to trepidation. She did not believe that El could pull out of a dive so steep, so fast. She tucked her head under her wing.

These creatures that the girls named "cherubs" have a peculiar feature that some of you have imagined certain animals in your world had anciently. And yet, it was one of which the cherubs themselves were largely unaware.

Inside the cherub's bodies are produced fatty compounds that have a heavier component, and a lighter component. Both components are what you would call "flammable." In addition to their ability to flash a blue light, the cherubs contain various points inside their bodies where electrical arcs can be produced, among which are locations along their teeth. If they expel these fatty compounds at the same time they apply this electrical spark, the compounds ignite and burn upon contacting the air. In this way, they can do what you would call "breathe fire." Indeed, it looks more like they are "blowing fire," but you understand the concept. And although neither of these two cherubs had ever done this before, the capability existed within them.

There are beetles in your own world, some of whom live out their entire lives without flying. Yet, they *can* fly, and when the need arises they do so very effectively. Similarly, although they had never done it, these two cherubs could blow fire very effectively. (Indeed, for reasons I will not go into, this ability that exists within cherubs is the source of your own mythology regarding fire-breathing creatures.)

And so as El dove downward and the ground approached fast, he opened his mouth, and felt a strange sensation he had not felt before. As he spread his vast wings and his dive turned into a terrifying swoop, out came a perfect stream of fire.

Raking across the forces of the Evil then, was a path of incendiary death. For not only were the Evil burned by the first blast of the flame, but the heaver component of the fluid stuck to their bodies and continued to burn.

El managed to turn so that the path of destruction missed Asherah at the last minute. But the effect proved so startling that the Evil fell to the ground and momentarily released the netting with which they had been holding her. Asherah too was startled, and she pulled her head out from under her wing and looked around. As she had many times before, she pulled away from her captors, but this time, she noticed she was loose. She ran out from beneath the netting and leaped into the air. She beat her wings, climbing steeply higher and higher into the air, where she was joyfully joined by El.

Speaking in their language they flashed quickly, and both ascertained the good news that they were each all right. For a moment, they experienced a reunion of happiness and relief.

But it was not all good news. El soon recounted the progress of the battle in the Plains of Wyoming and that events there did not go well for the animals. The pincer maneuver had been executed by the animals as planned, but to less-than-desired effect. The battle now was largely a free-for-all and El could not predict the outcome. Indeed, with these fresh forces of Evil massing below them, it did not bode well for the animals at all.

The Evil looked up as the two cherubs soared over them. And as they watched, the captains of the Evil realized that the cherubs flying overhead meant they had now been unsuccessful in maintaining the secrecy of their reserve forces, and they also realized that those two immense, powerful creatures were flying at an altitude completely beyond the reach of their own flying forces.

Realizing therefore that their aerial forces were now useless in this location, the Evil now immediately commanded them to fly toward the Plains of Wyoming to support the main battle, and the ground forces of the Evil in the Grand Canyon began to move in the direction of the main battle as well.

El and Asherah flew together far overhead. For a brief time, care was swallowed in a tenuous bliss as they plied the sky together, soaring with only the company of their true love beside them, as they had done so many times before. And yet, they could see the corps of the Evil below as they were marshalling and beginning to move in the direction of the main battle.

"El," Asherah asked, "have we anticipated this large force below that is now moving toward our friends?"

El paused for a long time. His quick mind had already anticipated their entire conversation. And you will soon see why he was in no hurry to continue it.

"No my love, we have not. With the arrival of these new forces below us, it is virtually assured that we will be defeated. That is, if this new force of Evil is allowed to arrive fully *intact*."

After another long pause, El looked at Asherah, and his eyes were sad. "Beloved," he continued, "I cannot allow this force below us to arrive intact. It must be attacked *here*."

Knowingly, Asherah looked back at El, and they continued to communicate with the flashing blue colors of their bodies. "But El, there is not time to summon any of our friends to attack these forces below us." She paused. "Of course, you know that."

For a moment, El felt his trepidation washed away, as he thought only of his love for her. From the time they had both been young, there had never been anything in his life he had wanted so much, as simply to be with her. Nonetheless, his path was now clear to him. His duty must outweigh his heart, and his life.

"My love," he said, "This will be the last time I will fly with you. I will attack them, *here*. But as you know, while I may be able to destroy many of them, I cannot destroy all of them."

He paused. It was quiet, except for the sound of the air rushing across their magnificent wings.

"But to do sufficient damage to their forces," he continued, "for me to be sufficiently aggressive in engaging them, I cannot possibly survive."

And Asherah turned away. She had known he would say this. But it still drew great pain nonetheless.

Yet now, El's countenance brightened as he turned to her, eyes gleaming.

153

"But you will survive!" he said. "Asherah, you carry the future of all of our kind within you, and you *will* survive! You can fly far away, and bear our young. Raise them, then return to this place in due time with all your forces. All will be well. We will prevail. All will be as it was!"

Asherah looked at El both knowingly and lovingly.

"No beloved," she said thoughtfully. "It will *not* be the same as it was. For you will be gone."

They soared high into the air, in perfect formation.

"Without you," she continued, "life will have no meaning for me. Without you, there is no future, no light, no life. If you are gone, the world will end for me. I will not leave your side, my love. But, you knew I would say that, even before I did. You knew I would not leave you."

El hung his head for a moment, then raised it again. He had persuaded her once to hide in the valley where she would have been presumably, far from the battle. He had assured her he would be all right. But this time, he knew he could not convince her. It was too obvious that he could not survive if he attacked all of the forces below them, alone. And so he knew he could not save her, for he knew he would not be able to persuade her to leave him this time. But he had needed to try anyway.

Nor had another, theoretically viable option been possible: That being the one where the two cherubs would simply *both* fly away, establishing a new land where they and their children could live in peace. Indeed, perhaps one day, they as an entire vast family of mighty cherubs could have returned *en masse*, by surprise, and saved the animals, freeing them from the inevitable enslavement by the Evil. But this very viable option, while it was known to both El and Asherah, was never even discussed. It would have meant death and a long time of great suffering for their friends.

As they both flew together, they knew what they had to do: the only hope of turning the tide of battle would be if these fresh forces below them could be destroyed or delayed, here, before they could reach the main battle. This would have the effect of disorienting and potentially discouraging the enemy, which could allow the battle to turn again in the animals' favor.

But neither El nor Asherah were under any illusions. They knew that were they both to attack the Evil's reserve forces, without any other support, that they would both be killed. And not just them, but all the little cherubs that were developing inside Asherah would also die. And with them, the future of all the cherubs who would ever live in New California would also end. There would be no more cherubs. And yet, what other way was there to save the lives of so many other animals?

And so, as El and Asherah climbed into the sky and soared there together as they had so many times before throughout their lives, they did not flash blue to each other, but remained silent, simply feeling the presence of the one they loved beside them, and listening to the rush of the wind. They had known each other so long that words were often unnecessary. And so, when El pointed his nose downward, Asherah did too. They would dive and make a final pass over their foes before they engaged them.

And as they did, the forces of Evil, every one of them, looked up together. As those two rare creatures dove toward them, all the forces of the Evil knew. For the Evil too, were old. They knew this was the end time of the cycle of life for the two great, blue creatures overhead. They said nothing, but all the Evil realized that they would first taste battle this day by killing the two remaining cherubs in this place. And in so doing, they understood that they would kill all the future cherubs that would ever be. When the full comprehension of this became clear to them, they raised their weapons, and shouted.

But as the two cherubs passed low and flew over them, the Evil did not attack. Instead, they lowered their weapons. And as El and Asherah climbed once again into the air for the last time, the Evil threw their weapons down, and to the dismay of their own captains, the forces of the Evil beat their chests in a token respect for the two cherubs. *This*, they thought, was truly bravery. *This*, they thought, was valor. It was sacrifice. It was courage. These things that the Evil had always been cynically told to value by their leaders were also things they had been told that animals did not possess. They had been told that all animals were *weak* because they were *good*. They had been told that animals had no strength, no courage, no ability to sacrifice. But now they could see for themselves that these things they had been told by their leaders were not true. And so they looked up and beat their chests and cheered, and they honored El and Asherah for a brief moment.

And when they had paid their tribute to the two, brave creatures overhead, the Evil became quiet and picked up their weapons. For while they now greatly respected the cherubs, their mission was one of conquest, not respect. Looking skyward once again, they waited eagerly for the coming moments, when they would destroy the last of the cherubs.

As they flew high above the Evil, Asherah saw the flashing of her lifelong friend.

"It is time," El said.

"It is, beloved," said Asherah.

"This is the end," he said. "Oblivion."

"We will go there together, my love" she replied. "With you, I am not afraid." And he could see her try to appear fearless, for his sake.

"You have always been with me Asherah. You are all that I have ever hoped to have; all I have ever hoped to be."

"You have always been mine, El. I am ever yours."

And as they turned and soared high in the air, her wing touched his. They exchanged a final glance, and they both knew that while the Evil could destroy their bodies, they could never destroy the love that bound them to each other. And then they dove toward their enemy, and their fate.

As they did, the two great Cherubs each flashed one last time to each other. And what they both said to each other was the same thing, although neither of them saw it.

On the ground below, a communication beetle saw, and recorded what they said. But this beetle was killed later in the battle. The only place these words are recorded is here, in this book that I am writing and that you are reading.

As El and Asherah dove toward their enemy side by side for the last time, what they said to each other was this: "Farewell, my love."

And since it was only the cherubs that flashed blue in this place, and therefore it was only because of them that the communication beetles flashed this color, this would be the last time a communication beetle would ever flash blue again.

At this point, the two cherubs determined that the heavy weapons should be the focus of their attack. El, still unable to allow Asherah to endanger herself, flew down first and set many of these weapons on fire. The sturdier of the weapons he clawed with his feet as he passed. Given El's strength, he was remarkably successful in this effort. He also successfully altered his tactics such that the Evil could not predict where he would strike, and therefore they were unable to succeed in their efforts to shoot him down.

However, finally on one pass, as he grabbed the top of one of the Evil's throwing weapons with his claws it did not give way, and his claws stuck in it. This flipped him over in the air, and he hit the ground hard. The Evil moved toward him fast, but he quickly immolated them with a stream of burning liquid, and once again took off. Nonetheless, this particular leg was now badly damaged, and would be of no further use to him. As he climbed into the air, Asherah noticed this, but said nothing. But now, seeing he was injured, she resolved to join him in all future attacks, whatever he might request of her.

Indeed, she knew the time had come for her great sacrifice as well. She was very powerful. She would destroy the Evil too.

Both cherubs now attacked together, and raked the Evil with twin tracks of flaming death. Many Evil spun and ran, on fire. And as they ran and collided with each other, they set others on fire as well.

Finally, after many more passes, the Evil took careful aim with some of their heavy weapons at the cherub who they perceived was the weaker of the two: Asherah. I do not take the time here to describe the irrelevant details of the weapons used in this battle, where those details do not pertain to this account. But in this case, I will state that this one was basically a spear thrower – designed to throw a large spear that was heavier than what a normal creature could carry.

And so on this pass, as they came low above the Evil, one of these heavy spears collided with the leading edge of Asherah's left wing. This caused her to spin partially in the air, and then crash to the ground, where the Evil ran toward her.

El, seeing this, swooped low, and spreading his wings he glided fast, barely off the ground, and his wings collided with many of the Evil who were running toward Asherah. This killed some of them, and knocked some of them off their feet.

But this also took a toll on El's wings. As he reached Asherah he could see what they had done to her.

He knew she would not fly again.

And so, neither would he.

For a while, both of the cherubs were able to keep the Evil at bay using their fire, and in the process they destroyed many of them. But eventually, their stocks of flammable fluids ran out. The heavier solvents were the first to go, leaving the cherubs only able to blow fire without being able to spray flaming goo that would stick to the Evil and continue burning.

Once they realized this, the Evil discovered they could fend off most of the damage by simply hiding behind their shields as the flame passed over them.

But El, grounded with his mate, began to emit his lighter flammable solvents without igniting them, and in so doing he would spread a layer of combustible gas around the Evil. Once it was in place, he would ignite it. The resulting explosion and fire once again did a lot of damage to the Evil. But this didn't last long. Soon, both El and Asherah ran out of all ability to produce flame altogether.

And so they spread their wings and charged the enemy and trampled many, all the while with the enemy inflicting deep wounds in the cherubs as they did so.

In this charging, the two became separated, which neither one noticed until El heard Asherah's cry. While the cherubs had been astonishingly successful in eliminating almost all of the Evil's heavy weapons (as well as a sizeable number of their soldiers) the Evil had once again focused on Asherah, training their remaining weapons on her. As El heard her cry, he turned and saw her being hit again and again. He spread his wings and charged with terrifying speed, killing Evil in a wide swath as he drove toward Asherah. Realizing his direction, the Evil ran in front of him and held up their heavy rods. Even so, they continued to fall as El charged forward, and yet, the metal rods took a heavy toll on his wings, and his progress slowed as he came nearer and nearer to Asherah.

But he never reached her.

On the Plains of Wyoming, the battle had turned decidedly in favor of the Evil once word came to the animals that there was a reserve force of them approaching. Nonetheless, the reserve aerial forces of the Evil were the first to approach, and the aerial forces of the animals made short work of them as they tried to enter the battle.

The battle then progressed like this: Now having almost no air power, the Evil concentrated their ground attack at weak points among the animals to great effect. The air power of the animals had so far been very effective against the Evil's aerial forces as well as against the Evil's ground forces. But the animals' aerial forces were becoming exhausted. And it is a truism, that while aerial forces can wreak damage on an enemy, sometimes spectacularly, they often are of only minimal effect in actually concluding a war, which task of necessity almost always falls to the ground forces to accomplish.

A decisive moment, and indeed one of desperation, occurred when two of the "pterodactyls" as they had been named, decided on their own, to remove Diane and Sally from the battle, which they did. Having removed them, the animals could then battle and sacrifice only for the sake of victory and with only that in mind, having assured themselves that both the two girls, and presumably the cherubs, were safe.

And as time passed, it became clear that something was irregular about the few reserve ground forces of the Evil that were now beginning to join the battle. Far from being the devastating force that had been expected, the reserve forces were ragged, and had almost no heavy weapons.

Suffice it to say, without any more detail, that the lack of a sizeable and effective reserve force discouraged the Evil and in turn, reinvigorated the animals, just as El had suspected it might. Ultimately the animals triumphed with a complete victory over the Evil. Indeed, the final act of war was accomplished by the animals with the use of their exhausted but still committed aerial forces in hunting down every single remaining Evil as they attempted to retreat. Once found, the remaining Evil were destroyed by the ground animals. They showed the Evil no mercy. And I would comment that while mercy is often a virtue, in this case the animals were right in showing the enemy none.

But the victory was not sweet, for the cost had been high. Many animals' lives had been lost. Yet, in spite of the cost in the loss of the lives of many animals, the first question on the minds of all the remaining animals was: Where are the two priceless cherubs, and the girls?

They didn't have to wait long to find out about the girls, who were retrieved by the pterodactyls, after which everybody started looking for the cherubs. A few knowing where El had hidden Asherah, this was where all the animals now went.

Although the communication beetles were asked repeatedly and intensely where the cherubs were, none responded. Indeed, none flashed blue at all. And although the animals did not know it yet, as I said, flashing blue is something no communication beetle would ever do again.

And so the animals all rushed en masse toward the place where Asherah had been hidden, in the valley of the Grand Canyon. Here, as they approached, the animals were astonished at the number of dead Evil and wrecked weapons, and they were perplexed by the odd scorch marks that seemed to be almost everywhere. As they moved through the canyon, the carnage all around became more and more clear. There were scorched and dead Evil everywhere, and large numbers of their wrecked heavy weapons. And yet, since the animals knew that none of their own forces had been deployed in that area, they wondered what had happened there.

Suddenly, overhead, the flying animals began screaming and they dove toward a place near the center of the valley where lay a large number of dead Evil and wrecked weapons. As the ground animals, together with the two girls, approached, they could see some Evil were still alive, and they were being attacked by the flying animals who were screaming wildly, frighteningly.

As they approached, some of the faster animals raced ahead. In the distance, in the melee of the flying animals screaming and diving from the sky and the faster ground animals all killing the remaining Evil, there was an ominous large mound in the center of it all. As the two girls ran as hard as they could, with their legs burning from the effort, they could see it was *two* large mounds.

Sally fell to her knees first. Then Diane screamed, and fell. As the few remaining Evil were at last all destroyed, the flying animals now ventured high into the sky still screaming, and the ground animals ran wildly.

Diane looked only briefly, then desperately buried her face in her hands.

For in the distance, Diane and Sally had both seen what the two large mounds in the distance were. They could see that they were blue. They were the bodies of El and Asherah.

~ ~ ~

TIME, if it exists at all in this place, passes much more slowly than it does in your world. But if it were accounted for after of the manner of the reckoning of your world, a great deal of time did pass in this place, after the great events that would forever after be called, "The Great Battle," and more reverently, "The End of the Cherubs."

Indeed it was centuries later, after the manner of your reckoning of time, that Sally and Diane were lying on one of the porches of one of the many spacious, beautiful homes – palaces really – that they and the animals had built since The Great Battle. This particular palace lay at the edge of a peaceful lake that stretched into the distant valley beyond. Huge trees framed the porch.

Except for a few very minor and really rather endearing squabbles that had happened between a few animals, the time had passed peacefully, idyllically, and happily. In fact, once the Evil had been destroyed, few spoke of it, and in time, fewer and fewer even remembered.

Diane, for her part, was wearing a tunic that she had been wearing for a very long time. Without day and night nor seasons to measure the time, it passed unnoticed. And because this world is so clean, everything tended to be clean. Even clothes that were worn for a very long time stayed relatively fresh. Her tunic had the appearance of a well-worn garment. Sally, for her part, had dispensed with wearing clothes altogether, centuries ago. And although she went around with nothing on, it really didn't matter. After all, they were still just two girls, and the animals took no notice of whether they wore clothes or not.

As Diane lay on the porch and smelled the sweet air, Sally leaned over her for a moment, then walked to the side and sat down, looking across the lake. It was quiet for awhile.

"So many things," Sally said, with a distant, sorrowful sound in her voice.

"What?" Diane asked, raising up on one arm.

Sally paused for a long time. In this place, one didn't take notice of long pauses the way they do in your reality.

"So many times," Sally continued, "I think that I can remember things. I think I can remember a time when things were not like this – a time when there was – when there was *badness* in the world. I can even remember a time when I had a mother and father, and there were other people like *us*."

Two communication beetles flew up and began to flash green.

Diane spoke. "It looks like some of them are having some games at the main castle. Should I send for some transport so we can go? Do you want to go?"

Sally looked over the lake, and there was a long pause again. "No," she said.

And one of the communication beetles flew away. But the other stayed, hovering.

Sally looked at it, and then unexpectedly, tears welled in her eyes.

"*Blue*," she said. "Flash *blue*."

But the beetle just hovered. Diane and Sally would never see the beetles flash blue again.

"I'd give *anything* to see one of them flash blue again . . ." Sally said, and her brow furrowed.

But Diane interrupted her. "Don't . . ." she said to Sally.

Tears appeared in Sally's eyes. "I'd give . . ."

And then after another long pause, the communication beetle flashed yellow. This time, the beetle was speaking for *itself*.

"Do not cry for what you have done, Sally. For it is true; I will never flash blue again. But although you caused the end of the cherubs, we gained something in return. We destroyed all the Evil forever. And more than this, we learned what Evil is. We learned to defeat it, to remove ourselves from it. This is a valuable thing to know. For to truly know the good, we must first meet the Evil. To know the sweet, we must know the bitter. And to know true happiness, we must first experience true sorrow." And the beetle flew away.

Sally cried for a little while, as Diane touched her gently on the shoulder.

161

Sally shook her head. "It isn't *true*," she said. "It *was* happy here before. I didn't give this world anything."

And then, after a long pause, she said, "I'd give anything just to see one of them flash blue – just blue, just once again. I'd give . . ."

And her voice trailed off.

~ ~ ~

And so now, I finish my record.

Having previously documented David's unusual skill with the Device, which he called the Space Sieve, I had completed the secondary purpose of this document. And now, having completed this chapter, I have finished the primary one. For the primary reason for this document was to record an event that has become increasingly known by my kind and indeed, by many creatures throughout the total expanse of all creation. For it was an event of such selflessness, such sacrifice, such strength, such courage, and such greatness that it has, and will be, described and re-told time and time again. The event of which I speak, was the willing, selfless sacrifice made by El and Asherah. For they could have fled. They could have preserved their lives. And in doing so, they would have received not a single note of condemnation from their friends. To the contrary, they would have received the gratitude of their fellows for preserving their rare breed for all future generations upon their world. Indeed, if they had left, if they had simply flown away, they would already have fought valiantly, and in leaving would have performed a final, vital act in preserving their very species. And even more, when they decided to stay, when they decided to sacrifice themselves as well as all their future posterity for the sake of the other animals, they could not have known whether their sacrifice would even make a difference. And yet, they stayed and fought the hopeless fight, knowing only that in so doing, they would have done all that they could have done. There is a saying you have: "No greater love has any man than this, that he would give his life for a friend." El and Asherah gave their lives, and the future of their kind, for their friends. And yet, they had no way to know whether their great sacrifice would even save their friends.

But of course, it *did*.

So having concluded the essential parts of this account, I am essentially, done.

Yet – and strangely – I feel marginally disposed to relate a few further notes. You will recall that I produced the present document as essentially an afterthought, as a by-product of my having made a document for those of my own kind after our own manner. But now, inexplicable as it may seem, I find I have an odd sense of concern for *your* welfare too.

Now that I have recorded this much, and understanding your sentimental way of looking at things, and your sensitivities, I feel compelled to write a few more lines that I feel will be of worth to you. I should say I feel "almost" compelled, because the truth is, my main reason for producing this document is finished, as I said. But now, in an odd way I feel I "owe" it to you to relate a few further facts that occurred as they relate to these matters, which I will now undertake.

❋ CHAPTER 16 ❋

ALPHA AND OMEGA

"I DONE TOLD YOU THIS IS YER PROBLEM!" Donna pointed at her husband Craig, "so git in there and see what's a-goin' on!"

Craig shifted nervously in the kitchen chair. "Okay, Donna. But you know it's more than a might worrisome to me. I ain't never seed the like."

"Well," Donna countered. "Yer the one's been gone to high school – so go git in there and figure out what's goin' on. After all, if we're gonna be his parents, we a need to be part of his life. We gotta know what all he's gittin' himself into."

Donna and Craig were two good people, if largely uneducated ones, who had become the unintended parents of a teenage boy, named Steven, whose parents had died in a tragic car accident. Donna and Craig were the closest relatives to the only child, who had come to live with them two years before.

"You know, to tell ya true, it's a fright to me, it is," Craig continued, "what with it sometimes makin' more noise than my old log splitter when it's a-runnin'."

But Donna was persistent. "Go on and git in there! He's just a little boy a-playin' with some ol' thing he's he done found."

Craig hesitated then headed toward Steven's room. Then he paused and turned back. "Donna, that ain't no toy. It's creepy. Why, you ain't seed all the strange things been happenin' round here lately."

"I did done seen that black box all the time, Craig. Done cleaned it too. Why, I know it's makin' a frightful noise right now and all. But it ain't nothin' but some little toy pianny or some such."

165

"But," he continued to protest, "I ain't never seed no pianny like that 'afore, what with all them flashin' lights. And you don't know, but late some nights when I've done stayed up, Steven's showed me things with it that I ain't never heard tell the like of. I done told Preacher, and he done said them thing's I seed is flat impossible. He said I'd best quit hittin' the 'shine. But I ain't been. I tell ya, that thing's got some kinda powers or something, sure as sure."

"Go on!" she urged, pointing down the hall. And so, he went.

As he came to the boy's bedroom door he noticed something odd. It appeared that there was a shoe on the door. But it wasn't that the shoe was painted onto the door, or that there was a shoe stuck to the door, but rather, it looked like a tennis shoe had been melted *into* the door. Craig smiled and tried to bulk up his courage, and then he opened the door.

"Steven?" he said.

The boy, Steven, was sitting in front of the Device - the Space Sieve – the exact same Machine that I have mentioned previously and which is one of the reasons for my producing this document. And as Steven sat in front of it with his fingers dancing on the glowing, shifting keys, its screen was ablaze with shapes and colors. To the left and the right of the Machine floating in mid-air were three auxiliary screens each, for a total of seven screens. Under each screen was a keyboard, and Steven, while turning his attention from one screen to the next, moved his hands upon the keyboards as they whipped toward him and than back again at his command. His toys and knick knacks on his dresser and other parts of his room jiggled about, and Craig felt what seemed to him like a breeze in the room. The window at the opposite side of the bedroom was open. It was a clear, sunny day outside.

You will recall that the former user of this Device – David – had lost track of it. And after he did, the Machine went to a landfill, where it was buried under tons of garbage.

You will also recall that when the Device originally entered your reality, it was as a result of its drifting there – a coincidence.

However in this case, its showing up where it did was no happenstance, but was by design.

This boy – the orphan Steven – who had come to live with his distant relatives, Craig and Donna – had found the Device resting inside a hedge of tall oleanders as he was walking down a dusty road one day. You see, it had been deliberately placed there for him to find. Steven had gone back to retrieve it, by pulling a wagon tied behind his bicycle. He had placed the Device on the wagon, and had hauled it home.

But unlike David, Steven did not learn how to operate the Device himself, nor could he have done so. For David to have figured out how to operate a Device such as this on his own was very, very rare indeed. By contrast, Steven was shown how to operate it.

But now I'm getting a little ahead of myself. You see, now that I am composing these concluding notes I can feel that I am almost done with this account. I suppose it is understandable that I would be feeling a little hasty. In spite of my acceding to a desire to relate these last notes, I *do* still so want to get this experience with your language over with.

Craig stepped into the boy's room and closed the door behind him. He really didn't want Donna listening to him as he tried to do something he feared he would be no good at. (Is this not a strange characteristic of humans? What creatures are there that one can find who are in many ways, more incompetent than you? And yet, because of your remarkable pridefulness, you feel hesitant in admitting you are deficient at anything, hating even worse to have someone *see* you being deficient at something.)

In any case, as Craig closed the door the light from the seven glowing screens lit his face as his jaw dropped. Stunned, he stood there, watching Steven's hands wildly moving from keyboard to keyboard like a genius plying a great organ for what he knew would be the final performance of his life. And indeed, so it was.

Passing in front of Craig's eyes on the various screens were wonders that he had never imagined, much less seen. He had come to talk to Steven about all the noise and mayhem that Steven was causing. But now that thought was far, far away. Craig's mind was now adrift – it was a leaf in the wind. There was nothing for him to think, and nothing for him to do, but *stare*. And as he did, his mouth slowly moved into a smile.

As he watched Steven's fingers move strangely upon the shifting keys, it was shocking to behold. But more than that, it was truly *wondrous*.

And at that moment, still unseen to Craig, to the side of room were two glowing beings. They appeared to be standing on the floor, but the soles of their feet were hovering a few inches above it. The man was blonde, the woman was dark haired.

But surely, you already knew that.

Sapentia leaned over to Actio. "I just can't begin to tell you how much of this I disagree with," she said. "Showing this boy how to operate this Machine – showing him all these functions . . . The other boy, David – who figured it all out – that was bad enough. But to actually *show* one of them . . ."

Actio didn't reply.

Sapentia continued. "I still can't understand . . ."

Actio turned to her. "A *commitment*," he said, and he turned back to watch Steven, "is a *commitment*."

"But Actio," Sapentia continued, "no one could ever have expected you to fulfill the commitment you made to those two boys. It was *impossible*. I knew that when you said it. I knew that when I asked you to say it to them."

"It was my fault," he said. "Ultimately, it was my responsibility." He turned to her. "That *alone* would have been reason enough." And he turned back to watch Steven. "But on top of that, I gave my *assurance*."

Sapentia turned back to watch Steven as he worked the Machine with the skill of a carefully tutored student. She looked back at Actio, then at the Machine again, and she said, very softly, while very faintly shaking her head, "Not *possible*."

Suddenly, the sound in the room increased. If you had been there, it would have sounded like a train was passing over the roof of the house at the same time that a great wave was crashing upon it, and although it was a sound that was very full and loud, it caused no pain. The light in the room grew intense as the screens all turned an electric blue-white, and the keys on all the keyboards flashed a blinding white light, like electric welders all striking a hundred arcs at once – like the corona of the sun flashing in the room – and yet no one had to squint, not even Craig.

Sapentia's face grew grim, and then her mouth opened. She stepped back, and placed her hand on Actio's shoulder. (For a being of Sapentia's knowledge and power to step backward in awe is no small thing, to say the least.)

Actio stood firm.

"That can't *be*," she said.

For in the middle of the room a spherical object had appeared. It resembled one of the ships of the Kex that I mentioned previously, but it was only as big as a large melon and was perfectly brilliant in color, as if it contained all the colors in existence at once, including both black and white, as well as all the other colors, at the same time.

Sapentia pressed her lips together, and they trembled in fear. (As I said, this is no small thing.) "Actio, tell me that's not what I *think* it is." And although, as I have said, these two speak in a language of clarity and beauty that you cannot comprehend, as she spoke, her voice cracked very noticeably.

"It _IS!_," he said firmly, if gravely, as he concentrated on what was happening.

As Sapentia spoke, she sounded very plaintive. "But no Actio, that can't _be_. No. It's just not _possible,_ Actio. If that is truly the _temporal nexus_ of that Machine, it _cannot exist_ outside of the enclosure of that Device, much less be _taken out_ of the Machine!"

The sphere hovering in the room flashed.

His eyebrows raised and then lowered. "It _is_ possible. Indeed, there it _is_. More importantly, it was the only way."

She shook her head. "Oh Actio, what have you done? That nexus cannot exist outside the Machine. For it to even be here is impossible. But given that it _is_ here, oh Actio, if that really _is_ the temporal nexus of the Machine . . ." and her voice trailed off.

"Indeed," he said. "I know the risk! But as I said, I have planned it all to the last detail! Everything that is occurring here in this room is happening just as I have planned it! There is not the slightest deviation!"

He pointed at Craig. "He will begin to move toward the boy. Then he will retreat." Just as Actio finished speaking, Craig did just that.

"There, you see?" said Actio. "I have planned everything to the slightest detail!"

At this, Sapentia moved in front of Actio and faced him. She grabbed his robe and pulled him up close. "Brilliant!" she said, fully earnest. "Absolutely brilliant! This is one of the greatest achievements ever performed! To have caused a Device such as this to disembody its own temporal nexus – it is an unfathomable accomplishment! You are truly amazing!" Then she clenched her teeth. "But Actio! Do you know why nobody has ever even _tried_ to do this?!"

He looked at her, and his teeth also clenched. "I _know_!" he said. "The risk is _great_! It is _immense_! But what stands to be gained – to be recovered – is also great! Please, I need you Sapentia! I need your support!" And he looked at her entreatingly.

She stared back at him for a moment then returned to his side. "Well," she said soberly, "I guess what stands to be gained must be important. After all, it's worth risking the complete annihilation of _this universe_."

Actio shook his head. "Not just _this_ one," he said, _all_ of them. _All_ the universes with which this Device has interacted."

Sapentia tried for Actio not to notice as she involuntarily raised her hand to her mouth in horror.

You see, what has happened here, is that Steven – following Actio's instruction – has freed the temporal nexus of his Device. For those of you unfamiliar with what that means, and indeed, for those of you who are insufficiently familiar even with your own language to *guess* what it means, I will tell you.

The temporal nexus is that part of the Machine that maintains all events relating to any action the Machine has taken in any universe that is time-constrained, such as yours is. You will recall that when Leland traveled back in time, he had no power to change time whatsoever. When he traveled back, everything happened just as it had before. But this Device has the power to change time (Indeed, it has changed the present and the future, has it not?) For it to do this, all of those changes must be stored, and indeed created, by the Machine's temporal, or time, center, or nexus. But the existence of the temporal nexus inside a Device such as this has always been only a theory. Indeed, it is to Sapentia's immense credit that she was able to recognize so quickly what it was that she was seeing, inasmuch as nobody had ever seen one before.

To be brief therefore, it is Actio's intention simply to destroy the temporal nexus of the Space Sieve. Theoretically, if he were to do this, it would be as though the Space Sieve never had existed. Obviously, given the events of this record that I am writing, for the Space Sieve to have never existed would have immeasurable benefits.

But there is one downside.

Rather than leave you to guess, I will once again have to explain. You see, when it was contained within the Space Sieve, this temporal nexus could only interact with the outside world through the controlling systems of the Machine. But now that it was outside, it could interact with your universe, indeed with *any* universe, independently. And indeed, in this unconstrained form, it was highly unstable.

"Actio," she said. "If this nexus becomes unstable, it will destroy this universe and all those others – not just for all time to come, but for all past time as well."

Actio didn't respond.

She looked at him. "You are *sure*, Actio?"

He nodded, determinedly. "I have calculated everything to the last degree. There is no possibility of error." And just then, he pointed at Craig, who was watching all of this, and Actio said, softly, "Wow," and then Actio shook his head.

Just as he did, Craig said softly, "Wow," and then he shook his head.

"You see," said Actio," I know everything that will happen, to the smallest detail."

And indeed, Sapentia, with her emotion rising, hoped he did.

In other words, to explain it again, one of two things is going to happen here. This is important, and I am writing this part of this account just for you, so please pay attention: Either Actio will succeed, and he will implode the temporal nexus, in which case it will be as though his Device had never existed. This will of course, have immeasurable benefits. The other possibility is that he will fail, in which case the temporal nexus will essentially detonate. This will annihilate all time within all time-constrained universes with which the Space Sieve has interacted. In other words, time within your universe will cease to exist, and your *universe* therefore, will *cease* to exist. There will be no more you, there will be no more Earth, there will be no more stars, or anything else in your universe. It will not "blow up" or anything so theatrical as that. Instead, it will simply *cease*. It will simply, no longer *be*. Or more accurately, to the extent one can be accurate using your language, your entire universe will simply, *cease to ever have existed*. Since time itself is integral to your universe, and since time within your universe will be annihilated, it will be as though your universe *never did* exist.

Imagine, in the blink of an eye, you, and everything you have ever known, everything you have ever seen, vanishes – and everything, no matter how far out in space, simply ceases. And moreover, try to visualize that not only does not one bit of it exist anymore, but it never will exist, and perhaps more difficult for you to understand, none of it ever will *have* existed. All history, as you call it, will never have been.

How is that possible, you ask? How could all this solid matter, all this energy, all of these things that you see and feel all around you and all of the things you see so far away in Space, simply cease?

Well, as you would say, it's easy.

You see, all of what you see is largely comprised of nothing anyway. Your bodies – solid as they seem to you – are mostly water. Even the most unyielding matter in your universe is largely comprised of nothing but empty space. You understand that even atoms are comprised of virtually nothingness. Energy is virtually nothing. And even *you* would have to ask, what is time? Although it is the very fabric of your lives, even time is essentially, nothing. As I have said, what you call past, present, and future, is all the same thing to me. And what is it all, if not almost nothing?

The temporal nexus of this Space Sieve has far and away sufficient interactive influence to annihilate your universe. Indeed, it can do it more easily than your morning sun can eliminate the morning frost – one minute it is there, so real and so visible, and the next minute – gone. Of course, in the case of the frost, it simply becomes water vapor. In the case of your universe, it will really be gone – and not just your universe, but many others. Indeed, the world they called "New California" would also be gone, and the two girls with it.

To be more succinct –

Actio succeeds: And it will be as if the Space Sieve has never existed.

Actio fails: And it will be as if nothing you have ever known in your universe has ever existed.

So you see, Sapentia was quite right to be concerned. I have to admit at that particular moment even *I* was a little concerned myself.

But from where you're sitting, there's nothing to be concerned about, is there? Even though we're talking here about the possibility of the complete annihilation of your universe and many other universes, from where you're sitting, you should have absolutely no concern at all.

After all, since you are in fact sitting there reading about all of this, you know how it all turned out, don't you? After all, you're still there, aren't you? Surely you had already realized that Actio would be successful, by virtue of the mere fact that you still exist!

None of this therefore, can have the slightest suspense for you, can it?

(And indeed, I have to tell you that regarding your universe and all these other universes, there were other beings [who I do not describe here] who were very interested in them and in how all of this was going to turn out. In truth, these beings take an *intense* interest in some of these universes. In fact, these beings were involved enough by this point that they had already taken steps to insure that Actio's success was already a forgone conclusion. But neither he nor Sapentia knew that.)

Just then, the temporal nexus became clear and increased in size, flashing violently.

"It's going *now* Actio!" she said.

"Watch the boy's glasses," he replied.

And at that moment, a shockwave emanated from the Machine and tore across Steven's, head and hurled his glasses to the ceiling, where they stuck, and then melted into it.

"Don't worry," said Actio. "He can do the rest by feel – and he's going to have to, because now that the Machine will begin to disintegrate his body, he will be unable to do it any other way."

Sapentia entreated, "But these creatures need their bodies – fragile as they are – to be able to live. ! Actio, is this boy going to . . ."

Actio turned to her and shook his head. "Is one boy's life really so high a price to pay, for the safety of all these universes?"

And may I add at this point: What is the big deal? In spite of all your pretentiousness, people in your world live and die as you say, like flies, every day, anyway. What's one boy? After all, he gets to save his own world. How many of you get to do that? And in reality, even though you think that it's all you *have*, how long do any of your short lives last anyway?

"This was part of my studies," said Actio. "It took a long time to find a boy who would have the courage of this – the courage to persevere – no matter the personal cost. No, this boy doesn't want to die, far from it. But he has both the skill to run this Machine, as well as the determination to see it through to the final conclusion no matter what!"

Just then, another shockwave emanated from the Machine. Craig staggered back, able to do little but stare, and watch. But momentarily, his mood changed, or his beloved pet, "Lady," had just poked its head in the bedroom window.

This animal was one of what you call a "dog." And may I say, I find it odd that you use the word "dog" as a general reference of great *derision*, while at the same time *loving* a few of them. In other words, while you use the word "dog" as a slur for almost anything, and while you often view other people's dogs with contempt, nonetheless, you develop a great attachment for your *own* dog. This is due to the fact that these animals have been bred for centuries to do nothing so well as flattering their own owners. And this they do energetically, and convincingly. Vain creatures that you are, you always take this personally. Thus, while you generally see dogs as vile creatures you see your *own* dog as much smarter than the rest. After all, *your* dog, unlike others, seems to recognize how wonderful *you* are, doesn't it?

"Lady!" Craig said, as he leapt to the window. Characteristically, the dog began to lick Craig's face, and Craig, characteristically, puckered his lips. There was a sense of relief to Craig to be playing with the animal, and thus to have a distraction from the bizarre goings-on in the room.

"How's my little honey?" he said, and he turned back to the boy. "Hey Scoot . . . uh . . . . I mean *Steven*, hey Steven, this little girl's a-wonderin' what's a goin' on in here!"

As Steven turned to look – and even though he couldn't see it clearly – he knew how Craig was kissing the animal, and it disgusted him. And as Steven looked, his attention waned from the Machine. There had been three auxiliary screens to either side of the Machine. Two of them disappeared.

Actio jumped.

"*Variable!*" he cried, with anguish in his voice. His jaw clenched and he became rigid and confused. He hadn't planned for this!

But Sapentia acted quickly. The situation was critical now, and in this time-constrained reality there was no time to lose. Her eyes fell on the dog and her hand went up to her mouth in concentration. Her lip flinched.

"YIPE!!" the dog called out, as it immediately broke away and ran out to a safe distance in the yard.

"What's a-matter honey?" Craig called. "Bee done bit ya?"

Sapentia's finger flicked.

"YIPE!" The dog let out another cry and tore across the backyard and ducked under the fence.

Sapentia lowered her hand. The variable had been removed.

Spinning now in three axes, and flashing wildly and blindingly, the nexus appeared to grow wild with fury. (But of course it wasn't growing furious. It isn't alive. It has no emotion. I just have to use these sorts of words to describe what is going on, since there is little other way to explain it to you.) It also appeared to be roaring – to be screaming at an ear-piercing volume. And yet, there was no need cover one's ears. It was perfectly possible to speak in a normal voice, and be heard.

"Steven?" Craig asked. Steven had already recreated the two screens, so there were once again seven screens and seven keyboards, which he was working furiously.

"Steven?" Craig asked again. "Whatcha doin' son? Ya . . . ya need'n any help there boy?"

Steven didn't look up. "It's all right Uncle Craig. I'm almost done. It's almost, almost ov . . ."

With a crash, the nexus flashed and increased in size for the final time. Partly involuntarily, Sapentia cringed, as did Actio. And indeed, Sapentia stepped back again, for she didn't want Actio to see she was trembling now.

The temporal nexus was now only moments from detonation – and you, and your universe, only moments from annihilation.

As Craig looked around, the room looked strange.

Back in the kitchen, as Donna reached for a pencil, it disappeared. She looked out the window. Somehow, everything looked odd, like in a dream.

174

Sapentia, now almost hysterical, could now do little but watch. She stood in silence, where Actio could not see her.

"This is the end," said Actio, as always, speaking in his own language, which I am having to translate into your crude form of communication.

He looked fondly at the boy. "You've done your part – goodbye, Steven."

And Steven vanished. Without giving you all the details, the light from the nexus appeared to dissolve him. As he disappeared, Actio took the controls of the Device himself. And as he did, Craig saw him, and then Sapentia, for the first time. But by now, Craig could no longer think, or move.

From his perspective, what happened to Steven was this. He found himself falling in a black void. While he sensed himself increasing in speed, there were at first no points of reference to be seen to prove he was actually falling. Then, below, he saw large, dull-brown spinning disks. They looked essentially like the undersides of huge, spinning tops. He was heading for one of them. As he landed and sprawled on it, near the center, the friction grabbed him and he turned around and around with the spinning surface. But soon he began to slide outward, to the edge of the disk. Unable to hold on, he slipped off, and was falling once again. Then, below him, another disk appeared as he fell toward it. He landed on this disk, held on, then was thrown off again, and so forth. While falling, and landing, and then being thrown off a succession of these disks, everything continually grew darker. Then finally, the darkness became total and there was nothingness. It was oblivion.

This is why Actio had to let Steven do the first parts of the work that needed to be done. Actio knew that he himself would have to do the last part. And if Actio had been annihilated as Steven had been, he would not have been around to do that. Could Actio have spared Steven, and taken his place, he would have done so. But it had not been possible.

And what Actio did now with the Space Sieve, he did quickly. With a sound like a huge chorus of screaming voices, and with trembling and terrible flashes of light, the temporal nexus of the Machine trembled, then imploded, and then, was gone.

In the same instant, the house that they were in vanished, Craig and Donna vanished, and Actio, Sapentia, and the Device were in an open meadow. The sky overhead was still clear, and the sun blazed in it. A single cow chewed its cud lazily at the end of the meadow, beside a fence that ran into the distance. The Space Sieve lay on the grass, on its back.

Except now, it wasn't black. It was a dull, cream color. If you had been sufficiently perceptive as David had been, you would have always felt that somehow, the Space Sieve looked *alive*. This contrast was especially vivid now, because now, it looked truly *dead*.

Sapentia smiled at Actio. "It's nice to see the sun, nice to see the grass too, and the fence, and the cow," She waved her hand expansively, "and the rest of this universe."

But rather than reply at first, Actio savored the moment. They both knew his accomplishment in imploding the nexus had been immense. But he was thinking about something even more important.

"Have you looked?" he asked.

"Yes," she replied. "When the temporal nexus was extant outside the Machine – when it was visible – I saw all that it contained. I saw all that had happened as a result of this Machine. I saw all that it did."

She looked at him very directly. "I assume it's all gone now, Actio."

But Actio was quick to correct her. "If I may say, my love, it was not the *Machine* that did any of it. After all, it is only a Device."

But Sapentia would not accept his argument. "Had it not been for your Machine none of it would have happened. Nonetheless," she continued, "I did see. The Machine is gone now, and all that it had done must now also be gone."

Somewhat chastened, Actio followed up. "But have you looked?"

"No," she replied. And after a pause she said, "I believe I know. But I want you to show me."

Then she chuckled. "For starters," she asked, "What happened to the house?"

(To help you understand, I will point out that Actio and Sapentia, using their own abilities, can travel to various points in time, space, and reality. As creatures advance, their knowledge becomes such that they can do many things that might otherwise appear miraculous. Yet, Actioand Sapentia cannot do all things. This is something few beings attain.)

The scene around them changed. They were standing in the air above an intersection. A car was hurrying through, clearly running a red light.

"This is the time and place where Steven's parents were killed," Actio said. "But look, now they made it safely. Oh, this is a coincidence," he continued, "the garbage truck that killed Steven's parents was the same one that was going to take away the Space Sieve when David's parents threw it away that morning. The delay caused when David ran out of the house to stop it, resulted in the garbage truck being in this intersection a little later than it would have been, and as the truck came through the intersection, hurrying, it was here when Steven's parents were running a red light. That coincidence – together with his parents running the light – is what killed them.

"But now, none of that happened. David never stopped the garbage truck because he never had the Device. Steven's parents were never killed. The Space Sieve never *was*."

Then around them, the scene changed again. And if you don't understand it – and I think you should have by now – Actio and Sapentia can travel backward and forward in your time as easily as I can, and indeed, as easily as they can travel from place to place, not only in your world, but in the total sphere of creation. And they knew where to go as well, having seen while the temporal nexus was disembodied.

Now, it was Christmas, five years hence. Steven was at his parents' house with his brothers and sisters.

"He's even cuter now than when I first saw him," commented Sapentia. "It looks like he's traded his glasses for contact lenses."

Actio continued. "His parents never died, so Steven never went to live with Craig and Donna, and it turns out those two never built that house we were in either. All that has ever been there was that field – and I suppose, the fence, and the cow.

As Sapentia smiled at him, the scene changed again. They were standing on the curb, outside David's boyhood home.

"This is the day the garbage truck picked up the Device in front of David's house – the day David ran out and stopped it – and the day it fell off the truck and hit the sidewalk." And Actio rubbed the sidewalk with his toes. "There's no chip in the sidewalk here. The Space Sieve was never here to chip it." And the scene changed again.

They were standing now in a far-away world. At least, it is far away for people from Earth.

Sapentia recognized it immediately. "This is the planet where Kito-Ono lived," she said.

"Yes, it is." Actio replied.

Surely, if you are not blinded by the hubris that is so typical for you kind, you would have anticipated that the interactions of the Space Sieve – while it existed – stretched far beyond your Earth and influenced the lives of many other creatures besides your own and beyond what I have recorded herein.

Indeed, it is a vast number of them. What Actio and Sapentia are investigating here then, is one of those other instances.

For your benefit then, this planet is called "Ono," and Kito-Ono was a great leader there. Some time previous, under his leadership, the people of Ono had defeated their foes – those who would have invaded their world and deprived them of their liberty if not their lives. The wars having ended, Kito-Ono had retired to a small house in a rural part of their world to live out the rest of his life with his wife and family.

But as a result of the inter-dimensional forces that were unleashed during the wars, the Device – the so-called Space Sieve – had come into this world and had been found by a girl named Shanna-Ono. She, like David, had gotten past the Tic, but she had never been able to achieve anywhere near the capability with the Device that David did. You see, there is a saying: "Just because you get past the *Tic*, doesn't mean you know *everything*."

Anyway, she managed to open an inter-dimensional rift – one that had been sealed after the wars. Opening it, using the Device, allowed a new enemy to emerge that attempted to conquer Ono. As a result, Kito-Ono had been forced to come out of retirement, to lead the people of Ono once again to the stars to fight for their world.

Of course, in most worlds – and indeed for most of your own Earth's history – it is the leaders who lead their people into battle. It is only in corrupt civilizations where a leader – or group of leaders – will argue for the benefits of having a war, and then for the leader or leaders to stay safely away from the battlefield, while others sacrifice *their* lives for the great causes that the leaders have put forth. Typically, if the cause is seen as being great enough for a leader to ask *others* to sacrifice their lives for it, the *leader* also is required to sacrifice – or at least risk – *his* life for it as well. You have a saying: "If it's good sauce for the goose, it should also be good enough sauce for the gander."

But the Ono were a good people, whose leaders fought alongside them. So during this new battle for Ono, the enemy had employed an algorithm that had revealed to them, based on the movements of all the ships in the battle, which ship was most likely to be piloted by the commander of the forces of Ono. In this way, it was unnecessary for them to crack the communication codes of their enemies to find the leader's ship. They could identify the leader's ship merely from the nature of the movements of all the ships. They soon identified the ship piloted by Kito-Ono and directed a preponderance of their fire on his vessel, destroying it early in the battle.

But far from disheartening the people of Ono, the loss of their great leader, Kito, had inspired in them a determination that was intense. For in addition to fighting for their world, their homes, their families, and their liberty, now they also fought for the memory of Kito.

And they drove their enemies from their skies.

"This is Kito's home," said Sapentia.

"Yes," replied Actio. "And there he is."

And sitting on the porch of a modest home, reading, was indeed Kito-Ono.

Sapentia smiled.

"There was no Space Sieve," said Actio. "None of it ever happened. When the war ended, the inter-dimensional rifts were sealed. There was never a Device here to reopen them. The Ono are secure, and Kito lived to an old age."

"And Shanna?" inquired Sapentia.

Actio smiled and wagged his head. "The Machine never *existed*, so it was never here for her to find," he said.

Now, Actio and Sapentia were standing on a vast prairie. This was the same one where the two Kex ships had cut the canyon-sized grooves into the planet surface when they were chasing the urchin ship that David had created to taunt them. But there were no canyons now.

"It looks natural," said Sapentia, as always, in her own language. "I like it this way better."

Actio nodded his agreement. "No Device. It was never here." He shrugged. "It was never anywhere."

The scene changed again. They were now in space above the Kex home world.

"It looks the same," observed Sapentia. "There are mo tributary vessels of the Barbarian Hoard in orbit around the Kex home world."

"Indeed," replied Actio. "The Kex are still a free people – still masters of their domain. They were never conquered by the Barbarian Hoard."

"Actio, I want you to tell me how it was that the Kex fell. I haven't looked. I want you to tell me."

"Well," he replied. "Early on, David had the presence of mind to set the Device so it would never do anything that would lead to his death or injury – this was first evidenced when they were at the Graveyard of the Gods – but sadly, he didn't think to set it to protect anybody else. Anyway, David caused quite a ruckus with the Kex, and as you well know, all those ships that were around him in space when he plunged Chip and himself into that sun – all those ships were just private vessels – friends of the families of the children who David and Chip had been frightening. While they were all very powerful ships, they were just pleasure craft of the Kex, not their far more powerful military vessels. Indeed, once, when an enemy of theirs continued to vex them, the Kex sent a fleet of military ships that sliced up the enemy planet like a piece of fruit, until it was just a spherical mass of magma floating in space. I have to hand it to the Kex: As far as directed energy weapons they really know what they're doing.

"Anyway, those ships that David overcame were only private vessels that came to see what was going on with the two little ships that David was pestering. The parents basically came to see what all the fuss was that their children were having.

"Well, the whole affair was disturbing enough that the Kex military that they immediately began to study the events – recognizing that David and the Device posed a potential threat to the Kex that was perfectly insurmountable and that could with impunity destroy the entire Kex civilization – and so they understandably felt it was their responsibility to do whatever was necessary to eliminate that threat. And David, who had still not perfected his use of the Device, in departing the Kex universe left a trail of wrinkled space that the Kex scientists eventually tracked all the way back to David's home universe, and to Earth.

"But these scientists realized it would not be easy, going and getting him, and securing the Space Sieve. It would in fact, take the combined power of two-thirds of the entire Kex battle fleet just to open a sufficient passage to be able to travel to David's universe.

"You know, some of these species are pretty good at some things, and then other parts of their technology are just so inferior . . ."

"Just go on with the story, Actio," she said.

"Well, they concluded that once their fleet had traveled to David's universe, it would be hopefully a simple matter to send a single ship, hidden in an electromagnetic drape, to David's planet to capture him unawares and take him back to the Kex home world – together with the Device. But their problem, was once they traveled to David's universe, for the Kex to return to their home universe would once again take the power of two-thirds of their most powerful ships, meaning of course that almost all of their vast battle fleet would have to travel *to* David's universe, in order to be able to travel *back*.

"So then it would follow," Sapentia interjected, "that once the Kex fleet left their reality, the entire Kex domain was then largely undefended and open for invasion by the Barbarian Hoard. They must have seen David as quite a danger to have been willing to take so great a risk, and apparently, a risk that ultimately would prove disastrous to their civilization. Once they left themselves wide open, their enemies lost no time . . . but Actio, that couldn't have been what happened."

"No," Actio corrected, "Actually, quite the contrary. The Barbarian Hoard did overrun the Kex, but the Kex never traveled to David's home world. For once the Device detected that the Kex were about to do so, because of the general directive that David had given it to protect him, the Machine basically 'took the initiative' and simply stopped the Kex from coming. It deactivated all the inter-dimensional drive capability from all of the Kex vessels, and it erased all related technology from all the Kex' data banks.

"As the Kex were preparing to jump into David's universe, they suddenly found themselves completely without *any* inter-dimensional capability whatsoever. And without this capability, they were at a huge disadvantage to their enemies who *had* this capability. The Kex had lost most of their mobility, while their enemies retained all of theirs. This disparity allowed their enemies to attack and retreat without the Kex being able to follow them, or even to predict where their enemies would attack next. The Kex were left to play a war only of defense. They could not take the battle *to* their enemies. It was only a matter of time before they were defeated and overrun."

"It's interesting." he continued. "The Machine could have done anything to fill the directive David gave it to protect him. What it chose to do was relatively minor, and quite unspectacular, nonetheless it was entirely effective in protecting David, to say nothing of changing the entire course of civilization in the Kex universe."

"Sometimes by small means, are large things accomplished," observed Sapentia.

Actio continued. "But now, none of that happened. The Space Sieve never existed. David was never here. The Kex never heard or dreamed of any of that. So here they are, still secure, still masters of their domain."

"Well I suppose then," she surmised, "the only reason David was able to *expire*, the only reason he was eventually able to *die* was . . ."

"He erased the memory of the Machine," Actio replied. "And then he abandoned it. Had David's order to the Machine remained intact, the machine would have continuously protected him as it did with the Kex, and as it did in so many other all other cases, even though David never realized it.

"Moreover," he continued, "it would have continuously maintained, repaired, and renewed his body. He would have lived forever."

"Hmmm." She replied. "It's a little confusing. Had David not wiped the memory of the Machine and his order remained intact he would have lived forever. But he did wipe the memory, so he died. But now, since the machine never existed and David never had it, he never gave it that order. So . . ."

Actio replied. "David lived - will live – out the rest of his life, and die, just as he would have done had there never been a Space Sieve. And of course, there never *was* a Space Sieve."

The scene changed again. Actio pointed to the tops of the trees that were lining the small park in which he and Sapentia were now standing. "David, when he was flying, and when he was pulling himself along in the branches in the tops of those trees over there, he broke that little twig off right there. But look, it's still there. David was never here."

Sapentia pushed him. "Okay, now you're teasing me," she said. But she looked at him with love and admiration. "Show me what I want to see. Show me the *important* things, Actio. You know those I wish to see."

And Actio and Sapentia found themselves in a large home near the Pacific Ocean. There were the sounds of children in the background.

"This is one of the last times David and Chip met in their old age, after their kind," Actio said.

As one of the children ran past them, (and of course, Actio and Sapantia could not be seen), Sapentia's eyes filled with delight as she saw the little boy.

"It's *David*!" she said.

And she looked at Actio. "But you said this was when they were older! It's David, and he's just a little boy. How?" she asked.

Actio beamed as he realized who it had been. "That little boy - it's David's *grandson*," he said. "The resemblance *is* striking."

"You know," he continued, "I really feel kind of strange showing you all this when you could perfectly well see for yourself if you . . ."

"Just you keep showing me," she interrupted.

Actio smiled. He was so fond of her. Who wouldn't be? I have to confess, Sapentia, is alluring.

"Well," Actio said to Sapentia, "then we'll want to go onto the balcony."

And as they walked, the little boy ran onto the large balcony, and up to two older men who were sitting there in chairs, talking, as they looked out over the sea. In the distance the seagulls were soaring.

"Amazing creatures," said David, "the aerobatics are awe inspiring if you think about it."

"Yes they are," replied Chip, "You know – Nature – everything around us – we take so much for granted. You seem to notice more than I do, David."

And for a moment, David and Chip just looked into the distance together, simply enjoying each other's company as they had done so many times before in their close friendship that had lasted through the many years.

"Just two old men," said Sapentia. "No 'Graveyards of the Gods' for them. They never traveled to any other planets; never saw any other universes. They just spent all the years of their lives as good friends - living, and experiencing. But they never had the Space Sieve."

Actio shrugged. "Neither of them would even know what one looked like."

"Grandpa!" The little boy ran up to him. "Grandma told me to tell you a long time ago that dinner's ready."

"Well we better get going then," said David to the little boy. "And when Grandma gets mad at your grandpa, you tell her it wasn't my fault that we're late!"

And as the little boy ran off, the two men got up and headed into the house.

"You know Chip," David said to him, "I've always liked evenings like this. We've had it pretty good, you and I."

"Yes," said Chip. "I've enjoyed being in the furniture business, although I never found that perfect chair that I somehow always imagined there should be. But I did okay."

"Well," replied David, and even in his advanced years his face still had a happy, boyish quality, and there was a twinkle in his eye, "the chairs you *did* sell were pretty good. I always liked 'em! In fact, I was thinking that anything better than that last chair you sold me would only have been possible in another universe!" And they chuckled.

"You know, David," he replied, "you were always the smartest person I ever knew."

"Yeah, I know," said David. "You *always* tell me that! But look at you. I should be the one flattering *you*!"

"Well," replied Chip, "you'll have to compete with my wife to do that. You know I can never get Diane to stop saying nice things about me."

"Yeah," said David, "Sally's the same with me. You know, I think I had a crush on her from the time we were just kids. We've both been very fortunate in a lot of ways. Having you as a good friend all these years – the times we've all spent together – you, me, Sally, Diane, our kids, the grandkids. It's been a great life. We've been very fortunate."

"Yeah," replied Chip, "of course my take on it," and he put his arm around his old friend and they headed in, "is that we've both been very blessed."

"So," asked Sapentia, "David married Sally and Chip married Diane?"

Actio nodded, and as he did, he prepared to take them to yet another place.

Sensing this, Sapentia stopped him. "Wait," she said, as they paused to watch the family go in for dinner. Then she nodded at Actio, and they were on a large plain. In the distance were two peaks. It was the world the two girls had named "New California," the peaks "The Two Alps," and the valley, "Shenandoah."

But there was no castle between the peaks, and none of those places had ever been so named. The girls had never been there to give them those names. Nobody had ever been there to build the castle. None of what the girls did in this place, ever happened. They were never here.

As Actio and Sapentia stood there, fully visible to all the creatures there, some of the creatures ran toward them, as a flurry of communication beetles flew up to them and swirled around. They were flying energetically, and they appeared haggard, to the extent that a beetle can appear haggard. And they were flashing wildly – a veritable fireworks show of communication beetles.

And then broad smiles spread across Sapentia and Actio's faces.

For, while the communication beetles were flashing many colors, the one they were flashing most of all, was the color *blue*.

Still, as the communication beetles flashed and spoke in the language of Actio and Sapentia, they were all saying different things – they were all relating the messages of a different creature, so much so, that it was impossible to understand what any of them were saying.

For each communication beetle that was flashing blue was carrying the message of a different individual baby cherub.

And as Actio and Sapentia looked, they could see there were thousands of them – tiny, blue baby cherubs were everywhere. They were flying and crawling. They were running and squawking. And all the other animals were having the times of their lives playing with them.

In the distance, something caught Sapentia's eye.

"Look!" She pointed.

In the distance were two large, flying creatures, almost at the range of visibility. "It's *them*," Sapentia said. "Actio, there they *are*!"

Far off, with the glow of the sky behind them two mighty creatures plied the air, far above the hectic affairs below. Their flight was powerful and magnificent, yet graceful and beautiful. They appeared to be enjoying themselves immensely.

And indeed, they were. Together as they flew, El and Asherah were enjoying a rare moment of peace, each of them in the company of their one true love.

"If you don't want to translate it for yourself," Actio said, "she is talking to him. He's saying that as much as he loves all their children, he misses the time he used to have to fly alone with her, and she is telling him that she agrees.

Actio paused. "Now she is telling him though, that even with all the cares that go with all these little children, she likes it this way better. He is agreeing with her."

"I know," said Sapentia. "I can understand their flashing. Let's just watch."

"Noisy as our little ones are," said El to Asherah, "our kind is preserved. Our children occupy the attention of the whole world."

"Yes," Asherah replied. "It's the way it has always been when the new ones are born."

She beat her powerful wings and climbed into the sky with El beside, matching her beat for beat.

"And as it will always be," he replied, and his eyes twinkled as he looked at Asherah.

Their wingtips touched momentarily, then they continued to soar as they had done so many times before – and as they would do so many times still to come – flying together – two longtime friends – in bliss and peace. Asherah broke to the side and tumbled, El following, and then they restored their formation and drifted away into the distance.

Sapentia turned to Actio, momentarily distracted from the tranquil scene by a disturbing thought. "I suppose that the Evil is still locked in the cave."

And she turned to Actio with a shocked expression on her face as he replied.

185

"No, it's *not*." he said.

And then he looked away. "I got rid of it," he said. "It's one of the last things I did while the Device was still working. I sent all of the Evil in this world into oblivion. I figured as long as something was going to be going finally and ultimately into oblivion, it might as well be *that*. It is gone, fully and completely." And he smiled.

Sapentia thought for a moment.

"Kind of neat," she noted. "I have a feeling those two flying creatures will become two of the most celebrated beings in all of creation for what they did – for the sacrifice they made. But of course, now that the Device is destroyed, they never actually *did* it. They never made their great and legendary sacrifice. And now, they never will. They will never even know about it."

Actio shook his head. "But they *would* have," he corrected. "Those two – the ones the girls called the "cherubs" – they have the capacity. They still have that level of greatness within themselves, even though they will never have to make the great and final sacrifice.

"And of course, they will never be called "cherubs" either, nor will they ever be called 'El' and 'Asherah'. There will never be anyone come to this place to name them that. We can still celebrate their greatness, but they themselves will never know."

Sapentia puzzled for a moment. "Does that not in some ways defeat the purpose?" she asked. "Can they be truly great, if they never are called upon to perform the great works?"

Actio thought for a moment, then shook his head. "Maybe," he replied. "I don't know. But it works for me."

Sapentia shrugged. "I guess, actually, I'm good with it too."

And as I now recognize that I am beginning to use some of your silly idioms to refer to their communication, Actio then said, "There's just one last thing I want to show you."

And as he spoke, they traveled a great distance in time and space, to Earth once again, to a certain Thanksgiving party.

In the main room of the house, the adults busied themselves with preparing the foods and drinks your kind find pleasant and which are customarily prepared and consumed on such an occasion, and while others of the party were occupying themselves with conversation, observation of various electro-mechanical devices in the home and so forth, four children were more or less running amok though the rest of the house. In this sense, they were both having the most fun and stood the chance of doing the most good, as little of interest was being accomplished by the parents, other than for preparing the meal. And indeed, the children's activities were far more entertaining as well. For the parents, while they could have been engaging themselves in interesting conversation regarding the intimate details and secrets of their lives, chose not to do so, as adults almost always choose.

Nonetheless, in the main room, Chip's father, Duane, and the rest of the group, laughed. Duane's wife, Ginger, had just related an entertaining joke. It was the one about the piano-playing mouse and the singing butterfly. She was always the life of any party, and Duane felt happy, as to simply have her nearby was all he ever needed to feel that way.

"But Actio," Sapentia pointed out. "I thought Duane's wife . . ."

". . .*died?*" Actio completed her sentence, "years before?"

"Well, it turns out," he continued, "that once, while in another part of this universe, the Device was operated by someone such that it caused an unusual ripple that intersected this world. This ripple momentarily interrupted the chemical function inside the bodies of some of the beings in this world, including Chip's mother. In a few of those cases, their bodies were unable to recover from this anomaly, so they died."

Actio held his hand to his chin, then flexed his fingers. "But there was no Device, so none of that ever happened. So here she is."

Duane reached over and squeezed Ginger's hand. She beamed back at him.

In another part of the house, four children, two boys and two girls had run down the hallway and had hidden in a closet. A few moments later they came out again, and as Sapentia and Actio watched, Sally, David, Chip, and Diane emerged from the closet, a collection of objects falling out with them. They quickly gathered it all up and put it back in again, then headed off down the hall.

"No Space Sieve to fall out of the closet." Sapentia observed.

"It was never here," replied Actio, stating the obvious. "It was never anywhere. It never existed. It never was."

They didn't say any more to each other – Actio and Sapentia – they just briefly chuckled at the antics of the children. And Actio, for his part, looked both relieved and satisfied.

And with that, the two of them headed off to a place of mutual interest, to continue their happy existences.

What all this means then, is two things. First, I am very near to the point of being able to conclude this ordeal with your language and to head off on *my* happy existence as well. Second, it means that except for the events I have mentioned here in these final notes – meaning the parts of this account after the time the temporal nexus was imploded – *nothing I have told you in this book ever actually happened.* Indeed, although it is difficult for you to understand – and I have no intention of trying to explain it to you – while the events of this document were very real and indeed, were important enough for me to document them, in another very real sense, they *never actually happened* at all.

And while your own universe at one point, came very close to being completely vanished to a state of non-existence and never-existence, in another very real sense, that never actually happened either.

If you want to contemplate that for a moment you are free to do so. Indeed, you might be well to do so, although by the time you do, I will be done with recording these events, and will be long gone.

I fear I am beginning to use your idioms far too much.

There is one final loose end and it regards the physical "shell" of the Space Sieve. To understand what happened to it I will relate a future conversation between Sapentia and Actio.

They were lying on a faraway shore, watching the waves and the creatures diving in the sea in the distance.

Sapentia asked Actio a question, the subject of which by now was only a distant, relatively unpleasant memory to her. "You know that Device you made – the terribly powerful one you had to destroy?"

He thought for an instant, then said. "Oh, you mean my Device? Yes, the Space Sieve?"

"Yes," she replied. "That's what the human called it."

"Of course I remember it," Actio replied. "What fun it was! But you say I destroyed it? No. I just imploded the temporal nexus."

"What?" she asked, her voice now tinged with concern and even a little anger. "You say, 'What *fun* it was?' It was responsible for the deaths of countless beings, and for ruining the lives of countless more. It damaged entire worlds!" Her eyes flashed. "Repairing the damage almost cost several universes! What do you mean it was *fun*?"

Actio's face now grew serious as well. "I'm sorry Sapentia; you're right! It *was* irresponsible. Sapentia, what was I thinking? My love, I assure you, I *am* so sorry for all of it!"

And indeed, he was truly sorry. In truth, he would have given his own existence if it had been necessary, to have made everything right.

Accepting his sincerity, she nonetheless followed up, "But it is inert now? Your Device is truly and eternally inoperative - dead?" she asked.

"Well yes," he replied, "In a very real sense it is dead. I imploded its nexus after all. You know what that means."

"Well, yes, I do know what that means," she replied. "And that's my problem, Actio. I was thinking, and it came to me just now."

She looked at him with an intelligent, endearing expression on her face. "Just imploding the nexus doesn't kill the Machine. All that would do, is make it as though it had never existed. But that's not the same as being completely destroyed. It's not oblivion, is it?"

"No," he replied sheepishly, "it's not the same thing, I suppose. But it's as good as if it was. "You see," he explained, "once the temporal nexus is imploded, then naturally, another one is immediately spawned inside the Machine. But *this* one *is* inert, inasmuch as the Machine has never been turned on, you see?"

"But if it *were* turned on?" she asked.

"Well even if it *were* to be turned on, it would all be new. The existing nexus cannot ever recreate the events of the previous one. It would be as though the Machine had come into existence at that very moment. It would have no prior history. The lives of David, Kito, the cherubs, everything – nothing would change from the way it is now. Nothing would change from the current, natural state."

Sapentia stood up. "And that's supposed to be a *comfort*?" she asked, and her voice was like the crackling of thunder across a wind-swept, stormy sky. "You mean somebody could activate it again and go rampaging across all of creation, but it's not so bad because this time it would all simply be *new*? And so now you offer this to me as an *assurance*?"

He also stood up now, and he raised his hands. "No." he said. "That's what I was trying to tell you. It cannot be reactivated. It's *locked*."

"*Locked*?" she replied, incredulously. "You mean its still *alive*, but *locked*?! Her adorable voice rose in pitch. "Actio, this is one of the most disconcerting things that you have ever . . . ."

"No, no," he assured her. "It's not a simple lock. You see . . . ."

"I don't care what kind of lock it is! I truly fear a lock is not good enough! I wish to asset with you my belief that the Machine should be taken apart immediately, and fully destroyed! Actio, I sincerely entreat you to insure that your Device is completely eliminated from existence!"

It had been so long that she had been worked up like this that they both were enjoying it, at least a little.

Actio smiled, and after pausing said, "I can't take it apart."

"Please Actio, I don't care what is required to do it." She replied. "I deeply wish that it be completely disassembled and destroyed!"

"I . . . I was trying to tell you love, I *can't* take it apart. It *can't* be destroyed. At least, I don't know how, you see, I made it out of the same thing *we're* made out of. It's immortal . . . indestructible." He looked at her, with his entreating eyes. "You see, the best approach is to *lock* it. Even were I to *hide* it or keep it safe somewhere, it wouldn't be as good as *locking* it."

And as she began to realize the futility, or at least the difficulty of pressing her point, she asked him, "Well, this lock – it is a *good* one?"

"Oh *yes*," he replied eagerly. "It's *very* complex - no, not just a *tactile* lock. No. It's a *chemical* lock, a *thermal* lock, a *tactile* lock, all *simultaneous*, and then once you get through *that* lock then there's *another* one. You see, once you get past *that* one then three objects appear above the Machine and you have to manipulate all three of them in just a certain way to . . ."

"Okay." She said. She was still disturbed, but was feeling that she had little choice but to trust him. "Okay, I'll take your word for it. But just tell me it's *safe.*"

"Oh yes," he replied. "It should be completely safe. Coming up with the key to the first lock set would be pretty hard to do, and the second lock – like I was telling you about the three objects above the Machine – the chances of getting past that are . . . well, and *then* you'd still have to get past the Tic. I know David did, but how many have ever . . ."

He paused for a moment before continuing. "You know, I *have* looked at many possible outcomes relating to the shell, and I have not foreseen that it will ever be reactivated."

But as Actio said this, I assume you surmised that were the Device to be reactivated it would change the future of any time-constrained reality with which it interacted, and this Actio would not have been able to see, for it would be something that did not presently exist. For while Actio could travel into what you call the past and the future, he does not have the ability to manifestly change either of them, nor to calculate how they could be changed in all possible outcomes. Of course there are beings that know these things, but Actio is not one of them.

Sapentia looked at him for a moment, a look of tension still on her face. But when he smiled at her, finally, she relaxed and smiled back too.

Now you might wonder where Actio chose to leave his Device. Perhaps in the core of a sun, or a black hole, you might surmise, and yet such places are exactly the sort where some beings go looking for strange objects, just as you might go looking in the bottom of a well. You see, beings, thought they might have very different abilities, are often not so different in other ways. And so, if you had a dangerous, yet adored, possession, would you necessarily seek to be forever rid of it? I would suggest to you that you might be well advised to do just that. But instead, you might choose a place for it where it would always be available to you should you choose to recover it, while still being away from criticizing eyes.

After all, what maker wishes to cast forever aside his greatest creation?

~ ~ ~

It was a clear, sunny day in front of Phosia's house. Everybody knew her. She was an endearing old woman who had placed a number of toilets in front of her house by the street as decoration. She used them as planters, and each one had flowers growing out of the bowl and out of the tank.

"Seems like a waste," she'd say, "to let something as beautiful as a torlet ever go to th' landfill."

And indeed, she knew what she was talking about, for she had spent many years having only an outhouse. And as a lot of people can tell you, if you've ever used an outhouse for a long time, you know what a beautiful thing a toilet truly is.

But as it applies to this story, at the end of her row of toilets in her front yard there was a strange, dull white box that looked like a small, upright piano – it was the Space Sieve. And since it didn't have any nice openings that a toilet has to put plants in, Phosia had placed them in pots on top of it.

You may be curious as to how the Space Sieve got there, at the end of her row of toilets. Actio had left it in the field where Craig and Donna's house had been, and someone had thrown it away. Phosia had happened to be at the dump one day disposing of some garbage and had seen it falling out of a garbage truck. Thinking it was a toilet, she rushed over to it. Naturally, she had been disappointed when she'd seen it wasn't a toilet, but she thought it was odd looking, and seemed lonely besides, and so she decided to give it a home.

"What d'ya got that thing over there fer? 'T'aint no torlet!" Her friends would say. But Phosia would patiently explain that she liked it anyway.

"Hated to see such nice workmanship go to the landfill," she'd say, "even though it weren't no torlet." And so she placed it there, at the end of her little row of toilets.

And for the most part, it seemed to fit in there just fine. If there was one drawback for Phosia, it was the fact that the bird droppings – when they fell on the other toilets – tended to blend in more with the white porcelain than they did when they fell on the Space Sieve. The Device, as she put it, "Weren't near as nice as them other torlets fer hidin' the bird plaster."

But it wasn't so bad, because she found they hose off easily enough. "Almost un-natch-rel how easy that thing is to hose off," she'd say.

And somehow it seemed at home there, baking in the sun with the flowers on top, just like all the real toilets beside it.

Phosia had a dog named "Daisy-Joe," who had a fondness for digging raw onions out of the garden and eating them. I know it is difficult to imagine how a dog's breath could be any worse than it ordinarily is, but you get the picture.

Anyway, one day ol' Daisy-Joe went a diggin' up and eatin' onions agin'.

And I find myself truly desperate for this to end as I am slipping further and further into your idioms.

So, after eating Phosia's onions and then sleeping for an hour, Daisy-Joe went over to its favorite place to relive itself. And while Phosia would never have tolerated one of her own children digging and eating her onions, much less urinating on her toilets, for some reason she let her dog do so.

As the dog searched for a nice place to "go" as you would say, it decided to go on the different one this time. As it lifted its leg beside the Space Sieve and relieved itself, it applied a very unusual mix of *chemicals* to the exterior of the Device. And it was at a certain *temperature*. At the same time, the dog began to *scratch* the edge of the device with its raised hind leg.

This *combination* it turns out, was precisely that odd combination of chemical, thermal, and tactile stimulus that Actio had set as the first *key* that could awaken the Device. He never could have imagined that an onion-eating dog could have produced this chemical, thermal, and tactile combination, but it is exactly what happened.

As a result, three solid objects materialized over the Device – the second key.

And the Device instantly turned black.

"Cain't believe you lettin' the dog go a-piddlin on yer torlets," Phosia's husband, Elmo, said, as the two of them rocked in their chairs on the porch. "Hey, lookit there," he continued, "at them funny lil' birds a twirlin' on top a-that black one!"

But remember, Phosia had set potted plants on the Space Sieve. So what it looked like then, was there, on top of the Device, were potted plants, and three colored, twirling objects. And perhaps strangely to you, it appeared these three objects and the potted plants were all occupying the same space – none was blocking the view of the other.

"Hey now," the thought just occurred to Elmo, and he pointed, "where'd you done git a black torlet – there on the end?"

"That's my new-un," she said. "But it ain't – hey – how come it's black!"

And just then, the dog too saw that the object had turned black. And when it then also saw the three strange objects hovering above the Machine, it took a safe distance, then ran off.

"Hey, Daisy! Daisy-Joe-dog!" Phosia called to it, as she got up and headed over to the Space Sieve. "Them's ain't *birds*, a-floatin' over'n it!" she said, and momentarily turning back, "I dcne told you that there thing weren't just no ordinary piece a junk!"

But as she turned back toward the Machine, the three objects were gone and the Device was a dull white again. For Actio, in his wisdom, had set the lock such that were the first key to be given, but the three solid objects – the second key – not quickly manipulated after appearing, they would disappear once again, providing yet another safety feature.

"What th"?" she said.

Her husband leaned forward. "Done told ya thems was *birds* atop it," he said.

"They done flewt away!"

She turned back to him. The hot afternoon sun was making her sweat. "You see 'em fly off?" she asked.

Her husband was getting irritated. It was a very hot day. "Yeah! I done seed 'em fly off. They done went over *there* someplace." And he waved his arm as he sunk back into the chair.

Phosia took his word for it having little other choice, and she came back and went into the house.

Sitting there in the sun, the Space Sieve remained inert, locked, powerless, unfeeling, and uncaring.

It was – it *is* – just a Device after all. It has no consciousness of any kind. If nobody wanted to use it, it neither knew, nor cared.

In the grass around it, the leafhoppers went about their business, trying to stay away from the jumping spiders as a mourning dove sat on the telephone line, and its tail moved faintly, in rhythm with its cooing. In the distance, the sound of an impact sprinkler could be heard.   Except for a few fluffy clouds, the sun blazed in an empty, blue sky.

It was what you would call a perfect day – and in fact, it *was* a pretty day – the sort of day that makes your world occasionally worth visiting.   And so, here I end.

Now at last, I bid you farewell.

And while you may have occasionally detected a feeling of condescension on my part toward you, nonetheless, I sincerely wish your journey will be a happy one, with much good learning and adventures along the way, until that bright day comes when we may all meet together once again.   And hopefully in that day, when you at last cast away that time which so binds you now, we can then experience life together as it truly is, and do so on a more equal basis.